MAGNOLIA

DIANA PALMER

THORNDIKE
CHIVERS

This Large Print edition is published by Thorndike Press, Waterville, Maine USA and by AudioGO Ltd, Bath, England.
Copyright © 1997 by Diana Palmer.
The moral right of the author has been asserted.
Thorndike Press, a part of Gale, Cengage Learning.

Thorndike Press® Large Print Basic.
The text of this Large Print edition is unabridged.
Other aspects of the book may vary from the original edition.
Set in 16 pt. Plantin.

LIBRARY OF CONGRESS CATALOGING-IN-PUBLICATION DATA

Palmer, Diana.
    Magnolia / by Diana Palmer. — Large print ed.
      p. cm. — (Thorndike Press large print basic)
    ISBN-13: 978-1-4104-3176-9
    ISBN-10: 1-4104-3176-2
    1. Love stories. gsafd 2. Atlanta (Ga.)—Fiction. 3. Large type
books. I. Title.
PS3566.A513M33 2010
813'.54—dc22   2010041630

BRITISH LIBRARY CATALOGUING-IN-PUBLICATION DATA AVAILABLE
Published in the U.S. in 2010 by arrangement with Harlequin Books, S.A.
Published in the U.K. in 2011 by arrangement with Harlequin Enterprises II B.V.
U.K. Hardcover: 978 1 408 49335 9 (Chivers Large Print)
U.K. Softcover: 978 1 408 49336 6 (Camden Large Print)

Printed in the United States of America
1 2 3 4 5 6 7 15 14 13 12 11

MAGNOLIA

To Russ and Carole McIntire with love

1

1900

The streets of Atlanta were muddy from the recent rain, and the poor carriage horses seemed lacking in spirit as they strained to pull their burdens along Peachtree Street. Claire Lang watched them, wishing she had the money to hire a ride back to her home, a good five miles away. The stupid buggy had hit a rock and broken an axle, adding to the financial worries that had plagued her for months. Will Lang had been so impatient for the motorcar part he'd ordered from Detroit that Claire had taken the buggy up to Atlanta to get the small part for her uncle from the railway agent. The buggy was old and in bad shape, but, instead of watching the road, she'd been looking for early signs of autumn in the gorgeous maple and poplar trees.

She'd have to get to her friend Kenny's clothing store the best way she could — and then hope that he could spare the time to drive her down to Colbyville, where her uncle lived. She looked at the caked mud on her high-topped shoes and the filthy hem of her skirts and grimaced. The dress, navy blue with a lacy white bodice and collar, was brand-new. Her cloak and parasol had protected the rest of her from the rain, and her hat had shielded her brown hair in its bun, but no amount of lifting had spared her skirts. She could imagine what Gertie would say about that! She was always untidy, anyway, puttering around in her uncle's shed, helping him keep his new motorcar running. Nobody else in Colbyville had one of the exotic modern inventions. In fact, only a handful of people anywhere in the country owned motorcars, and most of theirs were electric or steam. Uncle Will's device was fueled by gasoline, which he purchased from the local drugstore.

Motorcars were so rare that when one went past, people would run out onto their porches to watch. They were objects of both fascination and fear, because the loud noise they made spooked horses. But most people looked at the motorcar as a fad that would quickly die out. Claire didn't. She saw it as the future form of transportation, and she was thrilled to be her uncle's mechanic.

She smiled wistfully. How fortunate her life had been since she'd come here to live with her uncle. Her parents had died of cholera ten years past, leaving their only child without a relative in the world except Uncle Will. He was a bachelor, too, with only his African housekeeper, Gertie, and a handyman, Gertie's husband, Harry, to help run the big house where he lived. Since she'd grown up, Claire had done her share of cooking and housework, but her greatest joy was helping to work on that automobile! It was a spanking new Oldsmobile with a curved dash, and just looking at it gave her goose bumps. At the end of last year Uncle Will had ordered it in Michigan; it had been shipped by rail to Colbyville as soon as it was built. Like most motorcars, it occasionally choked and coughed and smoked and rattled, and from time to time its thin rubber tires went flat on the rough, deeply rutted dirt roads that circled Colbyville.

The townspeople had prayed for deliverance from what they said had to be an invention of the devil, and horses took to the fields as if driven by ghosts. The town council had paid a visit to her uncle the day after his motorcar arrived: Uncle Will had smiled tolerantly and promised to keep the elegant little vehicle out of the way of the carriage trade. He loved his toy, which had all but bankrupted him, and he spent all his spare time working on it. Claire shared his fascination. He'd finally given in and stopped chasing her out of the garage so that bit by bit, she'd learned about boilers and gears and bearings and spark plugs and pistons. Now she knew almost as much as he. Her hands were slender and dexterous and she wasn't afraid of the occasional "bite" she got when she touched the wrong part of the small combustion engine. The one real drawback was the grease. In order to work properly, the bearings had to be continually bathed in grease, which got on everything — including Claire.

Suddenly a carriage appeared on the street and Claire watched it draw near. When it was in front of her, it went through a puddle — splattering mud all over her skirts. She let out a groan and looked so forlorn that the driver stopped.

The carriage door opened and impatient dark eyes glared out at her. "For God's sake! Get in before you're even more soaked than you already are, you silly child!"

The voice, deep and familiar, had the power to turn her heart over. Not that he knew. Claire was careful to keep her feelings for her uncle's banker very close to her heart.

"Thank you, Mr. Hawthorn," she replied politely, smiling. She tried to make a lady-like entrance into his nice clean carriage as she folded the parasol and hiked up her skirts to the top of her shoes. But she tripped over the wet hem and landed in a heap on the seat, flushing because John Hawthorn made her so nervous.

Very dignified in his dark-vested city suit, he moved over to give her plenty of room, then rapped on the top of the carriage with his cane, signaling his driver to go ahead. "Honest to Pete, Claire! You attract mud like oats attract a horse!" He looked mildly exasperated as he surveyed the damage. "I have to get to the bank by opening time, but I'll have my driver take you down to Colbyville," he said, his dark eyes narrowing in his lean, handsome face. He had an innate fastidiousness, almost a coldness, with most women, as if he knew he was attractive to them and to maintain his distance. It had been the first thing that drew Claire's attention to him, a challenge to a woman's ego. But he wasn't cold with her. He alternately teased and indulged her, the way he would a very young girl. It hadn't

11

bothered her so much two years ago. Now it did.

She'd first become acquainted with him when he took a job at the bank owned by Eli Calverson. He'd already worked his way up to being a loan officer the year before the Spanish-American War broke out, and John, with an educated guess as to where Cuban-American relations were going, had left the bank in 1897 to serve briefly in the army. Because his early education had been at the Citadel, a military college in South Carolina, he was able to go in with an officer's commission.

Wounded in Cuba in '98 and discharged, John returned to the bank, and Claire really got to know him. They'd been acquainted for some years because of her uncle, who had made several small investments through John and had secured loans on the strength of them to buy land. As she got to know him, her attraction grew, but she realized that it would take more than her pleasant face, pale gray eyes, and slender young body to interest a man like John.

He wasn't merely handsome, he was intelligent. After graduating from the prestigious Citadel he went on to get a master's degree in business from Harvard. He was vice president of the Peachtree City Bank now, and rumor had it that the bank's president, Eli Calverson, since he had no children, had handpicked John as his successor. Certainly John's rise in the bank had been a rapid one.

But gossip had run rampant lately about the elusive John Hawthorn and the beautiful Diane, the new young wife of the bank's middle-aged president. At thirty-one, John was in his prime and a physical specimen other men envied. Eli Calverson was in his fifties and not particularly attractive.

Mrs. Diane Calverson was petite, blonde, and blue-eyed, with a complexion like cream. She was cultured, well bred, and said to be related to most of the royal houses in Europe. In short, she was any man's dream. She and John had a lot more than the bank and their connection to Calverson in common. Two years before, they had been engaged.

"You're a gentleman, Mr. Hawthorn," Claire said, with reserved politeness, although her eyes twinkled at him.

The corner of his mouth turned upward. Obviously, he was amused.

Her eyes went to the cane he carried strictly for ornamentation. He was fit and athletic, a tennis player, and she knew from the few dances her uncle had escorted her to that John could dance better than most men. He smelled of some exotic cologne. It drifted into Claire's nostrils and made her heart race. If only he'd notice her. If only . . . !

She straightened out her wet skirts, frowned at the mud caked on them. Her laced-up shoes were full of it, too; it would take hours with a scrub brush to get them clean again. Oh, dear — and Gertie had only just stopped fussing about the grease on Claire's white shirtwaist!

"You look very untidy," John remarked gently.

She flushed, but her chin lifted. "If you'd walked three blocks in the rain in long skirts, I suppose you'd look untidy, too."

He chuckled. "God forbid. It was grease last time, wasn't it?"

She cleared her throat. "Uncle and I were changing the oil in his Oldsmobile."

"I've said it before, Claire . . . that's not fit work for a woman."

"Why not?"

He sighed. "Your uncle should speak to you," he said. "You're twenty years old. You need proper grounding in etiquette and social life so that you can behave like a proper lady."

"Like Mrs. Calverson, perhaps?"

His face was impassive. "Her manners

14

certainly leave nothing to be desired."

"Indeed they do not," she agreed readily. "I'm sure Mr. Calverson is very proud of his wife." She studied her hands. "And probably *very* jealous of her."

His head turned. "I don't like insinuations," he said in a dangerously soft tone. "Are you presuming to lecture me?"

She arched her brows. "Why, sir, nothing was further from my mind. I mean, if you wish to become the subject of vile gossip and risk your position at the bank, who am I to interfere?"

His scowl was intimidating. Imagining he'd once looked at his troops in just that way, she wouldn't have blamed a single one of his solders for deserting. His voice was still soft, and more chilling for it, when he asked, "What gossip?"

"Perhaps I shouldn't have spoken," she said, giving him a nervous smile. "You can let me out here, if you please. I have no desire to be strangled on the way home."

He did look angry, but he never seemed to lose his temper, especially not with Claire. "I haven't given anyone reason to gossip," he said.

"You don't consider a candlelight supper, alone with a married woman, scandalous?"

He looked surprised. "We were hardly

alone. It was at her sister's house, and her sister was present."

"Her sister was upstairs asleep. The servants knew it and told everyone else's servants everything they saw," she told him flatly. "It's all over town, John. And if her husband hasn't heard it yet, it's only a matter of time until he does."

He made a rough sound under his breath. He'd been careless in his obsessive desire to be alone again — just once — with Diane. Her marriage to Calverson had been an act of vengeance — when he'd refused to ask his people for a large advance on his inheritance for an elegant wedding and an expensive honeymoon. He'd joined the army by then and was certain that he would see action. She'd promised to wait . . . but, within two months of his having been in Cuba, Diane apparently had found Calverson too handy, too rich, and too old not to drag to the altar.

John came from old money in Savannah, and he stood to inherit millions. But he refused to ask for a penny of it, preferring to make his own living. He was doing that now, thanks to his salary and some small investments. Calverson's support had given him an edge, although he knew his family background and his Harvard business degree had helped influence the man in his favor. Losing Diane had changed John, had made him cold. Now her marriage of less than two years seemed to be in trouble. She'd beseeched John to come to her sister's house for a meal so that she could ask him for help. How could he have refused, even with the risk of scandal? But the urgency of the situation seemed lessened upon his arrival, because whatever her motives had been in inviting him, she'd told him nothing. Least of all did she ask for any sort of help. She had only said that she regretted her marriage and that she still had a tenderness for him. But now they'd caused this terrible gossip that would threaten her good name, as well as his.

"Are you listening to me?" Claire persisted, dragging him back to the present. "It isn't just your reputation you're risking, it's Mr. Calverson's and hers — and even the bank's."

He gave her a hard look. "I'm not risking anyone's reputation. But I can't think how this problem, if it is a problem, has anything to do with you, Claire," he remarked coolly.

"That's true," she had to admit. "But you're my uncle's friend as well as his banker. In a way, you're my friend, too. I would hate to see your reputation compromised."

"Would you, really? Why?"

She flushed and averted her face.

He leaned back, watching her with faint affection and touched by her concern. "Do you have a secret regard for me, Claire? A tendresse?" He teased her softly. "How very exciting!"

The flush grew much worse. She watched feverishly as the familiar Gothic lines of the bank came closer. He would get out of the carriage — and she would be alone with her embarrassment. Why, oh, why, had she opened her mouth?

He saw her gripping her purse with both hands. While he disliked her intrusion into his privacy, she was just a sweet child whose observations shouldn't upset him. He indulged her more than any woman he'd ever known. He'd have thrown a man out of his carriage for less than what she'd just said to him. But she had a kind heart and she cared about him. It was difficult to be angry about that. She kindled protective feelings in him, too.

If it hadn't been for Diane, he could well have cherished this child. He leaned closer as the carriage began to slow down. "Well, Claire," he persisted in a deep drawl, "are you besieged with tender feelings for me?"

"The only feeling I have right now is a consuming desire to lay an iron pipe across your skull," she said under her breath.

"Miss Lang!" he said with mock outrage, and made it worse by chuckling.

She turned and glared at him, her gray eyes sparkling with temper. "Ridicule me, then. You make me ashamed that I was ever worried for you," she said flatly. "Ruin your life, sir. I will never concern myself with it again."

She banged against the ceiling with the handle of her parasol and was out of the carriage before he could do anything more than call her name.

She fumbled the parasol open and got onto the wooden sidewalk, which was a relief from the mud, at least. In front of the bank, which was about to open, she spotted Kenny Blake, a friend of hers from school days, and ran to greet him.

"Oh, Kenny! Thank goodness I found you! Can you give me a ride home? Our buggy's axle broke."

"You're not hurt?" he asked.

She shook her head. "Just a little shaken, that's all." She laughed. "Fortunately, it was very near the blacksmith's shop and the livery stable. I was able to get help, but they were so crowded that nobody could spare the time to drive me home."

"You could have hired a coach."

She shook her head with a rueful smile. "I haven't any money," she said honestly. "Uncle spent the last little bit we had on new spark plugs for the motorcar, and until his pension comes, we have to be very careful."

"I can make you a loan," he offered. And he could have, because Kenny had a very good job managing a men's clothing shop in town.

"No, you can't. Just give me a ride."

He grinned, and his plain face lit up. He was medium height, blond, blue-eyed, and very shy. But he and Claire got along well, and he wasn't shy with her. She brought out all the best in him.

"Wait until I finish my business in here, and I certainly shall," he assured her.

She let go of his arm, feeling cold eyes on her back. She glanced around at John Hawthorn in his expensive suit and bowler hat, his silver-headed cane in one hand as he leaned elegantly on its length and waited for Mr. Calverson to unlock the door from the inside. Calverson trusted no one except himself with that key. He was very possessive about things he owned — something that John would have done well to have remembered, Claire thought.

At the stroke of nine, Mr. Calverson opened the huge oak doors and stood aside to let the others enter. His eyes were on his gold pocket watch, which was suspended from a thick gold-link chain. He nodded as he closed the case and stuck it back in the watch pocket of his vest. He looked rather comical to Claire, the short, stout little man with his flowing blond-and-silver mustache and his bald head. She really couldn't imagine any woman finding him attractive, much less a beauty like Diane. But then, only John thought she'd married old man Calverson for love. Everyone else in Atlanta knew that Diane had expensive tastes — and that her family's ruined fortunes had left her, at the age of twenty-two, with no tangible assets save her beauty. She had to marry well to keep her sisters and her mother in fancy clothes and insure that the elegant mansion on Ponce de León kept running smoothly. But Mr. Calverson had more money than she could ever spend. So why was she risking it all for a fling with her old flame John?

"The bank isn't in trouble, is it?" she asked when she and Kenny were in his buggy on the way to Claire's home.

21

"What? Why, certainly not," he said, shocked. "Why do you ask?"

She shrugged. "No reason. I just wondered if it was solvent, that's all."

"Mr. Calverson has managed it quite well since he came here a few years past," he reminded her. "He's prosperous . . . anyone can see that."

So he seemed to be. But it was a little strange that a man who came from farming stock should amass such a fortune in so short a time. Of course, he did have access to investment advice, and he foreclosed on land and houses and such.

"Our Mr. Hawthorn was glaring at you," Kenny remarked.

"He gave me a ride and insulted me."

His hands jerked on the reins and the horse protested loudly. "I shall speak to him!"

"No, Kenny, dear. Not that sort of insult. Mr. Hawthorn wouldn't soil his hands by putting them on me. I meant that we had a sort of disagreement, that's all."

"About what?"

"I'm not at liberty to discuss it," she said stiffly.

"Well, it's not hard to guess about what," he remarked. "Everyone knows he's panting after the bank president's wife. You'd think the man would have more pride."

"People in love seem to lose it rather easily, and she was engaged to him before she married Mr. Calverson."

"If she's risking her little nest to see John behind her husband's back, maybe there *is* some worry about money," he remarked. "That young woman doesn't miss a step."

"If John loves her . . ."

"A scandal would ruin him in Atlanta. Not to mention her good name. Her people were always mercenary, but there was never a breath of scandal about them."

She remembered John coming home wounded to find Diane comfortably married. John had been in a terrible state at the time, stoic and unapproachable in his recovery. Claire had gone with Uncle Will to see him in the hospital, having heard the gossip about his badly broken engagement. At eighteen, Claire had felt the first stirrings of love for the wounded soldier who bore his pain with such courage and had even won a medal for bravery.

"It must be terrible to lose someone you love that much," she remarked, and thought of herself, because she'd loved John for almost two years . . .

"There's a circus coming to town very soon," Kenny said. "Would you care to go with me to see it on Saturday?"

She smiled. "I should like that very much, Kenny."

"I'll ask your uncle for his permission," he said, beaming.

She didn't tell him that her uncle was much too modern for such things, or that she didn't feel that she needed permission to do what she liked. Kenny was nice and uncomplicated, and he took her mind off John. Anything that could accomplish that made the day worthwhile.

Uncle Will just had finished fixing a leaky radiator. Kenny said his piece and left while Claire was changing into a clean skirt and blouse and shoes. Grimacing, she gave the dress to Gertie.

Gertie sighed. "Miss Claire, you have a gift for soiling clothes," she remarked, a twinkle in her eyes.

"I do try to stay clean," she told the older woman. "It's simply that fate is after me with a broom."

Gertie chuckled. "It seems so. I'll do what I can with this. Oh, and I won't be here on Sunday. I'm going to meet my father at the station and go with him to a family reunion."

"How is he?" Gordon Mills Jackson was a

famous African trial attorney in Chicago and very well respected.

"He's as wicked and devious as ever," Gertie said, laughing. "And my brother and I are very, very proud of him. He faced down a lynch mob a few months ago and rescued a farm laborer from a rope. The man was innocent, and Daddy defended him successfully."

"He'll be a Supreme Court judge one day," Claire predicted.

"We hope so. Can you manage by yourself on Sunday or would you like me to see if I can find someone to cook for you that day?"

"I'll do it myself. You taught me how to make chicken and dumplings, after all, and I'm not so squeamish that I can't kill the chicken."

Gertie looked dubious. "Suppose you let your uncle do that part for you. He's much faster than you are."

"Well, I have to ease up to doing it," she said, defending her procrastination.

"He doesn't. You'll spend enough time dressing it fit to cook."

"You're right, I suppose."

"I'll have something on the table in a couple of hours for lunch. No guests?"

Claire shook her head. "Kenny had to get to work. It will only be Uncle and me."

As Claire walked toward the workshop, she called, "I'm back. Need any help?"

Her uncle leaned out from under the front of the car. "Hallelujah! You're just in time! I had to fix a leak in the radiator. Hand me a wrench and those hoses, and then bring me those new spark plugs!"

It took about two hours to get the new part in place, the plugs in, the gaps set, and the timing just right. Her uncle had to take one of them out and worry with it until it fit properly, but just before lunchtime the engine was running prettily.

"It works! You've got it going!" she exclaimed.

He stood up, his white hair darkened with grease from his big hands, a huge smile under his thick silver mustache. "By golly, I sure have! Thanks to you, girl! It was a great day for me when you came to stay. I had no idea what a mechanic I'd make of you."

She curtsied, ignoring the grease spots on her formerly pristine blouse and her face. "Thank you."

"Don't let your head get too big, though. You didn't replace the last screw in the boiler when you put it back."

She groaned. "I got interrupted by Gertie."

"That's right," Gertie called from the porch. "Blame it on me."

"Don't eavesdrop," Claire called back.

"Stop talking about me and I won't. Lunch is ready."

Gertie went back into the house, and Claire shook her head. "Uncanny, isn't it — how she always knows when I'm blaming her for some —"

Her uncle broke in. "Let's go for a spin."

"It's pouring rain. Besides, Gertie's got food on the table."

He sighed angrily. "Just my luck, darn it! When I've got it running right! Why don't they make tops for motorcars?"

After they ate, the two of them sat in the parlor while the rain beat down outside.

"Why did Kenny bring you home?" he asked suddenly. "Where's the buggy?"

She drew in a long breath. "The horse took it over a rock I didn't see and busted the axle. Now, now. It won't cost so much to have it replaced . . ."

Her uncle's husky shoulders slumped. "Oh, dear. Oh, dear, dear," he murmured. "And I've spent the last money we had to buy that new motorcar part, haven't I?" He looked up. "Why, Claire! I have a thought — we can sell the horse and buggy now," he

27

exclaimed. "We have a horseless carriage that runs!"

She grinned. "So we do."

He let out a sigh. "Gasoline is very cheap at the druggist's, so it won't be expensive to run it. And the extra money will pay off the last big mortgage I've had to take out on the house." His face assumed a blissful expression. "Our troubles are over, my dear. They're quite —" He stopped. His face seemed an odd gray color and he clutched his left arm. He laughed shortly. "Why, how very odd this feels. My arm has gone numb, and I have a very hard pain in my — in my — in my throa . . ."

He looked at her as if he was seeing right through her and suddenly pitched forward, right onto the rug.

Claire ran to him, her hands trembling, her eyes huge and tragic. She realized at once that this was something more than a faint. He was lying so still, not breathing, and his skin had gone a ghastly gray color. But worst of all, his eyes were open and the pupils were fixed and dilated. Claire, who had watched pet dogs and cats and chickens die over the years, knew too well what that meant . . .

2

In the space of two hours, Claire's life changed forever. Her uncle never regained consciousness. Her frantic telephone call from a neighbor's house to the doctor brought the family physician within minutes.

"I'm very sorry, Claire," Dr. Houston said softly, with a paternal arm around her shoulder. "But at least it was quick. He never knew a thing."

Claire stared at him with dull eyes.

"Gertie, bring a sheet, please, and cover him," he asked the housekeeper, who was quiet and solemn.

She nodded and went away, returning quickly with a spotless white sheet. Fighting tears, she put it lovingly over Will.

That made it all final somehow, and Claire felt her eyes welling with tears. She brushed at them as she began to sob. "But he was so healthy," she whispered. "There was never anything wrong with him. He never even had a cold."

"Sometimes it happens like this," the doctor said. "Child, do you have family? Is there anyone we can get to come and help you sort out the estate?"

She looked at him blankly. "We only had each — each other," she said, faltering. "He never married, and he was my father's only living sibling. My mother's people are all dead, as well."

He glanced at Gertie. "You and Harry will be here, won't you?"

"Of course," Gertie said, coming forward to put her arms around Claire. "We'll look after her."

"I know you will."

He filled out the death certificate, and, by the time he finished, the coroner came and a horse-drawn ambulance took the body to the mortuary. It was only then that Claire realized her position. The doctor and the funeral home would have to be paid. The sale of the buggy and horse would barely cover it. The house was mortgaged; the bank would surely foreclose.

She sat down heavily on the love seat and clenched a handkerchief in her hand. Her beloved only relative was gone; she was soon to be penniless — and homeless. What could she do? She tried to calm herself; after all, she had two skills — sewing clothes and repairing motorcars. She designed and made gowns for rich society matrons in Atlanta. That she could do, but there wasn't a motorcar in nearby Atlanta, so working on them was no solution.

A renewed wave of panic left her momentarily in tears. But they soon were dried by Gertie, who reminded her that she had few equals with a needle and thread and the fine Singer treadle sewing machine in the bedroom. Claire made all her own clothes, designs of her own creation that most people thought were store-bought because they were so richly and lavishly embroidered and laced.

"Miss Claire, you could work as a seamstress anytime," Gertie assured her. "Why, Mrs. Banning down on Peachtree Street can't make clothes fast enough to meet the demand. I bet she'd hire you in a second to work for her. Said she thought your pretty blue suit was a Paris fashion, she did! And she knows you sew for Mrs. Evelyn Paine."

That made Claire feel a little bit better. But, still, the prospect of a job and an income was only that — a prospect. She was afraid of the future, and trying hard not to let it show.

Barely an hour later, people who knew and loved Uncle Will began filling the house. Claire's pride and self-control were sorely tested with condolence after condolence. Women brought platters of food and desserts, and jugs of iced tea, and urns of coffee. Everything was taken care of in the kitchen, with Gertie's supervision. Kenny Blake came early and would have stayed, but Claire knew his business depended on the personal service he gave his customers. He needed to keep his shop open for long hours, too. She promised she would be all right and sent him back to work. They came all day and into the evening, until at last a familiar but unwelcome face showed itself at the door.

Claire's eyes were red with tears as she let the bank president, Mr. Eli Calverson, and his beautifully dressed and coiffed blonde wife into the house.

"We're so sorry, my dear," Diane Calverson said in her cultured voice, extending a graceful hand in a spotless white glove. "What a terrible tragedy for you, and how unexpected. We came the moment we heard."

"Don't worry about a thing, young lady," Mr. Calverson added, pressing her hands in his. "We'll make sure the house is sold for

the highest possible price, so that there will be a little something left over for you."

Claire wasn't even thinking properly as she stared at the old man, who had the coldest eyes she'd ever seen.

"And he did have that infernal motorcar, as well," the banker continued. "Maybe we could find some buyer for it . . ."

"I won't sell it," she said at once. "The buggy and the horse are at the livery stable and they can be sold, but I won't part with Uncle's horseless carriage."

"It's early days yet, my dear," Mr. Calverson said smugly. "You'll change your mind. Diane, have a chat with Miss Lang while I speak to Sanders over there. I believe he's had his eye on this property for quite some time."

"Now just one moment —" Claire began, but the banker had already walked away.

"Don't worry your head about it, dear," Diane said languidly. "Leave business to the men. We women were never meant for such complicated things as that." She looked around. "You poor thing. What a drear place. And you haven't even a decent dre to wear, have you?" she asked gently.

Claire had been too upset to change old dress she'd worn to work with Uncl the garage. Still, she bristled at the wom

remark. She had dresses upstairs that would have made Mrs. Calverson's Paris import look tacky by comparison. "My uncle had just died, Mrs. Calverson. Clothes were not much on my mind," Claire said.

Diane shook her head. "Nothing is more important to me than to be correctly dressed, whatever the occasion. Really, Claire. You should go and change before other people come."

Claire gaped at her. "My uncle died only hours ago," she repeated, loud enough for her voice to carry. "I hardly think my clothes matter just now."

Diane actually blushed as heads turned toward her. She made an awkward little gesture and laughed nervously. "Why, Claire. You misunderstood me. I never meant to demean your ensemble. And certainly not on such a sad occasion."

"Of course you didn't," John said quietly, joining Diane at Claire's side. Claire hadn't even noticed his arrival and her heart jolted at the sight of him, even through her grief.

He took Diane's arm, staring down with concern at Claire. "I'm very sorry about your uncle, Claire," he said gently. "I'm sure that Diane is, too. She was only concerned for you."

Claire searched his lean, hard face and

wished desperately that he would defend her so valiantly. If only she could lay her head on his shoulder and cry out her pain. But his comfort seemed reserved for Diane. One more thing to add to her burdened spirit.

"I haven't misunderstood one single word, Mr. Hawthorn," she said. Her eyes went to his hand on Diane's arm. "Nor one single action."

They both looked uncomfortable. He moved quickly away from Diane, but not before Mr. Calverson had seen and noted the byplay. He came back to join them, taking his wife's arm with a look that spoke volumes.

"Come over here, my dear, and meet a new client of the bank. You'll excuse us, I trust?" he asked John coldly, then turned and led his wife away.

"You'd better be careful, hadn't you?" Claire whispered. "He isn't blind."

John's eyes darkened with distaste. "Be careful. I'm not the same tame breed as your pet clothing-store manager."

She lifted her chin, angry at his pointed reference to Kenny, who was a darling but hardly a man of action. "Do you want to snap at me, too? Well, go ahead," she invited. "Diane's had a ripping go at me already about my clothes, and her husband is busy trying to sell the roof over my head so that your bank doesn't lose a penny on the loans you made to Uncle Will. Don't you have anything hurtful to say to me? It would be a shame to waste this opportunity. You should always kick people when they're down!"

The mettle in her words contrasted painfully with the wobble in her voice and the sheen of tears in her gray eyes.

"Excuse me. I don't feel well," she said in a husky tone, and went quickly out of the room, into the hall. She leaned, resting her forehead against the cool wall, while sickness rushed over her. It had been such a long, terrible day.

She heard the door behind her open, then shut. The voices in the parlor receded as footsteps sounded. She felt the pull of a steely hand on her upper arm, turning her, and then she was pressed against scratchy fabric. Strong, warm arms held her. Under her ear, a steady, comforting heartbeat soothed her. She breathed in the exotic cologne and gave in to the need for comfort. It had been a very long time since her uncle had held her like this when her parents had died. In all the years of her life, comfort had been rare.

"My poor baby," John said softly at her

temple. His hand smoothed over her nape, calming her. "That's right. Just cry until it stops hurting so much. Come close to me." His arms contracted, riveting her to him.

She'd never heard his voice so tender. It was comforting and exciting all at once. She pressed closer, giving free rein to the tears as she cried away the grief and fear and loneliness in the arms of the man she loved. Even if it was only pity driving him, how sweet it was to be held so closely by him.

A handkerchief was held to her eyes. She took it and wiped them and blew her nose. He made her feel small and fragile, and she liked the way his tall, muscular body felt against hers.

She pulled slowly away from him, without raising her head. "Thank you," she said, with a watery sniff. "May I ask what provoked you to offer comfort to the enemy?"

"Guilt," he replied, with a faint smile. "And I'm not the enemy. I shouldn't have spoken to you as I did. You've had enough for one day."

She looked up at him. "I most certainly have," she said angrily.

John searched her fierce eyes and wan face. "You're tired," he said. "Let the doctor give you some laudanum to make you sleep."

"I don't need advice from you. I doubt anyone close to you has ever died," she said miserably.

His eyes flared darkly as he remembered his younger brothers, the frantic search of the cold waters for bodies, the anguish of having to tell their father that they were dead. "Then you would be wrong," he said abruptly, dismissing the painful memories. "But loss is part and parcel of life. One learns to bear it."

She wrung the handkerchief in her hands. "He was all I had," she said, lifting her gaze to his. "And if it hadn't been for him, I should have ended up in an orphanage, a state home." She drew her shoulders up. "I didn't even get to say goodbye to him, it was that quick." The tears came again, hot and stinging.

He tilted her chin up. "Death isn't an end. It's a beginning. Don't torture yourself. You have a future to contend with."

"Grief takes a little time," she reminded him.

"Of course it does." He pushed back a strand of unruly hair from her forehead. As he moved it, he noticed a smudge of grease. Taking the handkerchief from her hand, he wiped away the smear. "Grease smears and dirty skirts. Claire, you need a keeper."

"Don't you start on me," she muttered, snatching the handkerchief away.

His lips curved in a semblance of a smile. He shook his head. "You haven't grown up at all. Instead of teaching you to work on motorcar engines, Will should have been introducing you to young men and parties. You'll end up an old maid covered in grease."

"Better than ending up some man's slave!" she shot right back. "I have no ambition to marry."

John cocked his eyebrow in amusement. "Not even to marry me?" he chided outrageously, grinning at her scarlet blush.

"No," she replied tightly. "I don't want to marry you. You're much too conceited and I'm much too good for you," she added, with a twinge of her old impish nature.

He chuckled softly. "That tongue cuts like a knife, doesn't it?" He took a slow breath and tapped her gently on the cheek. "You'll survive, Claire. You were never a shrinking violet. But if you need help, I hope you'll come to me. Will was my friend. So are you. I don't like to think of you being alone and friendless, especially when the house is sold."

She looked vaguely panicked, and John understood why at once.

"I won't own anything, really, will I?" she asked suddenly. "Uncle Will mentioned that he'd just taken out another loan . . ."

"So he did. The bank will have to foreclose on the house and sell it. You'll get anything over the amount necessary to pay off your uncle's debts, but frankly I doubt there'll be much left. The motorcar will have to go, too."

"I won't sell it," she said through her teeth.

"And I say you will."

"You have no right to tell me anything. You're neither my banker nor my friend!"

He only smiled. "I'm your friend, Claire — whether you like to admit it or not. Mr. Calverson won't act in your interest."

"And you will? Against your employer?"

"Of course, if it becomes necessary," he said surprisingly.

She dropped her gaze to his expensive tie. He sounded very protective. He'd always been protective of her. She'd never quite understood why. "I won't sell the motorcar, all the same."

"What will you do with it?"

"Drive it, of course," she said. Her eyes lit up. She lifted them to his. "John, I shan't have to sell it! I can hire it out to business-men, with myself as the driver! I will start a business!"

He looked as if she'd hit him in the head. "You're a woman," he pointed out.

"Yes."

He took an exasperated breath. "You can hardly expect me to condone such a hare-brained scheme."

She drew herself up to her full height. It didn't do any good. He still towered over her. "I'll do as I please," she informed him. "I have to make a living for myself. I have no means of support."

He studied her curiously. Several things were becoming clear to him, foremost among them that he was about to land himself in one hell of a scandal because of Diane. Her husband was very suspicious — and if what Claire had told him was accurate, he was being gossiped about. He couldn't afford to let one blemish attach itself to Diane's good name.

His eyes narrowed. Claire wasn't at all bad to look at. She was spunky, and she had a devilish sense of humor. She had a kind heart, and even passable manners, and most of the time she delighted him. He had a soft spot for her that he'd never had for any other woman. Besides all that, she worshiped him. "You could marry me," he suggested wickedly. "Then you'd have a husband to look after your interests as well as a roof over your head."

She felt the ground go out from under her feet. It was the oddest sensation, as if she weren't touching the floor at all. "Why should you want to marry me?"

"It would solve both our problems, wouldn't it?" he drawled mockingly. "You get the husband of your dreams," he said, smiling at her blush, "and I get a respite from gossip that could ruin Diane's good name."

Diane's good name, she noticed, not his own. He was still putting the woman above his own reputation. And the unkind remark about her infatuation for him hurt. She hated having him know how she felt.

"Marry you?" she replied haughtily. "I'd sooner eat an arsenic casserole with deadly nightshade sauce!"

He only smiled. "The offer stands. But I'll let you come to me when you've discovered that it's the best solution to your problem."

"I'll drive the car and make my living!" she said belligerently. She knew she wasn't facing reality, and she almost added that she could support herself equally well if not better by becoming a seamstress. However, since he knew nothing of that particular talent, she thought it best to keep it to herself for the time being.

He shrugged. "Drive the car, by all means," he said, turning to leave, "but, just remember, no self-respecting businessman is going to permit himself to be driven through the streets of Atlanta by a woman." He gave her a rueful smile. "I'll be waiting to hear from you, Claire. When your situation is desperate enough, come and see me."

"I'll never do that!" she said to his retreating back.

It was all bravado. She didn't know how badly she might end up, or what measures she might be forced to take. But how dare he make her such an offer of marriage — so cold and calculating that she got chills down her back just thinking of it! He *couldn't* believe she'd accept such a proposal — without even the pretense of warmth or affection!

He *could* believe it because he cared so much for Diane. She didn't have to hear him say that to know the truth of it. He loved the woman more than anything, so to save her the vicious gossip of society dames, he would sacrifice himself on the altar of marriage to another woman. It was rather noble and heroic, except that Claire would also be making a sacrifice to marry a man who didn't love her. She knew how he felt about Diane. That wouldn't change. She

43

would be a fool to link her life to his.

But what if she could make him love her? asked a tiny voice deep inside her mind. What if by living with her, sharing things with her, being around her constantly, he could learn to love her? There might even be a child, she thought with a scarlet blush, and surely he would feel something for the mother of his son?

She put the thought away as quickly as she entertained it. He might be able to make love to her, as men were known to be capable of it with any woman. But he would be thinking of Diane, wanting Diane. How could she bear his kisses and his embraces when she knew he wanted someone else, even if the someone else didn't want him back?

The answer was, of course, that she couldn't. She had to pick up the pieces of her shattered life and become independent. There would surely be a way. If her uncle's beloved motorcar wasn't the answer she would think of something else. Then let Mr. High-and-Mighty Hawthorn come calling with his infamous proposals!

For two weeks after the funeral Claire only went through the motions of living. Kenny came once and offered to do anything she needed done, including trimming the hedges. She didn't take him up on his offer, because she didn't want to raise his hopes. He had a mild crush on her, but she had no love for him, only friendship.

She missed her uncle terribly. Money was already a problem. She'd had to let Gertie and Harry go, a blow to all three of them, and not done without a tearful parting and promises to keep in touch. They easily found work, because locally they were known as hard workers. That, at least, took some of the burden from her conscience. The house was sold; Mr. Calverson had sent word that he had a buyer who wanted to move in within the month.

Claire would receive two hundred dollars as her part of the sale, but that would quickly be gone, because the funeral expenses had to be paid out of it.

She had tried to find clientele for her motorcar enterprise, but as John Hawthorn had predicted, businessmen didn't flock to her door to become clients. In fact, she was brushed off unceremoniously. She did back the motorcar out of the drive and run it around the block, dressed in the long white driving coat and goggles and cap her uncle had always worn. Young boys threw rocks at her, and she frightened a horse into jumping a hedge. Afterward she parked the motorcar in the garage and locked it away.

She had briefly considered work as a seamstress in a local fabric and notions shop, but the woman Gertie had suggested as a potential employer had just taken on a new seamstress and had no need of help. The only alternative was to sell her designs door-to-door or find a shop owner who would let her do alterations. Kenny came to mind, but she had no wish to sew men's fashions, much less do alterations on them.

Sewing at home was a good possibility, except that the house would soon be gone. The chickens were hers, and the eggs they laid, but where would she take them to live in order to keep getting her egg money from her regular customers?

John had predicted that she'd have to come to him for help, and she was almost to that point. Only pride held her back. Pride was very expensive, though, and she was running out of money fast.

She'd only just put up her cloak and hat when there was a knock on the front door. She went to open it and found John on the doorstep.

Her heart skipped, but anger overrode attraction. "Women run brothels and board-

46

inghouses!" she raged, shaking her finger at him. "If they can run one sort of business, certainly they can run others!"

"Are you planning to open a brothel?" he asked, with faint amusement. "I shouldn't advise it — not in Colbyville." He leaned down. "However, if you do, I promise to be your first customer," he whispered.

She flushed to her neckline. "You know very well that I had no idea of doing any such thing! I was merely making a point," she added, while the thought of being in John's arms in bed made her knees weak. He was only joking, of course. "What do you want?"

He smiled gently. "I wanted to see how you were," he replied. He searched her eyes. "I've been keeping up with you through your neighbors. You seem less than prosperous at the moment."

She folded her hands over her waist. "I can find a job when I'm ready."

"The house has to be vacated by the end of the month. Surely you were informed of this?"

"Yes," she admitted reluctantly.

He'd expected her to fold up after her uncle's death. In fact, he'd had every reason to believe that she'd approach him for help. She hadn't. In fact, she hadn't approached

47

anyone with her hand out. The extent of her pride surprised him, when very few things did anymore. Past experience had made him far too cynical about human nature. He remembered the very moment in Cuba when all his illusions vanished forever. The sight of human beings rounded up like cattle in the Spanish general's concentration camps had sickened every man in his company. A large number of those prisoners had died before American troops invaded the island.

But even worse than the sight of those wretched men was the horror of the USS *Maine* going down in Havana Harbor only two months before his unit was shipped to Cuba. His two younger brothers had been on board that ship. It was he who had influenced them to join, he with his officer's commission and his medals. Now Rob and Andrew were dead. At the boys' funeral, his father had cursed him until literally running out of breath. He'd had to have permission from his commanding officer to return to Savannah from Tampa, where he was temporarily stationed, to attend it. Soon after that, his unit was sent back to Cuba to fight when the war against Spain was declared.

He could hear his mother weeping, see the pitying looks in the eyes of his young remaining brother and sister. He could feel the cold, hateful eyes of his father and hear the vicious admonition that he would never again be welcome at their Savannah home. Even later, after he was wounded and shipped to New York to muster out of the military, it was to an Atlanta area hospital that he eventually was sent, by his own request. And his father had not permitted his mother to come and visit him, even to correspond with him during his convalescence. He still hated the man for that alone. Claire had come often to see him then, he recalled, his gaze moving to her face. He'd lost everything he loved, even Diane, and Claire's gentle presence had meant so much. He'd never even told her that.

"Why do you look like that?" Claire asked unexpectedly.

He blinked. "How do I look?"

"As if you had nothing of hope left in you," she said, with keen perception.

He laughed without humor. "Did you think me fanciful?" he taunted.

"I thought . . . well, it hardly matters, does it? I suppose losing the one thing in life you love would harden any man. I'm sorry for the things I said about Diane," she said, surprising him. "I know you can't help the way you feel about her."

He moved as if she'd stung him. "You see too much."

"I always have," she said, with a sad smile. "I don't have close friends because people like to keep secrets."

"I can imagine that it's hard to keep them around you."

She sighed. "Sometimes." She looked around the barren room. "Do you think the new owners might need someone to keep house for them?" she asked absently.

"No, they have their own servants. What sort of work do you want to do?"

"All I know how to do is cook and clean," she replied. "Oh, and work on motorcars, of course. And I sew a little," she added, with a secret smile.

He glanced at her. "Every woman sews a little. And working on automobiles is hardly a viable skill when there are so few of them around. In fact, I seem to recall that your uncle had the only gasoline-powered one in these parts."

"One day there will be many."

"No doubt. But your need is more immediate."

She let out an angry sigh. "What a world we live in, where women have to fight to be allowed any sort of work save washing, typing, sewing, or waiting on customers in shops."

He sighed to himself, remembering Diane saying languidly that she had no interest in being anything except a loving wife. Why had she married Calverson? Now she knew what a mistake she'd made and it was too late. Too late! It hurt most of all to remember that he'd introduced her to Calverson, when he went to work at the bank for the first time, fresh out of Harvard.

He glanced around. Most of the furniture was already gone, sold to pay bills. "Do you have anyplace to go, Claire?"

Her spine stiffened. "I'll find someplace before I have to leave here."

He saw the fear behind the pride. She wasn't going to admit defeat, regardless of what it cost her. He admired that independent spirit.

He stuck his hands in his pockets and sighed. "Marry me," he said, with sudden seriousness. "It will put an end to all your troubles and most of mine."

Her heart jumped with pained pleasure, but she refused to give way to it. She glared at him. "I said no before and I'll say it again. You only want me to be a blind, a camouflage, so you can carry on with your married woman!"

51

His black eyes narrowed. "You don't know me at all, do you? Turn it around, then. Would you marry me and cheat on me with some other man?"

She stiffened. "It would never occur to me to do anything so dishonest."

"Nor would it occur to me." He stared into her pale gray eyes and saw that nothing short of the truth would sway her. "Let's have it out in the open, then. Yes, I love Diane," he said, taking his hands out of his pockets and moving a step closer. "Some part of me will always love her. But she's married and I can't have her honorably. Anything less than that would destroy her reputation and mine. The only sensible thing to do is make a new life for myself. You and I aren't strangers. We've known each other, casually at least, for several years, and quite well for the past two. You have qualities I admire. We might not have the most passionate marriage of all time, but I think we can deal very well together. Right now, both of us are extra people in the world."

She hadn't expected him to say that. She expected coaxing and even a display of passion to make her fall in with his plans. His honesty left her without a defense.

He looked at her slowly, deliberately, until

she blushed. One eyebrow lifted slightly. "You might enjoy being married, Claire."

"If I marry you, it will be — it will be just as friends," she stammered. "I won't — That is, I can't . . ."

"You can't share my bed," he said for her, and the smile grew larger. "All right. We'll leave it like that. For a while, at least."

"Forever!" she exclaimed, embarrassed.

"Why, Claire. How red you look!"

"You stop teasing me!" She shifted nervously. "And you must promise."

He put his hand over his heart. "I promise, most sincerely, that I won't ask you to do anything that makes you feel compromised. Will that suffice?"

She unbent a little. After all, he was doing her a tremendous favor to offer her the protection of his name and the security of a home.

"I don't want to be her stand-in, you see," she mumbled, under her breath.

"I can understand that," he told her. "I hope that you'll always be so honest with me. In return, I'll promise never to lie to you." His dark eyes were very intent. "I think we'll get along."

She sighed wearily. "It seems an unlikely sort of business."

"Given time, it may prove a blessing for

us both. What sort of ring would you like?" he added, with a smile. "And suppose we shock Atlanta by getting married at the end of the month?"

She almost gasped. "The end of the month? It will cause a scandal!"

"Probably, but a nice one."

"I have no one to give me away." She nibbled her lower lip and looked up at him, not realizing that she was capitulating. "You have family, surely. Will they want to come?"

"My family lives far away," he said stiffly, not wanting to tell her why he couldn't invite them to his wedding. "They won't be able to come."

"Oh. I see." She sighed. "I shall have to walk down the aisle alone."

He smiled. "You'll be a lovely bride, Claire. And I promise, it will be a very small wedding. Only the necessary people."

She didn't give that another thought, for the moment. Oddly, it never occurred to her just who the necessary people would be . . . until it was too late.

3

Because Claire had been so devoted to her uncle, and so involved in helping him, she hadn't tried to make friends of the few other single women in the community. She felt that lack keenly as she was helped to get ready for the wedding ceremony by an excited Gertie. At least she had someone who was "family" at the most exciting event of her young life.

"I wish your uncle could see you now, Miss Claire." Gertie sighed. "You look pretty as a picture."

"Of course I do — the veil covers my face!" Claire teased, smiling. She didn't have a traditional wedding gown. She wore an elaborate white silk-and-lace dress that she'd made for a debutante's coming out. The debutante had decided at the last minute that she didn't want it. It was Claire's size, so she'd kept it for herself. She was glad now that she had. With the

addition of a huge white hat with a conceal-
ing veil, and the small bouquet of autumn
flowers that Gertie had picked for her and
threaded with a silver ribbon and white lace,
Claire looked the picture of a modern bride.

"That wasn't what I meant, and you know
it," Gertie scolded. She straightened a fold
of the long flaring skirt. "There. You look
perfect. Mr. John will be ever so proud."

"Mr. John" hadn't looked as if he felt very
proud of her when he'd glimpsed her briefly
at the front door, Claire thought miserably.
For the past three weeks he'd been very attentive and courteous, taking her out to
poetry recitals and musical concerts every
night. He'd been a charming companion.
His affection for her was as evident as it
had ever been . . . but that was all. There
was simply nothing more. There had been
no kisses, no effort to make their relationship anything more than friendship. And
today, when the ceremony was to take place,
he suddenly looked haunted. Claire had a
sudden fear that he might have second
thoughts at the altar — a picture of herself
being left there forming in her mind.

"Why, your hands are trembling!" Gertie
exclaimed, taking both of them in hers to
warm them. "Now, child, don't get over-
wrought. Honestly, marriage is very nice.

Harry and I have been together for thirty years, and we've been so happy. You'll be happy, too."

Claire met the gentle, laughing dark eyes evenly. "Yes, but Harry loves you."

Gertie gnawed on her full lower lip. "Sometimes love comes later."

"Or not at all," Claire added, remembering that John had invited his employer — and wife — to the wedding. John might be worried that the gossip about Diane and himself brought some of these people to the wedding out of sheer curiosity. Surely that was what made him look so concerned — not regret for having asked her to marry him! She had to think that he was glad to be marrying her or she'd go mad.

In fact, John was trying not to see Diane, so beautiful in her glorious white-and-black-patterned dress, so elegant. She was smiling, but she looked worn, and her husband wasn't smiling at all. John had worried about her since the day of Claire's uncle's funeral. Eli had been quite brisk with her, and hostile toward him, as if he'd heard the gossip about them and was angry. John had wanted to talk to Diane badly, to find out if she was being mistreated by her husband because of the wild rumors. But he hadn't dared approach her for fear of making the whole situation worse. But today, she'd detained him at the back of the church while they were momentarily alone. There had been tears in her eyes.

She tugged at his sleeve and coaxed him into an empty room. "I never dreamed you'd actually go through with it. Oh, don't! Don't!" she pleaded, clinging to his arms. "John, you simply can't go through with it! I was wrong. I made a terrible mistake. I admit it freely. I married only to spite you. But what if my marriage were suddenly dissolved and you were tied to Claire? You have to stop the wedding!"

"What are you talking about, Diane?" he asked, holding her tight by both upper arms. "You're still my friend . . ."

The fire in his eyes thrilled her. She leaned into his body, giving him all her weight, and lifted her face. "It isn't friendship I want. I love you!"

His breath caught in his throat. "You said . . ."

"I lied! I was trying to make the whole terrible situation easier for you, but now I must speak. I must. John, you mustn't go through with this. I'll promise anything, *anything* . . . if you'll walk out of the church. Anything, my darling," she whispered boldly.

He thought he might scream. Her eyes promised heaven, her lips . . . He bent toward them, pulled by invisible strings. And then he suddenly realized who he was — and who she was — and where they were. He drew away, slowly, reluctantly. Perspiration beaded above his upper lip. "It's too late," he bit off.

"No!" she said. "You could walk out!"

"How?" he demanded through his teeth, tormented by the anguish on her lovely face. She loved him. She still loved him! And he was about to be married! "Diane, half of Atlanta is out there. I cannot!"

She looked at him through tears. "I was a fool! Only recently have I realized how much I love you. But there's no reason for you to ruin your life, as well. John, you don't love her. You love me!"

"I know." He groaned, holding her hands tight. His black eyes adored her. "I love you more than my life!"

She pressed closer to him. "My marriage may not last much longer," she whispered urgently. "I can say no more, but I may be free sooner than you realize. John, you have to stop the wedding. There cannot be two spouses between us. There's something I simply must tell you about Eli —" She caught sight of her husband coming along the hall and sprang away from John. She was laughing by the time Calverson joined them. She recovered so quickly, John thought — much more quickly than he could.

"Oh, John. What a story!" she said, dabbing at her eyes. "You simply must tell Eli!"

Her husband relaxed when he saw the tears of laughter on her face. "Later, my dear, later," he said, nodding toward John. "This fellow has some marrying to do." With that, he took her arm and drew her across the threshold.

She looked over her shoulder at John, her eyes wild and desperate and pleading.

John was distraught. Diane hadn't said a word to him in weeks. Now, at his wedding, she was declaring her love, begging him to forgo this marriage, promising a future for them, insinuating . . . what? And he, who loved her, and now knew for certain she loved him, was on the verge of marrying another woman. Instead of one barrier between them — her own marriage — he was creating two.

Was he mad to marry Claire, when he didn't love her? His eyes sought Diane's across the room and his pained expression brought a sad but reassuring smile to her lips. He turned away, miserable. Diane . . .

his love, his life! He was losing her forever, because of his need to stem foul gossip about her and his pity for Claire. Why hadn't he realized in time how deeply he was committing himself with this marriage? He hadn't thought there was a chance of Diane's marriage ending. Now there *was* the possibility — now, when it was almost too late! There could be no easy divorce, no quick annulment of his marriage to Claire even if Diane should suddenly become free, because that would create twice the gossip. Of course, they could go away . . .

There was still time, he told himself. He could stop this, right now. He could go to Claire, tell her that he hadn't been thinking straight, that despite his compassion for her situation, he didn't love her and couldn't marry her. He could do that!

He even made the attempt. He joined her as she entered the church sanctuary, his feelings in turmoil.

She gave him a clear, uncomplicated look, something akin to worship in her soft eyes as she stared up at him, flushed with delight.

His lips parted to speak the words that would end the farce. But somehow, looking into those soft gray eyes through the thin white veil, he couldn't find the words. He just stood there, speechless. She looked so pure, so untouched, so innocent. So much in love, he thought bitterly. And suddenly, the thought of hurting her was insupportable.

"Is . . . something wrong with my dress?" she asked worriedly.

"No," he replied curtly. He glanced back at the full church and made a rough sound. "Wait for the music, Claire," he said stiffly, and turned to go back down the aisle to the altar, where the minister waited to marry them. He was disgusted with himself. Pity was no excuse for marriage. His heart was forever Diane's, now more than ever.

Good Lord, would he ever forget what Diane had just confessed to him? Would he ever forget the torment in those beautiful eyes? How could he have thought to marry Claire when a simple loan of money would have done equally well? But sanity had come far too late to save him. He could hardly walk out of the church now, with half of Atlanta's most prominent citizens watching. The scandal would ruin him . . . and Claire. He had to go through with it.

Claire heard the music start and she walked down the aisle, all alone. There was no one to give her away; there were no bridesmaids, no attendants. It was a church wedding, but more funereal in tone than joyous. John had looked angry, unhappy. She glimpsed Diane through her veil and saw the woman looking straight at John with a curious, drawn expression. She still wanted him, it seemed. And a split second later, she saw John's head turn helplessly toward Diane, saw his tormented gaze rest on the other woman.

As she stopped by his side and the minister began speaking, Claire's heart raced. John was in love with Diane, and, judging by the way she was looking at him, it was reciprocated. Diane loved him, too! Claire felt trapped. John was as helpless in his emotions as she was in her own.

She loved him, but it wasn't going to be enough, ever. He'd live with her, someday he might even make love to her and they might have children. But he'd be dreaming of Diane, loving Diane, wanting Diane, every minute of every day — just as she wanted him. It was going to be an empty triumph and a hollow, heartless marriage. And she'd realized it too late, overwhelmed as she had been with grief for her uncle and hopeless love for John.

The minister asked John if he took Claire to be his wife; he replied "Yes," in a terse, forced tone.

The same question was put to Claire. She

63

hesitated. At that instant, she felt John's hand grasp hers, hard. She said the word without conscious volition, flushing. He put the ring on her finger, and the minister concluded the service, adding that the groom could kiss the bride.

He did, to give him credit, lift the veil from her face and look at her, but his expression was troubled. He bent and barely brushed his cool, firm lips against her own, in a kiss so very different from the one she'd hoped for, dreamed of, wanted with every thread of her being.

He took her arm and they walked down the aisle to the standing congratulations and happy cries of the audience. Only Diane didn't cheer them on. John glanced at her miserable face once and felt his heart go cold. He looked away. He walked out the door without a single glance backward.

They arrived at John's apartment late, after the boisterous reception. It might have been fun, except that Diane looked like a grieving widow, and John's forced smiles wore on Claire's nerves. By the time it was over, Claire felt as if she'd been shaken to pieces.

The apartment was nice. It was on Peachtree Street, in a very pleasant neighborhood, with trees lining the road out front and plenty of them around the yard. Claire wished it were light enough so that she could see more. Tomorrow, she'd look at that shed John had told her about. She could keep Uncle's motorcar there.

She hesitated in the doorway of the upstairs floor of the sprawling, late-Victorian house where John lived. There were fancy sofas and chairs in the parlor and curtains at the windows. There was a large ashtray, with a half-smoked cigar in it, and a fireplace in which a fire burned briskly, because some September evenings were cool even this far south.

"This will be your room," John announced in a subdued tone, twisting the crystal doorknob of a door that led off the parlor.

She walked into it. It was small, but neat, with an iron bedstead painted white and a damask coverlet on it. There was a washstand with a pitcher of water and a large bowl on top of it, along with a mirrored dresser and a chifforobe. All anyone could want, she thought hysterically, except for a husband.

"Thank you for not insisting that we share a room," she said discreetly, and without looking at him.

"It isn't a hardship, since we don't have a normal sort of marriage." Angry, guilty, he knocked his hand against the dresser, welcoming the pain. "I must have been out of my mind!" He looked at her fully then, with eyes so bitter and full of agony that she felt his emotions bite into her body.

Her fingers clutched the lace curtain. "I didn't trap you," she reminded him curtly. "You convinced me that it would be for both our sakes."

"Yes, I did," he replied honestly, getting his feelings under tenuous control. "It was an act that we can both spend our lives regretting!"

She didn't know what to say. He looked destroyed.

He closed his eyes and opened them again. He felt as if he'd aged twenty years. "Well, it's done. We must make the best of it. There's no need for us to be much together. You can keep the apartment tidy and I'll go out to work each day. I often work late into the evening, even on Saturdays. We have church on Sundays. Occasionally I go to my club to play tennis."

Apparently she wasn't to accompany him. "I should like to have my uncle's motorcar moved here," she said proudly.

He sighed and made an odd gesture with a lean hand. "If we must." He had no heart for argument. Diane's lovely tear-filled eyes haunted him.

"We must," she replied firmly. "Furthermore, I want my wheel."

His eyebrows lifted. "You ride a bicycle?"

"Certainly I do. Most young ladies have wheels these days. It's wonderful exercise. There is a bicycle club in the city."

"It's dangerous," he said, concerned for her daredevil schemes. First a motorcar, now this. "A woman racer fell off her wheel and was injured. And I understand that in at least one city it has become illegal to ride a wheel at night unless it is properly lighted, so that it won't frighten carriage horses."

"I know all that," she replied. "I'll certainly obey all the rules. In any case, I don't ride at night."

He stuck his hands in his pockets and studied her carefully. He really didn't know her at all. She was his friend. But she was also a stranger who would now share his life, even though it was only a partial sharing. He wasn't sure how he was going to like this.

Neither was Claire, despite her hunger for his love. She grimaced. "Is there indoor plumbing?" she asked.

"Of course. Down the hall," he replied. "And you have access to the kitchen, but Mrs. Dobbs supplies all meals. You may check with her about the schedule and ask for any particular dishes that you like. She's quite accommodating."

"I'll do that."

She took off her hat, replacing the big pearl-tipped hairpin through the fabric. Without it, she looked fragile, and very young.

She wounded him, looking like that. None of this was her fault. He scowled as he thought how disappointing a day it must have been for her. He hadn't done anything to make it easier. In fact, he'd been openly hostile most of the time, because of what Diane had said to him, because of that stricken look on Diane's face. He could hardly bear the pain.

"I'm sorry," she said unexpectedly, lifting her wan face to his eyes. "I knew that you wanted to back out of the wedding today, and it was too late. You didn't think this far ahead, did you?"

There was no use lying to her. He could see that at once. His chin lifted and he sighed heavily. "What I thought no longer matters. We must make the best of what we have."

She wanted to laugh hysterically. It wouldn't help. Her gaze slid over his lean, handsome face with wistful regret. It would be a barren sort of life, without love or the hope of anything more than resentment and tolerance on his part. She must have been as crazy as he to have agreed to such a sterile arrangement.

"Why did you marry me when you still love her?" she heard herself ask.

A muscle in his jaw twitched. "As you said, Claire, I never thought very far ahead. I felt sorry for you; perhaps for myself as well. And what difference do our feelings really make now?" He shrugged in resignation. "She's married, and so am I. Neither of us is low enough to forget those vows, made before God." He looked worn, weary, almost defeated as he spoke. He turned away. "I plan to have an early night. It might benefit you to do the same."

"Yes, it might. Good night."

He felt so guilty that he couldn't look at her as he closed the door.

Alone in the dark later, Claire gave way to tears. She'd had such great expectations about her marriage, only to find that her husband was full of regrets and bitterness. If only Diane hadn't come to the wedding! But now she was bound to John in a marriage that he didn't want, and it was far too late to do anything about it. Just the thought of divorce made her ill. It was a stigma that no woman would want to have to live with. But a loveless, sterile marriage would be so much worse. There would be no kisses, no shared pleasure, not even the consolation of a child. She put her fist to her mouth to stem another burst of tears. Really, she had to stop crying. Broken dreams happened to everyone. But lately it seemed that her entire life had become one long trail of them . . .

Friday came, and Claire's spirits had lifted a bit, because she'd cleaned out the shed behind the apartment house for the motorcar. Mrs. Dobbs, the landlady, had agreed only after much coaxing. Like many people, she was a bit afraid of the modern inventions, especially those that moved by themselves.

Claire had John's driver take her down to Colbyville to drop her off at the house her uncle had owned. She dusted off the motorcar and climbed aboard. A kind neighbor had helped her tie her wheel onto the back with ropes. She donned her goggles and waved goodbye.

It was like being freed from bondage. She zipped along the rutted streets toward Atlanta, grinning as she sat high in the seat in her long white riding coat and goggles,

70

and the cap that went with her uncle's regalia. The clothing might be too big for her, but she was quite capable of driving the car. Horses grew nervous at the unfamiliar noise, so she slowed down when she spotted a carriage. She didn't want to spook anyone's horse. Many people were killed in runaway buggies, not only because of automobiles, but also because they unknowingly purchased horses unsuited to the task of drawing a carriage behind it. There was some skill involved in picking a proper horse for such duties.

The wind in her face made Claire laugh with sheer joy for the first time during the single week of her marriage. John pretended that she wasn't there, except at breakfast and supper, when he was obliged to acknowledge her as they shared a table with the elderly Mrs. Dobbs. Unaware of the true nature of their marriage, she was forever teasing them and making broad hints about additions to the family.

The good-natured teasing didn't seem to bother John. She wondered if he even heard it, so preoccupied did he seem. But it disturbed Claire. It was stifling to pretend all the time.

Here, though, in the motorcar, whizzing down the rough dirt road at almost twenty miles per hour, she didn't have to worry about appearances. She was so well covered in the driving gear that she wouldn't have been recognizable to people who knew her. She felt free, powerful, invincible. The road was clear of other vehicles, so she let out a whoop and coaxed even more speed from the motorcar.

It had a natty curved dash, spoked wheels, and a long rod with a knob that came up from the box between the front tires, which was how the driver steered it. The engine was mounted between the rear tires, with the gearbox under the small seat. It now zipped along the rough roads smartly, although it had had no end of problems, which Claire and her uncle had needed to deal with on a daily basis. For one thing, the boiler tended to overheat, and in fact, Claire still had to stop every mile and let it cool down. The transmission band snapped with irritating regularity. Oil that had to be splashed over bearings to prevent their overheating constantly leaked past the piston rings and fouled the spark plugs. Brake problems abounded. But despite all those minor headaches, the little engine chugged merrily along for short spells, and Claire felt on top of the world when she drove.

She loved driving in Atlanta, past the elaborate traps and carriages. It was a city of such history, and she herself had been part of two fairly recent celebrations in 1898. The first had been the United Confederate Veterans reunion in July, to which some five thousand visitors had flocked to see the grand old gentlemen parade down Peachtree Street in their uniforms. She recalled old General Gordon sitting astride his grand black horse in the rain as the parade passed by him on the thirty-fourth anniversary of the Battle of Atlanta. The moment, so poignant, had brought tears to her eyes. The Northern newspapers had been disparaging about the event, as if Southerners had no right to show respect for ordinary men who had died defending their homes in a war many felt had been caused by rich planters who were too greedy to give up their slaves.

But controversy dimmed in December of the same year, when another rally was held. Called the Atlanta Peace Jubilee, it was to celebrate the victory of America in the Spanish-American War. President William McKinley was there, and Claire actually got to see him. John had been in the hospital at the time, and Claire had gone to tell him all about the excitement of seeing Confederate and Union war veterans celebrating side by side.

In fact, just this past July, Claire and Uncle Will had joined John at the Aragon Hotel at a reunion attended by veterans from both Union and Confederate forces. There, she thought, was a truly touching event as old enemies reminisced together and tried to bury the past.

In what seemed a very short time, Claire was home, maneuvering the little vehicle past Mrs. Dobbs's towering white Victorian house. She guided it carefully into the shed and disengaged the engine, wrinkling her nose at the fumes from the gasoline. The burning oil was equally obnoxious to the nostrils. She fanned at the air, keenly aware of the stains on her uncle's long driving coat and on her face, as well.

She climbed out and patted the open seat lovingly. "There, now, Chester," she cooed, using her own pet name for the mechanical creature she loved with all her heart, "you're home at last. I'll be out to clean your plugs later." She grimaced as she noted the knots that secured the wheel on the back. "And I guess I'll have to bring a knife, to free that," she murmured to herself. It was unlikely that she was going to be able to enlist John to untie the complicated sailor's knots that

Uncle Will's neighbor had used to tie on the bicycle. He had so little time to spend with her, even in the evenings. Especially in the evenings.

She closed the shed up, twisted the wooden knob that secured it, and went toward the back of the house, stripping off the car coat and goggles on her way. She walked down the hall, intent on reaching the upstairs apartment without being seen in her deplorable condition, her once pristine skirt and blouse splotched with dust and dirt and oil, her face grimy, her hair disheveled from the goggles and driving cap.

Just as she gained the hall, she unexpectedly came face-to-face with her husband and two men in business suits.

John looked at her as if he didn't recognize her — worse, as if he didn't want to recognize her! His dark eyes grew darker and he took a visible breath.

"Claire, come and meet Edgar Hall and Michael Corbin, two of my colleagues. Gentlemen, my wife, Claire."

"How do you do," she said, with a smile, extending a grimy hand — which they both shook without apparent distaste. "You'll have to excuse the way I look; I've just been driving my uncle's motorcar up here from Colbyville. It took most of the morning."

"You drive a motorcar, Mrs. Hawthorn?" one of the men asked in surprise.

"Yes," she replied proudly. "My uncle taught me."

He gave John a speaking glance. "How . . . er . . . interesting and unusual."

"Isn't it?" she replied. "If you'll excuse me, I'll just go and get cleaned up."

"You do that," John said, looking as if he were dying to say more.

She made her escape, painfully aware of the shocked and disturbed glances she was getting.

". . . not wise to let your wife be driving that contraption around," one of the men, the older one, said as she reached the top of the staircase. "What will people say?"

She didn't wait for John's reaction. Men! she thought angrily. If a woman took off her apron and did anything intelligent, it shocked them speechless. Well, they were due for a few more shocks, if she had her way. And that included her reluctant husband!

But her bravado lasted only until John came into their apartment. The very sharp and deliberate way he closed the door was disturbing.

"I won't have you driving that contraption around the city," he said shortly.

"Because it isn't ladylike and your friends don't approve?" she taunted, eyes sparkling with bad temper.

"Because the damned thing is dangerous," he returned. "Don't drive it alone again."

"Don't you puff up at me like a rooster with ruffled feathers," she shot back. "I'll do what I please. I'm not your slave . . . or your property."

The scowl grew darker. "You're my wife, for my sins. I'm responsible for you. That thing is a death trap!"

"No more dangerous than a horse," she informed him. "And the opinion of your colleagues matters not one whit to me!"

"Nor to me," he said irritably. "My concern is for you, not public opinion."

Her heart jumped. "Truly?"

"Truly. And I don't want you talked about," he added quietly, searching her eyes. "Some measure of decorum is called for. Your social status is higher now than it was when you lived with your uncle. You will have to conform, just a little."

She felt sick inside. The old freedom-loving days of her youth seemed to have died with her uncle. Now she had to conform to fit in with polite society. How in the world would she manage that dull sort of life, after the wonderful days with Madcap Will?

She caught hold of the back of a graceful wing chair and held on to it for support. "I see," she replied, staring at John as the full impact of the shift in her life hit her — and the difference in her husband. He wouldn't have been overbearing like this with Diane. If she'd wanted to ride naked down the streets of Atlanta in a motorcar, he'd probably have said nothing about it. But then, he loved Diane. And while he was concerned for Claire, it was for her reputation. God forbid that more gossip should be added to fan the already blazing fires.

John let out a long sigh. Claire's sudden pallor enhanced his guilt. "Certain sacrifices have to be expected in a marriage like ours."

"My sacrifices, of course," she said, nodding curtly. "You'll go on as before, working fifteen-hour days and mooning over Diane."

The attack caught him off-guard. "Damn you!" he snapped.

He seemed to implode, Claire thought. His eyes blazed at her, his stance threatened.

She lifted her chin and moved toward him, utterly fearless. "Would you like to hit me? Go ahead. I'm not afraid of you. Do your worst. I've lost my uncle and my home and my independence. But I haven't lost my pride and my self-respect, and nothing you can do will take those away."

"I don't hit women," he said icily. "But I won't have you driving around in that motorcar alone. Try it again and I'll cut the tires off the damned thing."

"John!" she burst out, shocked at hearing him curse not once but twice in less than a minute.

He smiled coldly. "Do you think that because I work in a bank I don't react like a normal man to things that anger me? I wore a uniform for several years, Claire, between graduating from the Citadel and going to Harvard. I was working in Atlanta when I reenlisted — long enough to fight in Cuba — but at one time, I never envisioned a life outside the military. I learned to conform to civilian life, because I had to. You'll learn to conform to high society, because you have to. There's been more than enough gossip about us already."

He hadn't spoken to her like this before — and now he was making himself a stranger to her. She cleared her throat.

"I had to get Chester here, didn't I?"

"Chester?" he asked, scowling.

She made an awkward motion with her hand. "My motorcar."

His eyes twinkled. She was an odd woman,

he mused, full of spice and vinegar, but she gave a pet name to a piece of machinery.

"I won't drive it." She finally agreed, although it was like giving up a part of herself. Apparently the cost of her support was going to be the suppression of her personality. "I can ride my wheel when I need exercise, I suppose."

"You needn't sound so tragic. I only wish you to act like the wife of the vice president of one of the most prestigious banks in the South," he said, "instead of a little girl playing with dangerous toys."

Her gray eyes glittered. "A motorcar is hardly a toy."

"For you, it is. Why don't you spend some of this abundant free time you seem to have making friends or visiting or buying yourself some new clothes?" he asked irritably. "You're living in the city now, not feeding your chickens and washing clothes like a countrywoman."

In other words, she had to behave as if she were good enough to be married to a bank officer with a Harvard degree. She felt pure dislike for him.

"I shall try to give good value, sir," she said haughtily, and curtsied.

He looked as if he might like to give way to a string of curses, but before he could utter them, Claire beat an orderly retreat to her room and slammed the door behind her.

A minute later, she opened it again, red-faced and furious. "Just to set the record straight, I was driving Chester up from Colbyville with my wheel tied on to save you the freight charges. And also for the record let me tell you that I have no intention of terrorizing Atlanta or shocking your friends with Chester. I shall ride the trolley!"

And she slammed the door again.

John stared at the closed door with mingled reactions, the strongest of which was amusement. Claire was spirited, all right. It was a pity his heart was Diane's, because in many ways, Claire was his match.

He didn't really mind her playing around with the car, but only when he was with her, to protect her from her reckless nature. Besides, she had to learn to conform to his lifestyle. It wouldn't hurt her to be tamed, he thought, just a little. But all the same, he had to fight the very strong impulse to follow her into her bedroom and continue the argument. He found her stimulating in a temper. He wondered if the passion in her could be physical as well as verbal. Perhaps one day he'd be driven to find out.

4

After a sleepless night, Claire finally decided that if her husband wanted her to become a social butterfly, it might be to her advantage to accommodate him.

She'd never been a social climber, but she did have acquaintances among Atlanta's elite. The foremost of these was Mrs. Evelyn Paine, the wife of local railroad magnate Bruce Paine. She called upon her early one morning, cards in hand. But since Evelyn was in, there was no need to present her maid with the requisite two cards from a married woman, one for Evelyn, and one for her husband. Cards were only presented if the host or hostess was unavailable. And most cards carried an "at home" legend, stating when the holder would receive guests. Today was Evelyn's "at home" day.

She was received in the small parlor and given coffee and delicate little cakes while Mrs. Paine sprawled on her satin-covered divan in an expensive and beautiful silk-and-lace wrapper. She and Claire had met through Claire's uncle and found that they had quite a lot in common. Under other circumstances, they would probably have been close friends; Claire hadn't sought friendship because of Evelyn's higher social status. But Claire's skill with a needle had caught Evelyn's eye, and Claire had made any number of original gowns for her — and never used her relationship with Evelyn in any way to open doors for her. Now, however, she felt obliged to approach anyone who could help her make the best of her new place in society as the wife of a bank executive. John might not want her as a true wife, but she was going to show him that she was no shrinking Nellie, just the same. She was as good as any of his haughty friends, including the adored Diane!

"My dear, it's such an unexpected pleasure to see you," Evelyn drawled, smiling lazily. "I was about to call on you and see if you could design something very special for me for the Christmas ball at the governor's mansion. You see how much time I'm giving you to create it; it's almost three months away."

"I daresay I can do something very special with so much time," Claire promised.

"Then what can I do for you?"

Claire clutched her purse. "I want to join some societies," she said at once. "I'll work hard, and I'm not afraid to approach strangers for contributions. I'll bake cakes and pies, man stalls at bazaars, do anything I'm asked within reason."

Evelyn raised up on her elbow. "My dear, you sound positively frantic. May I ask the reason for this sudden flurry of ambition?"

"I want my husband to be proud of me," she said simply.

"Well, that is a laudable goal!" Evelyn sat up, stretching. "I do know several people on committees, and they always need volunteers." She smiled mischievously. "Count on me. I'll make sure you get the proper introductions — and to the very best people."

"Thank you."

Evelyn waved a languid hand. "No need for that. We women have to stick together."

Claire very quickly found herself in demand. Her days were full from morning until late afternoon, baking for cake sales, sorting clothes and whatnots for the fall bazaars, and wrapping bandages with her church group to send to the military in the Philippines and China for Christmas. She kept the apartment spotlessly clean, as well, and even found time to help Mrs. Dobbs bake. She felt obliged to do that, since she was having to borrow her landlady's woodstove to make her contributions to her various societies.

Mrs. Dobbs was impressed by the sort of women who began to call on Claire for tea. The names read like the roster of Atlanta society. The landlady began to dress more formally — and even to help Claire set up the tea tray, using her own best silver.

"I must say, Claire," Mrs. Dobbs told her one afternoon, "I'm very impressed with the company you've been keeping. Imagine! Mrs. Bruce Paine right here in my house! Why, her family and her husband's were founding families of Atlanta, and they keep company with people like the Astors and the Vanderbilts!"

"I've known Evelyn for several years," Claire confided. "She's a fine person, but for obvious reasons, I never tried to become a close friend."

"Well, that's all changed with your marriage, since Mr. Hawthorn is well-to-do and holds the position he does at the Peachtree City Bank."

Claire didn't exactly know that John was well-to-do, although he never seemed to lack money. He didn't discuss finances with her. She did know that his position at the bank was an important one. "Yes, I know. That's why I've tried so hard to find my way into the right social circles, so that I wouldn't make him ashamed of me."

"My dear," Mrs. Dobbs said gently, "no one would be ashamed of such a hardworking, kind young woman."

Claire flushed. Mrs. Dobbs always made her feel better. It was just as well that the starchy woman had been out of the house the day John and his business colleagues came home to find Claire in such a disreputable condition. "You're the kind one, Mrs. Dobbs — to give me such freedom in your house."

"It's been my pleasure. I must tell you, I've enjoyed the little savories left over from your efforts. Where did you learn to cook so well?"

"From my uncle's housekeeper," she recalled. "She was a wonderful cook — of the 'pinch of this and dab of that' variety."

"Now, I'm just the opposite. I can't cook without my measures." There was a knock at the door. "Ah, that will be your callers, Claire. I'll let them in."

Claire greeted Evelyn and her friends, Jane Corley and Emma Hawks, and introduced them to the flustered, beaming Mrs. Dobbs.

It made the landlady's day. She went off to bring in the tea tray in an absolute delirium of pleasure.

Later, after tea and cakes, Evelyn brought out a sketch from the leather writing case she carried.

"I'm no artist, but this is what I thought I'd like you to make me for the ball, Claire," she said, and handed the rough sketch to the younger woman. "What do you think?"

"Why, it's lovely," Claire said, nodding as she considered fabric and trim. "But this line, just here, won't do. A peplum is going to make you look chubby around the hips, which you certainly are not," she added with a grin.

Evelyn's eyes widened. "Why, you're right. I never noticed."

Claire took a pencil from the small porcelain bowl on the occasional table and erased the line. "And if we just add one flounce to the skirt, here . . ." She made another few strokes with the pencil, while Evelyn watched, amazed.

"There," she said, finished, and handed the sketch back. "What do you think? In black, of course — with silver trim and black jet beads on the bodice, just here?"

Evelyn was wordless. "Exquisite," she said finally. "Just exquisite."

"I've never seen anything so beautiful," Emma Hawkes exclaimed. "I buy all my clothes in Paris, but this is — this is extraordinary. How very talented you are, Claire!"

"Thank you," Claire replied demurely.

"Yes, I want this," Evelyn said immediately. "And I don't care about the cost."

"You will." Claire winked. "It's going to be quite expensive."

"Anything worth wearing to the governor's ball should be," came the reply.

Emma nibbled on her lower lip and glanced at Claire. "I suppose it will take all your time to make Evelyn's gown . . . ?"

"Not at all."

Emma brightened. "Then could you do one for me as well?"

"And one for me?" Jane added.

"Not of this design!" Evelyn cried, aghast.

"Certainly not," Claire said. "Each gown will be individual, and suited to its wearer. I'll work on the sketches and you can come Friday to approve them. How will that do?" she asked Jane and Emma.

"Wonderful," they said in unison, beaming.

Claire had very little free time after that. If

she wasn't baking or helping with some worthy charity, she was buried upstairs in her room with the sewing machine and what seemed like acres of fabric, sewing madly to meet her deadlines.

Of John, she saw little. That suited her very well, given their last conversation. She was still bristling from his disapproval. He seemed to avoid her afterward, but he chanced to come home early one Friday, and, since Claire's bedroom door was open, he went to speak to her.

The sight that met his eyes was a surprise. "What in God's name are you doing?" he asked curtly.

She'd been sewing an underskirt for Evelyn's gown, and thank God she had the rest of the project safely hidden in the closet. She didn't want John to know that she had a separate income from the household money he gave her. Her independence was sacred, and she wasn't sharing the news with the enemy.

"I'm making myself a dress," she said calmly.

His eyes narrowed. "You aren't living with your uncle now, Claire," he said. "You don't have to manage with homemade clothes. Go down to Rich's and buy yourself some clothes. I have an account there."

"I like to sew my own things."

His gaze went over the plain blue dress she was wearing, which was one of her older ones. It was faded, but very comfortable to work in. "So I see," he replied mockingly. "But that's hardly the sort of thing you need to wear in town."

Her chest rose and fell angrily. She'd make herself a gown for the governor's ball, too — and then he'd see something!

"Where in town did you have in mind?" she asked coolly. "You haven't take me out of the house since we married over a month ago."

He scowled. "Has it been so long?"

"It seems like much longer," she returned quietly. She pushed back a loose strand of brown hair. "If you don't mind, I'm quite busy. I'm sure you have some exalted function to attend, or a dinner with colleagues."

He leaned against the doorjamb and studied her. It hadn't seemed like a month. Claire had been conspicuously missing from their apartment — and his life — every time he looked for her lately. He'd supposed that she spent her time shopping, but she seemed to have nothing to show for it. There was the fabric she was working on, but it seemed an odd choice for a day dress . . . or for any kind of dress. It looked more like a slip.

His eyes darted around her room and found it neat and clean, but with very few obvious signs of occupation — save for the brush and hand mirror on her dresser, and the small porcelain powder and jewelry boxes.

"I hardly see you," he said absently.

"A blessing, I should think, considering the opinion you have of me and my wardrobe," she murmured as she continued to apply pressure to the treadle under her feet to move the needle along the seam.

He stuck his hands deep in his pockets, drawing the fabric taut against the powerful muscles of his thighs. "Well, one or two people have remarked upon the fact that we aren't seen at social functions. I suppose we should be more outgoing."

"Why?" she asked, lifting clear gray eyes to his. "Does someone think you've murdered me and buried my body in the garden?"

His mouth twitched. "I don't know. Perhaps I should ask."

She took the fabric from under the needle and cut the thread with her small pair of scissors, holding the seam up for critical inspection. "I'm quite content with my life as it is," she said, not looking at him. It made her heart skip to see the long, power-

91

ful lines of his body in that unconsciously elegant pose. He was so handsome. It took her breath away to look at him at all, but she couldn't let him see. She'd had quite enough taunts from him about her helpless attraction to him.

"Don't you miss pretty clothes and parties, Claire?" he asked.

"I've never had either, so why should I want them?"

He considered that for a minute. It was true. She'd never had much in the way of material things. Now she had access to them through him. So why wasn't she taking advantage of it? Diane would have. She'd gone on a shopping spree immediately after her marriage to Eli Calverson that still had tongues wagging today.

"Buy a new gown," he said abruptly. "There's a party at the Calversons' next Saturday evening, and we've been invited. Apparently Eli thinks you've had long enough to grieve for your uncle and become accustomed to marriage with me. He wants to introduce us both to a new investor. A very important one."

"Why us?"

"Because I'm vice president of the bank, Claire, and investors keep us solvent. This gentleman is the head of an investment firm, and he's very thick with Eli. Apparently, he's rich as Croesus."

"How nice for him. But I don't want to go to the Calversons'."

He took an impatient breath. "I've told you that I have no back-door dealings with Diane!"

She looked at him steadily. "So I should go with you and spend the evening watching you eat your heart out over the sight of her? No, thank you."

His eyes flashed angrily. "It would be far better than to spend the evening here, watching you eat your heart out over me," he countered icily.

She threw the underskirt down on the floor and got to her feet, her gray eyes like lead bullets as she went right up to him.

"I am not eating my heart out over you! I hardly see you, in any case. I have no secret hankering for such a conceited, overbearing —"

Suddenly he reached for her and pulled her against him. In his leaning position, she found herself pressed intimately to his long legs — in between them, in fact — with his arms wrapped tightly around her. The look on her face amused him, taking the heat out of his anger.

"Don't stop there," he invited, with a

smile. "Do go on."

She wanted to, but her heart was beating too rapidly to allow speech. The whalebone corset she was wearing constricted her breath enough, without the added pressure of his embrace. She could barely breathe at all.

Her hands pushed weakly at his chest. "Let go," she said faintly. "I can't . . . breathe."

"Relax, then."

"It's the corset," she whispered, pushing as hard as she could.

He loosened his arms. She felt his hands tracing the bones, his thumbs brushing up under her breasts in the muslin chemise that contained them above the edge of the corset. The light, teasing pressure made her stiffen with unexpected pleasure.

He was looking intently at her, watching her reactions as his lean hands teased her body.

His thumbs slipped higher with each movement. "Is this better?" he asked, and his voice was suddenly deeper, huskier.

She realized she was shaking. Her hands were clutching at his hard arms through his suit coat, and she couldn't even manage speech. The feel of him so close, the touch of his hands, made her knees weak. She loved him so much that even the lightest caress was heaven. She hadn't the will to pull away, despite the shame her easy capitulation caused. She wanted his touch too much to protest.

His lips brushed her forehead. He could sense her struggle. "I'm your husband. It's all right to give in to me, Claire," he murmured deeply. "God knows, I've given you little enough since we married. It's no hardship to pleasure you. I won't do anything to frighten or hurt you. Relax, now."

Her hands trembled where they clung to his arms. She wanted to deny that he was pleasing her, to tell him to let her go, but she couldn't. She had no pride. She moaned in anguish, drowning in the need to be touched by him, held by him, wanted by him.

He understood. He was as helpless in his passion for Diane as Claire was in her need of him. In that one way, they were very much alike. It hurt him in an odd, new way, to see her suffer for his touch. He felt her need and ached to fill it.

His lips hovered at her eyelids, closing them tenderly. His hands moved to the tips of her breasts and found the nipples hard and warm.

She jerked back, but he drew a breath and

shook his head, stilling her instinctive withdrawal. She met his eyes for an instant and found deep fires burning there.

In the silence of the room, the ticking of the clock on the mantel was unusually loud. Outside, the steady *clip-clop* of a horse and the grinding wheels of a carriage behind it could be heard. Above all that, Claire's heart made a rocky rhythm that was audible to the man holding her.

Her response, her reaction, made him dizzy. Diane was so experienced that his touch only made her purr like a kitten. Claire was altogether different. He didn't have to ask to know that she'd never permitted any other man to touch her like this. She'd probably never been kissed, either. The knowledge shook him.

He watched what he could see of her downcast face while he teased her hard nipples, feeling her body tremble with each new caress. She liked what he was doing, but she was too shy to admit it, or let him see it.

His hands slid up to the buttons at the high collar of her dress and, one by one, began to unfasten them. She stood before him, perfectly still and silent, so caught up in the excitement of her first caresses that, he knew, she was incapable of movement or speech.

When he had the bodice unfastened to her waist, his warm, strong hands slid inside the neckline and spread the fabric before they eased down over the soft muslin of her chemise. He heard her breathing stop and then start again, jerkily, felt her hands contract even more on his arms. Smiling indulgently, he moved his hands slowly under the muslin and down, down until he had her soft, pretty little breasts warm and throbbing in his palms. He heard her gasp and felt his own body go rigid, and he laughed with surprise at how easily little Claire had aroused him.

"Oh, you . . . mustn't!" she whispered frantically, pulling at his wrists.

"Claire, you're my wife," he whispered, ignoring her protests. His hands became even more warm and caressing and his lips brushed against her forehead, her temples, her nose. "This is part of marriage," he continued softly, as his mouth moved down to poise, teasingly, just above her lips. "This is how a man expresses tenderness." His mouth eased down right over her own, lightly brushing until he made her lips part. "Yes, that's it, sweetheart. Open your mouth," he coaxed against her lips, and then he moved closer again, and kissed her as a lover.

Claire had never experienced such sensations. She trembled as his mouth became part of hers, lost in the pleasure his hands were arousing on her naked breasts, adrift in the sheer sweet anguish of his hard, insistent kiss.

She never wanted it to end. She whimpered from the force of the pleasure he inspired in her. She felt his hands on her upper arms, guiding them up around his neck. She felt his body shift, so that she was completely between his long, powerful legs. His free hand slid down to the base of her spine and pushed her hips into the sudden hard thrust of his. Her head spun. She knew nothing of men's bodies, but his felt different all at once, and her legs started to tremble. There was a burst of heat in her lower stomach, along with a thrill of pleasure that brought a shocked gasp from her mouth.

He lifted his head and looked into her wide, stunned eyes. Holding her gaze, he deliberately moved her hips against his and felt her shudder with need.

As she struggled to speak, his gaze fell to her bodice. Gently, one lean hand came up to pull the muslin down, baring the hard red peaks of her firm breasts to his eyes.

His breath caught. "Oh, God, Claire!" he whispered roughly. Desire for her over-whelmed him.

She had no idea what had caused him to look so violent. He sounded shocked, and the hands gripping her waist were hurting her. "What's wrong?" she whispered shak-ily, because he looked as if he were hurting.

"Don't you know?" He lifted dark eyes filled with heat and pain to meet hers.

She hung there, frightened, fascinated, with the sound of her heartbeat loud in her ears. She wanted to ask him what she'd done wrong, but as her lips parted to make the words, there was a sudden loud knock at the door of their apartment.

John actually jerked, as if he'd been hit. His hands contracted and suddenly let go. He moved away from Claire as if it hurt him to walk. His movements were stiff and awkward as he went to the apartment door and opened it just a crack.

"Yes?" he asked curtly.

"Oh . . . Mr. Hawthorn . . . I didn't hear you come in . . ." Mrs. Dobbs was flustered by the bite in his voice. "I wanted to you that I've set the table in the f ing room for you and Claire this I'm having some women friends bridge and we'll be taking our meal in the kitchen."

He seemed stuck for a reply. After a minute, he said, "We could very easily have our meal up here, so that it wouldn't inconvenience you."

"I wouldn't hear of it," she said cheerfully. "You both can come down whenever you're ready. I've made a cherry pie especially for Claire. I know how much she likes it."

She was gone with a wave of her hand.

John closed the door and leaned his head against it, fighting against the most powerful desire he'd felt since his youth. Claire didn't understand what she'd done to him, and he was certain that he didn't want to tell her just yet. He was still coping with the shock of it.

When he turned, she'd redone her buttons and was picking up the underskirt from the floor. He stared at her as if he hadn't ever seen her before. It stunned him that she had such an effect on him. Perhaps it was the soft, helpless devotion and longing in those gray eyes that kindled his desire to such a feverish pitch. Being loved was affecting, apparently. But what disturbed him most was that he should feel such a powerful hunger for anyone other than Diane.

It must have been a fluke, he told himself

as he moved toward the doorway, back in control now and angry at her submission and his response to it.

She glanced toward his angry face and away again, still hot inside. "You needn't look as if the whole thing was my fault. I never held a gun to you to make you touch me. And I don't need your pity, either, while we're on the subject." She was seething with humiliation. Her eyes sparked with temper. "I'm not dying for your kisses, and I won't beg for them!"

He recognized the hurt under the words. She was more vulnerable than any woman he'd ever known, but she was fiercely proud and didn't like people to see her weaknesses. He understood that feeling.

"It was a moment out of time," he said gently. He felt protective of her. "Don't agonize over what happened."

Nervous, she wrapped and unwrapped the underskirt in her hands.

"Aren't you hungry?" he asked after a pause. "I hardly had time for lunch. Mrs. Dobbs made you a cherry pie."

"I like it."

He smiled indulgently. "I know."

She averted her gaze and put the skirt down. "I suppose it wouldn't hurt to eat something." She looked in the mirror and grimaced at the way his hands had disarranged her hair into wild tangles, the way his lips had made hers swollen. She groaned in sweet memory.

"Claire, we're married," he emphasized, watching her carefully bundle her hair. "People expect us to act like it occasionally."

She lowered her gaze. "You don't want to be married to me. You said so."

"I also said that we might as well make the best of it," he added. "A few kisses won't make you pregnant," he teased wickedly.

"John!"

He enjoyed her scarlet blush. He enjoyed so much about her. His eyes glittered with sudden intentness as he watched her complete her toilette. He'd never given much thought to her place in his life. He'd been far too busy mourning Diane. But now, as he looked at Claire, he felt the first stirrings of pride in possession. She belonged to him. She was innocent and kind and mischievous, and she loved him. There had never been a man, because she wanted only him. It went to his head like wine. Diane had flirted, withdrawn from him, in a game of love. Claire had no knowledge of such games. She was completely honest and open with him, devoid of coquetry. How very different she was from the sleek, experienced women who had walked through his life. For a moment, he wondered how it might have been if he and Diane had never met, and he could have come to Claire heart-whole. Perhaps he would have fallen in love with her.

As it was, he felt a sudden, fierce attraction to Claire — and possessive and protective of her. As he stared down at her flushed, dear face, he wondered why he'd never noticed that little dimple in her chin, or the way her mouth curved so sweetly. Her figure was all a man could ask for, nicely rounded — even if a bit on the thin side. She wasn't beautiful, but she had beautiful qualities.

He fought a stirring of desire for her that rose like a tide in his blood. How unexpected, to feel that for his own wife. What might happen if he gave in to it fully?

There was Diane, though. He turned away from Claire, more confused than ever.

5

Claire learned new things about John every day. He was a studious, quiet man for the most part. He liked to play chess and he loved railroads and trains. Often when he was home, she found him standing on the balcony watching the trains go slowly down the tracks toward the freight yards. She wondered if he'd ever entertained dreams, as many boys did, of becoming an engineer. But he didn't talk to her of his past at all.

He did let things slip from time to time that he must have learned during his military career. He knew which medals were which, and how to distinguish one uniform from another. He knew quite a lot about military history, reading a great deal, she noted, about strategy and tactics. And he seemed to relish perusal of his collection of biographies about great military leaders.

He was fastidious to a fault about his personal appearance. His hair was always clean and combed, his fingernails immaculate and trimmed. His shoes were so polished that they reflected. The crease in his trousers was perfect. He never looked disheveled or rumpled — all due, she guessed, to that military background that he wouldn't talk about.

There was so much that she didn't know about him. She wondered if there had been women besides Diane in his past, and reasoned that there probably had. He looked at her with a sort of sensual wisdom from time to time that made her knees go weak. He hadn't learned that in banking. And he was careful to open doors for her, help her into carriages, walk to the street side of her on the infrequent occasions when they strolled together on nice fall days. His family must have taught him exquisite manners. He also had a strong sense of right and wrong, and he was honest to a fault.

But he kept his distance. There were no more passionate kisses or even familiar touches. They were as apart as if they'd never married. He'd withdrawn from her at a time when they were just beginning to grow closer.

Part of her understood his attitude. He loved Diane. Perhaps in some queer way it made him feel that he had been unfaithful to Diane when he had kissed Claire, even though Claire was his wife. It was so sad that he'd married her in the first place, feeling so deeply and strongly about someone else.

The real tragedy was the way Claire felt about him. She loved him with all her heart. There had never been any other man in her thoughts, in her life. He knew that. It probably flattered him. But on the other hand, it must have been unpleasant, as well, to have the responsibility for someone's happiness, when it was a woman he didn't, couldn't, love.

And despite his courtesy, the everyday things that any cherished woman would expect from her husband weren't forthcoming. He never brought her flowers or little, inexpensive presents. He never sought her out, just to talk. He never took her to the opera or the theater or even out for a meal unless it was connected somehow with the bank's business. He never commented on her clothing or paid her compliments.

Only once did she get a glimpse of the real man that John was under the intangible mask he wore, and that was when a tall, lean, very dark-haired man in a military dress uniform came by the apartment house and asked for him.

Claire stared at the man as if he weren't quite real. "Well, my husband is at work. At — at the Peachtree City Bank," she said falteringly.

The man, very formal, with his cap tucked under his arm, smiled at her faintly; his green eyes glittered with amusement. "You are his wife? I must say, it delights me that you aren't fair and petite, madam. The last time I saw John, he was mourning his ex-fiancée and threatening to shoot her husband."

That was news, and not welcome news. Claire's face fell.

"Forgive me," he said quickly. "Permit me to introduce myself. I am Lt. Col. Chayce Marshal, United States Army." He presented her with his card and made her a formal bow. "I have been serving in the Philippines. I was wounded and only have recently recovered enough to go back to duty and assume my next post, but I wanted to call on John before I left the city. I have very little time."

"May I offer you tea or coffee?" she asked more wistfully than she knew. It was a very lonely life that she led outside the small circle of women with whom she worked on charitable events.

He smiled. "It would be a pleasure. I don't

suppose that you could send word to John?"

"Why, yes, I could," she said. "Mrs. Dobbs has a telephone. I'll ask her to contact the bank and tell him that you're here."

He grinned widely. "That would be wonderful."

She went to find Mrs. Dobbs, to ask for a pot of coffee, which he said he preferred, and for sliced cakes. It was almost midday, so Mrs. Dobbs also offered a meal, which he declined.

Mrs. Dobbs rejoined them shortly with a tray of cake and coffee.

"Mr. Hawthorn was delighted to hear of your arrival," she told the army officer, "and he's on his way home right now."

"Thank you," he said. "And for such a lavish feast, as well."

"This is just some pound cake and some freshly baked bread," Mrs. Dobbs murmured, blushing. "But I hope you find it edible."

"Don't be silly, Mrs. Dobbs." Claire chuckled. "Everything you cook is delicious."

"How very kind of you." The older woman beamed. "Well, I'll be in the kitchen if you need me."

She left, and Claire poured coffee for herself and the colonel.

"How long have you and John been married?" he asked.

"Let me see. It's the second week of November . . . Almost two months," she replied.

"I see. Well, do you own this house, then?"

"No. John has rooms here on the second floor," she said conversationally. Her face was lowered as she poured coffee into the thin china cups, so she didn't see the surprise on her companion's face. "He said that a house was unnecessary."

"Thank you," he said, and picked up his cup without adding either cream or sugar. His green eyes were thoughtful as they searched Claire's wan face. "Have you known him long?"

"Several years," she said, surprising him further. "My uncle died recently, but he and John were good friends as well as banker and client. When my uncle died, I was left destitute. John proposed and I accepted." She looked up with a smile. "So you see, it was not an affair of the heart with us. It was . . . a business relationship."

He had to bite back a comment.

"Forgive me," Claire said. "It was the way you looked, as if you couldn't understand why John would marry someone as plain as me."

He was taken aback by her frankness. "I could hardly think of you as plain," he said gallantly. He studied her with unblinking intensity. "I can't imagine John marrying any woman out of pity alone."

"Nor did he," she replied. "There was scandalous gossip about him and his now-married ex-fiancée."

"I see." He smiled. "It pleases me that you trust me enough on such short acquaintance to be so honest with me."

"Honesty is a fault of mine," she confessed. "I never feel the need to dance around unpleasant topics. Even if I offend people, they know exactly where they stand with me."

He burst out laughing. "Do you know, that's why John and I became friends when we were first in the service together. He spoke his mind and so did I. We were kindred spirits. I don't believe I've ever heard him tell an overt lie. I don't think he could."

She had to admit that he'd been just as honest with her about his feelings for Diane. She sipped coffee for a moment. "Was John a good soldier?"

"A good officer," he corrected. "And yes, he was. Few men are more suited to the military life than John. It hurt him to give it up, I think. But he couldn't bear the memories."

"What memories?" she asked quickly.

He smiled. "No, you don't. I won't share John's secrets with you. He must do that himself."

"Then I can assure you, I'll live out my life without knowing. He tells me nothing about himself."

"You are newly married," he pointed out. "Wait a few years."

"And you think it will bring him to speak about himself?" She laughed coolly. "Hardly. Everything I know I have learned by observation. He likes military history," she recounted, "also biographies and railroads."

"Yes." He smiled. "He knows most of the railroad lines in this part of the country and their routes, as well as some of the engineers who run the trains. He has some expertise in the area of colonial Georgia history, as well, and a working knowledge of skirmishes between the Georgia militia and the Creek and Cherokee and Seminole Indians."

She smiled. "How exciting."

"You might ask him to tell you about the 'red sticks' one day, when you need a topic to help pass the time."

She leaned forward intently. "Red sticks?"

"Renegades who left their tribes and

formed a confederation to try and defeat the whites who were taking over their ancestral lands. For instance, did you know that *Baton Rouge* means *red stick?*"

She caught her breath. "Why, how very interesting! And he likes ships, too. He has an intricate model of the *Cutty Sark* inside a bottle."

"Yes, he built it."

She all but gasped. "That tiny thing?"

"He loves sailing," he told her. "The sea haunts him. But he never liked the navy because it would involve spending too much time away from land. John was a keen horseman and loved to ride before the war. He was a cavalry officer."

"I don't think that he rides now," she remarked.

"He had a bad experience with a horse in Cuba," Chayce Marshal said slowly. "It balked at the lines and was shot out from under him. His leg was pinned and the Spanish Army got a little too close." He shrugged. "Several of us went to his rescue, but he never forgot the incident. I think he hates horses now."

"I didn't realize there were horses in Cuba."

"We shipped mounts over for the officers," he told her. "Sadly, many of them were eaten in the days after the war when food was so scarce and people were starving."

"I read the dispatches in the local paper when the war was raging in Cuba," she told him. "They were full of sad stories. And it sounds as if it was much worse in the Philippines."

"It still is," he said shortly, and for an instant, the horror of that continuing conflict was in his eyes. What he'd seen was no fit talk for women's ears. Cuba had been bad, but the Philippines was hell itself. "I deeply regret being denied a chance to go back there and support my men. It was a wicked thrust of fate that I should have been wounded."

"Aren't you going back?" she queried.

He shook his head. "I have an uncertain temper and the courage of my convictions," he said amusedly. "I made enemies of all the wrong people — and now I'm being assigned as instructor to a bunch of green cadets. Pray God I can instruct them well, so that they don't go into battle and die as so many of the young cadets under my command did."

"Yes." She searched his face. "It must have been a terrible time."

"It was. War is never glorious, Mrs. Hawthorn. It is only a facade of glitter over an

113

ugly, red wound." He chuckled. "Forgive me. I become fanciful."

"Oh, I could listen to you all day. How very knowledgeable you are!"

He stopped feeding her facts and studied her animated face. She was pretty when she was excited, and she was the best female listener he'd ever encountered. "Lucky John, to have so willing an audience," he murmured.

"I expect he's always had a willing audience when it comes to women," she said bitterly.

He cleared his throat and sipped some more coffee, unwilling to put his head into that particular verbal noose.

"I've embarrassed you," she said at once. "Forgive me. I do tend to ramble."

"Dear lady, I've spent most of my life in the military," he said, giving her a droll smile. "I don't think I can be embarrassed anymore. However —" he paused, his eyes twinkling "— please feel free to try."

"Why, Colonel . . . are you flirting with me?" she asked demurely, and colored.

It was unfortunate that John should come in the door at that particular moment. Claire's red cheeks and the colonel's teasing expression didn't improve his disposition one bit. It had been an altogether dif-

114

ficult morning and it seemed bent on worsening.

But he kept his irritation to himself and went forward — with every appearance of happiness — to meet his old friend.

"Chayce!" he said, holding out his hand.

The two men shook hands and patted each other on the shoulders warmly.

"God, it's been such a long time," John said.

"Two years," Chayce said. He sighed. "It's good to see you again. I'm on my way to Charleston, and I thought I'd look in on you as I passed through Atlanta."

"Charleston?"

Chayce smiled coldly. "I'm to teach cadets," he said. "Ironic, isn't it — after years on the front lines of battle! I made some enemies in Washington by speaking my mind, you see."

"I'm not surprised." John chuckled. "You never were one to pull your punches."

"I made my support of William Jennings Bryan a little too well known, and I joined the anti-imperialist movement. The senior officers felt that I should have kept quiet. McKinley has just won the election and I am disgraced."

"Your political views should be your own business," John remarked. "I say that even

115

though I supported McKinley."

"Yes, because of Roosevelt getting the vice presidency. Served beside him, didn't you?" John nodded and Chayce said, "Well, we can agree to disagree."

"Just what I was about to say!" John sat back and took the coffee cup that Claire had filled for him. He didn't meet her eyes. He was too unsettled. She'd never flirted with him, but she seemed to find no difficulty doing it with Chayce, who was a ladies' man for real. "What will you teach?" he continued.

"Strategy and tactics," Chayce replied. "I've learned a lot from some of the career soldiers I met while I was serving in Arizona, and then in the Philippines. Many of them were veterans of the Indian wars out West." He spoke intently. "You'd be amazed at how canny those Plains Indians were in battle. And Geronimo led the U.S. Army a merry chase until his final surrender in '86. I was stationed in Arizona, but I never fought Indians." He sighed. "Although I served with men who did."

"I remember one of them — Jared Dunn, who lives in New York City. I had a card from him at Christmas last year."

"So did I," Chayce recalled fondly. "Dunn was a character. I hope he's put his gun away for good now."

"His service revolver, you mean?" Claire interjected.

Chayce chuckled. "No, his six-gun. Dunn was a gunfighter and then a Texas Ranger. I think you might say that he led a colorful life before he settled down to practice law in New York City."

"I wouldn't call him settled," John said. "He still has a reputation for shooting straight when it's called for, and he takes a lot of cases outside of the city."

"Not a job I'd like," Chayce remarked. "The law is dry as dust. I much prefer the military life. Don't you miss it?" he fired at John suddenly.

"I miss it every day I draw breath," John replied curtly. "But I can't go back, and you know why."

"Time heals all wounds," Chayce said solemnly. "And your record was exemplary. I spoke with one old colonel who said he still mourned your decision not to reenlist after you were mustered out, when you decided to go to Harvard."

"Colonel Wayne?"

Chayce nodded. "He was an exceptional commander. He knows more than I ever will have time to learn about frontline skirmishes." He shrugged. "But he likes his

Montana ranch and has no interest in moving East."

"How are you going to tolerate Charleston after Arizona?" John asked.

Chayce grimaced. "About as well as Geronimo and his Chiricahua Apache liked being marooned in St. Augustine, I expect. Desert dwellers don't cotton to damp rot."

"Charleston has its good points. I lived there for several years and loved it," John recalled.

"You loved the sea," Chayce reminded him. "I remember hearing you talk about all the sailing you used to do with your father and brothers as a boy. But I hate it."

"You'll have plenty of years to learn to love it."

Chayce sighed. "I hope not."

"Give it time. You'll work your way back into favor one day."

Chayce shrugged. "So they say."

He stayed only a little longer and then declared that he had to be on his way, so that he didn't miss his train.

"It's been swell seeing you again," he told John as they shook hands out on the sidewalk where a carriage had been summoned and was waiting for Chayce. "Take care of your wife. She's a treasure."

"Thank you, Colonel," Claire replied, with

a smile. "It was a pleasure to have met you. Do stop by the next time you come this way."

"Perhaps by then you'll have a proper house and a yardful of children," Chayce remarked, but he was looking at John, not Claire, when he said it. "Please thank Mrs. Dobbs for the delicious cake, Claire, and keep well. So long."

John pulled his pocket watch out and glanced at it. "I'll share your carriage. I have to get back to the bank," he said. He glanced at Claire. "I'll be late. Don't wait supper."

He climbed in beside Chayce. The door closed. The carriage took off down the street. Claire stood on the sidewalk looking after it. She'd learned something new about her husband, but it would do her no good at all. If he'd cared for her, she'd have learned those things from him, and not had to find them out from his old friend Chayce.

Amazingly, the next day John actually took her riding. He left his office just after noon and hired a carriage with a driver.

"I thought it might be nice for you to get out of the house for a bit," he explained when she appeared shocked by his suggestion.

"We — we never go anywhere together," she stammered.

"What about the bank social Saturday night?" he asked.

She smiled. "Well, there's that."

He handed her into the carriage and climbed in beside her, his eyes approving of her black suit with its natty white trim and her matching hat. She had incredible dress sense — when she wasn't working on that silly automobile or riding that cursed wheel. She only rode it around the property, but she often fell off, and it was a high one. He felt guilty about puncturing one of her tires and then lying about having no time to get it patched for her. She wouldn't know that he was concerned for her welfare. More and more, the idea of Claire being hurt in any way, physically or emotionally, was disturbing to him.

They talked about Atlanta and its tempestuous past, talking about more recent events like the unusual house on Peachtree Street, the "house that Jack built," and the famous Tally-ho wagon of the Driving Club that a retired military man used to carry pretty debutantes and visiting dignitaries racing along the streets. The coach was pulled by white horses and regal in its livery, and a silver trumpet sounded its approach.

"What a fabulous city this is," Claire said.

"And what a future it has," John replied.

"We make long-term as well as short-term loans to businesses, and we're showing huge profits." Well, on paper, at least, he added to himself, putting aside some nagging worries about the bank's finances that he wasn't going to share with Claire.

"Oh, John, look!" She grabbed his arm unconsciously, wincing as she saw a carriage just ahead of them collide with a dog and knock it to the roadside. It kept going. "The animal! How could they leave it! John, do stop," she pleaded.

"Of course we'll stop," he said, equally incensed. He banged on the top of the coach with his cane, tossed his hat aside, and unbuttoned his jacket and discarded it before he followed Claire out of the carriage. He rolled up his sleeves on the way.

The animal was yelping in pain. John knelt beside it and his hands gently felt for breaks in its ribs and legs while it tried feebly to snap at him.

"It's his leg," John said after a minute. "I'll need a splint and some gauze."

"It's in pain."

"Yes, I know. But there's very little I can do about that," he said apologetically.

"Beauregard!" a sobbing, elderly voice called. A tiny little old woman with white hair came down the path from an imposing brick home. She leaned heavily on a cane. "Oh, dear. Oh, dear," she said, wiping away tears. She looked at John helplessly. "Will he die?" she asked resignedly.

"Certainly not," John said gently. "He has a broken leg and he's in some pain. Have you gauze and something I can use for a splint?"

"Oh, are you a doctor?" the old woman asked.

"No, but I've patched up enough wounded men in my time. I know what to do. I'll carry him."

"You'll get dirty, young man," the old lady said worriedly.

He chuckled. "Yes, I probably will."

He bent and picked up the poor animal, very careful not to jostle him any more than necessary. The animal was still whimpering, but he was no longer trying to bite.

Claire's eyes adored her husband. She'd always thought him a kind man, but seeing this tender side of him made her heart ache. All the way to the house, she reassured the worried owner of the dog, recalling her own pets who had survived worse mishaps. By the time they reached the elegant house, the old woman had stopped crying.

"I can't thank you both enough for stopping," the old woman said as they walked

122

up the steps. "Beauregard was given to me by my late husband. He's all I have. I saw that carriage hit him and drive on. I know whose carriage it is, too. It belongs to that commercial banker, that Wolford man."

"Our competition." John chuckled. "Yes, I know him."

"He would not loan a starving beggar a nickel," the lady said. She glanced curiously at John. "And to which bank do you belong, young man?"

"I am vice president of the Peachtree City Bank," he replied.

"Ah." She smiled.

John didn't understand that smile, but he quickly became too occupied with the poor dog to analyze it. They put the animal on the porch, and when the materials he required were fetched, he set the animal's broken leg securely.

"He lives in the house," the elderly lady said. "I'll keep him warm and fed and watered — and I won't let him move around any more than necessary. I can never thank you enough."

"This may sound wicked," John said, "but if you can give him a little whiskey, it might help the pain."

She grinned. "I have several bottles of my husband's best. I shall take your advice."

She petted the dog gently. He was lying still, shivering a little, but not whimpering.

"Here," John said, picking the animal up once more. "Show me where you want him."

She led the way inside, with Claire and John right behind her. On the way, a huge painting over the fireplace caught Claire's eye and she flushed as she recognized the subject. She didn't say a word as she watched John place the animal gently on the rug at the hearth, where a fire was going.

"Old bones get cold. He'll be happy here." The old lady extended a hand, which John kissed with gentle sophistication, smiling at the elderly woman's quick flush.

"I hope he does well."

"Thank you for your help, young man. It won't be forgotten."

"It was the least anyone could have done."

"Yes, but no one else did it." She showed them both to the front door and watched them down the drive with a smile.

"Do you know who that was?" Claire whispered frantically to him before they reached the carriage.

"Of course I do," he said. "But I didn't when we stopped. She's quite a character. And stories are still told about her husband. He was a Civil War general."

"Yes, I know, I've read about him." She also knew that the elderly lady was the richest widow in town.

He chuckled. "I had no idea whose house that was, or whose dog. Poor old Wolford. If he only knew whose dog he abandoned to its pain . . ."

"She smiled."

He nodded. "A kind but vengeful woman. His bank will suffer, I'm afraid."

"And so it should," Claire said hotly. "Imagine! Hitting the poor animal and just driving on!"

He stopped at the carriage, pausing long enough to thank the driver for waiting so patiently.

"No problem at all, sir," the man said stoically. "I seen what happened. It takes a heartless man to leave an animal in such pain."

"Yes, it does," John agreed. He put Claire into the carriage and climbed in beside her. The front of his shirt was soiled and wet. He unbuttoned it a little to move the wet part aside.

Claire's eyes were drawn to his broad, hair-roughened chest, and she couldn't help but stare. She'd never seen a man without his shirt.

He cocked an eyebrow and chuckled.

"Life is all lessons, isn't it, Claire?" He caught her hand and drew her closer in the cozy confines of the carriage. His fingers guided hers against the muscular wall of his chest into the thick mat of black hair.

Her fingers jerked at first, but he flattened her palm there and moved it sensuously on his warm flesh. His breathing changed suddenly.

She looked up into his dark eyes and found them smoldering.

"You . . . like it?" she asked uncertainly.

"I like it." He took the other hand and put it with the first, but the gloves irritated him. He stripped them off and tossed them onto her lap before he placed her bare hands against him. His chest expanded with the feel of her flesh against his.

"Yes, that's how I wanted your hands on me," he said, bending his head. He kissed her, his mouth half open, teasing, demanding.

"John?" Her voice was a bare squeak.

"Claire!"

He caught her to him, turning her across his lap. The kiss became deep, invasive, and he moved her hands on his body until she understood what he wanted. His heartbeat shook both of them. Seconds later, he drew back slightly and guided her lips down to his chest, arching back, shivering as he felt them on his bare skin.

The sudden jolt of the carriage made them draw apart. They looked at each other as the carriage began to slow, then realized almost simultaneously that they were nearly home.

Claire jerked away from him, flustered and wide-eyed.

"It's all right," he said, with more composure than he actually had.

She retrieved her hat from the floor while he pulled his sleeves down, buttoned his wet shirt, and put his jacket and hat back on.

Their appearance left much to be desired. He liked her disheveled. His body was aching from frustrated desire, but he felt both affection and amusement as he looked at Claire's guilty expression.

"No one will lecture us about the way we look. We're married," he said, teasing.

"Yes." She pulled her gloves back on with fumbling hands.

He touched her cheek gently. "You are a delight to kiss, Mrs. Hawthorn," he said softly. "You look adorable."

She flushed and smiled, confused as she'd never been.

He chuckled. "And now we really had better go inside."

He paid the driver and helped her out, his eyes unusually tender. He even held her arm as they went into the house, pausing only long enough to speak to Mrs. Dobbs before going upstairs.

But once they were in their apartment, John suddenly grew remote. He realized he'd forgotten Diane altogether for the afternoon, and wondered how he could have done such a thing. He smiled vacantly at Claire and went to his own room with the excuse that he had to clean up.

When he emerged, he was the man he'd always been — courteous and friendly, but detached. Claire wondered if she'd dreamed the whole episode in the carriage. It was a sad end to a wonderful day.

6

Over the next few days, Claire noticed a definite shift in her relationship with her taciturn husband. After his friend's visit and their shared adventure in the carriage, John seemed much more approachable — almost watchful. They had most meals together now. But the growing camaraderie vanished when she asked if they were going to the governor's ball at Christmas. He suddenly clammed up as if she'd asked him for state secrets.

She couldn't know that it was painful for him to consider that annual event, because his parents were always invited. He hadn't seen them since his abrupt departure from home two years before, and he was reluctant to resurrect old wounds in a public place. But his presence would be expected as an officer of the largest bank in the city — and the one, incidentally, favored by the governor himself.

Because Claire knew nothing of her husband's background, she had no idea how it affected him to be an outcast in his family — or even that he was an outcast. Her fears were that he might be ashamed of her somehow, and that was why he didn't want to go to the ball. She wasn't really in his social class, and he'd never seen her properly dressed for an evening out. Perhaps after seeing her grimy from working on the automobile, and even in her comfortable day clothes, he might think she lacked proper dress sense.

Well, she had every certainty of showing him how carefully she could dress and groom herself, because she already had the design and the cloth for her own gown. She would make something that would raise eyebrows, something even more spectacular than the gowns she was sewing for Evelyn and the other society women. She'd show her husband, by hook or crook, that she could compete with his lovely Diane!

He hadn't mentioned the other woman recently. She knew that he occasionally saw her, because she often accompanied her husband to the bank. But he never mentioned either Diane or any dealings he had with her. As he'd promised at their wedding, he wasn't going to cheat on Claire.

The sad thing was that he didn't love her, Claire reflected. She'd married hoping for a miracle, but her marriage had only led to more heartache. And now that she knew how it felt to be kissed by her elusive husband, things were ever so much worse for her. He had only kindness and teasing affection to give her, while she hungered for him and loved him more fully than before. Life, she thought wistfully, could be so difficult.

Saturday arrived, and Claire steeled herself for an evening with the Calversons and the investment-firm owner whom Mr. Calverson was courting.

Claire hadn't had time to make herself a dress for the occasion because she was so involved sewing Evelyn's, Jane's, and Emma's dresses for the governor's ball, so she'd taken John's invitation to heart and bought one for herself at Rich's on Whitehall Street. The store's elegant black-and-gold interior had delighted Claire's sense of fashion and color, and the plate-glass windows that adorned it were filled with exciting displays.

Enchanted by her surroundings, she found the very dress she was looking for, a deep emerald green with jet beads and a lacy overlay on the low-cut bodice. The straps were velvet and satin, the trim around the bottom of the gown in the same jet beads as the bodice. The dress had been quite expensive, but it turned her gray eyes green and enhanced her complexion. She stared at herself in her long oval mirror with fascination. She didn't look so bad when she dressed up. She had her mother's marcasite-and-onyx necklace and earrings, too, which matched her gown beautifully. John was going to be surprised, she thought.

And he was. He stared at her in their parlor with narrow dark eyes that took in every line of her slender body in the well-fitted dress.

"Where did you get that?" he asked abruptly.

"Rich's. Do you like it?"

Like it! The silhouette of the gown enhanced her perfect hourglass figure, and the neckline drooped to show the soft curves of her white breasts. Her arms were bare, as he'd never seen them, and they were round and white and soft above the white gloves she wore with her gown. She hadn't used lip rouge, but her pretty lips were red just the same, and her cheeks were pink with excitement. In her hair, she wore an egret, a heron plume on a jet-jeweled comb. She was breathtaking and very stylish, for a woman who'd been raised in the country, outside society.

"You look very nice," he said formally.

She could have said the same about him. Dark clothes suited him. He was devastating in white tie, but she was too shy to tell him that.

"Thank you," she said politely, gripping her small purse.

"Shall we go?"

He opened the door and escorted her down to the waiting carriage. She was very nervous and kept picking at her purse for something to keep her hands busy. She wasn't overly fond of Eli Calverson, and she had grave misgivings about John's reaction to Diane. Claire knew that she might look passable in a nice gown, but she was no match for the elegant and beautiful Diane. Only love would have given her the edge, and she didn't have John's.

"How many people will be there?" she asked after a long silence, broken only by the sound of the horses' hooves on the cobblestone street.

"Just the Calversons, Mr. Whitfield and his wife and son, and us."

"Oh."

"It's a small, intimate gathering, not a party," he returned gently, flicking lint from his sleeve. He glanced at her approvingly. "Oh, and one other thing, Claire," he added, leaning toward her with a wicked smile. "Please refrain from making remarks about the motorcar."

She glared at him. "Why?"

"Because Calverson thinks they're inventions of the devil, that's why. Bankers have to bow to convention to get business. Speaking of which," he said suddenly, "do you remember the dog whose leg I mended?"

"Yes."

"Well, the lady who owns him withdrew every penny she had in old Wolford's bank and deposited it in ours." He chuckled at Claire's delighted expression. "That will show him to take a little more care with his driving."

"Indeed it will. How delightful for your bank!"

"Calverson thought so, as well. Although," he added, "I would have stopped just as quickly had she been a poor woman."

"I knew that already, John," Claire said. Her soft eyes lingered on his face, and he had to forcibly tear his own away from that adoration. He found himself thinking less often of Diane lately, although his heart was still sore from her loss. Claire was a charming companion. At times, he wondered what

134

it would be like to have a real marriage with her. He thought more about it when he didn't see Diane. He had been looking forward to tonight's dinner, in any case, because his heart fed on the mere sight of her. But Claire's appearance made him feel a sense of pride in his young wife. She would turn heads tonight.

It didn't take long to get to the huge Calverson mansion. It had gingerbread woodwork and turret rooms, and it looked like a castle. As Claire mounted the front steps on John's arm, she thought that it would never suit her; it was far too flashy. But Diane needed a showcase, and certainly this was it. Crystal chandeliers blazed through every long window, past exquisite white curtains. Even the staircase inside was hand-carved mahogany.

Diane came to meet them, barely managing a curt greeting for Claire before she went to John with her heart in her eyes and looked up at him with a hand on his sleeve.

"I'm so glad you could come,' she said in her soft, husky voice. "Both of you," she added reluctantly, glancing at Claire. "Mr. Whitfield's business is so important to us right now. I hope you'll both do your best to make him feel at home in Atlanta, and with the bank."

"Certainly we will, my dear," John said. His tone of voice was different when he spoke to Diane. His eyes as he looked at her were suddenly hungry and hot and full of pain. He tensed, because he hadn't expected the feeling to rise in him so powerfully.

Diane saw it and her own eyes sparkled. She smiled coquettishly. "Why, John. You mustn't look at me that way," she whispered quickly, glancing toward the parlor door and totally unconcerned with Claire's reaction to the byplay. "We must be careful. Eli already suspects —"

Before she could say another word, Eli Calverson came out into the hall to greet their guests, motioning impatiently for a hovering maid to take their coats. Diane took his arm and smiled up at him lovingly.

He flushed — and his good humor seemed to return. He patted Diane's small hand and smiled at her before he turned to greet John. "There you are, my boy. Glad you could come. And how nice to see you again, too, Claire. You're both looking well," he said pleasantly, shaking John's hand before he turned to kiss Claire's. His eyes narrowed unpleasantly as he looked at her. "I do hope you don't plan any trips in that motorcar in the near future, Claire. It could play havoc with Mr. Whitfield's sensibilities. And we wouldn't want to do anything to upset him, would we? It wouldn't help John's position at all."

It was a veiled threat. She wished she could tell this fat toad what she thought of him. She didn't dare. Her feathers were already ruffled from Diane's tragic-queen performance. She smiled instead. "I haven't much time for motorcars these days, Mr. Calverson," she said, with quiet dignity.

"Glad to hear it," he returned, and smiled more broadly. "Come in and meet our guests."

He propelled them past Diane and into the parlor where a tall, silver-haired man was waiting. He looked bored and half out of humor. His wife, an insignificant little blonde woman dressed in pink, sat quietly on the velvet-covered couch, looking haunted. A tall, very good-looking young man about Claire's age lounged with one hand on the mantel. He looked toward the newcomers and the boredom abruptly left his face. He smiled at Claire.

She was taken aback when he came forward as the introductions were made and possessed himself of Claire's hand.

"No one told me that Mr. Hawthorn had

such a lovely daughter," he said, oblivious to the sudden shocked silence around him. "I'm Ted Whitfield, and I certainly hope to see more of you while we're in Atlanta," he added, kissing her hand.

A viselike hand on her arm pulled her back to John's side. He glared at the younger man, assailed by a surge of jealousy that shocked him. "I'm John Hawthorn. And this is Claire. My wife," he added deliberately.

Ted wasn't the least perturbed. He only grinned. He looked rakish, with his blond hair and blue eyes and handsome face. "Is she, now? Well, well."

"Ted, mind your manners," Mr. Whitfield said abruptly.

"Sure, Daddy," he drawled.

"John is our vice president," Eli continued, a little shaken by Ted's unexpected behavior. "A worthy addition to the bank. He's a Harvard graduate, you know."

"I'm a Princeton man, myself," Ted said.

"Which class?" John asked, with a mocking smile.

Ted looked uncomfortable. "Well, I haven't actually graduated yet."

"Oh?"

Amazing, Claire thought, listening, how easily John could imbue that word with shades of contempt and hauteur. Her husband was still very much an unknown quantity. He intimidated the younger man without even trying.

"But Ted is at the top of his class, aren't you, my darling?" Mrs. Whitfield purred at her handsome son, glaring at John. "He's very intelligent," she added for good measure, her face flushed with irritation.

"Obviously," John drawled.

"Would you like a drink before dinner?" Eli asked abruptly, staring pointedly at John.

"I don't think so," John replied, glancing with raised brow at the brandy snifter in Ted's hand. The look and the implication were enough to make everyone more uncomfortable, especially Diane.

Claire was surprised at the way John behaved toward Ted. The boy was young and harmless, but John seemed to find him offensive. Diane, on the other hand, was kindness itself to the young man, putting herself out to make him feel at home. Claire wondered if she was doing it on purpose, to chastise John for his rudeness to Ted on Claire's behalf.

The dinner was an ordeal for Claire. Noah Whitfield seemed very straitlaced, and his conversation was limited to financial talk that went right over Claire's head. Diane hung on every word, although Claire was certain that the woman didn't understand anything about money except the spending of it. Perhaps her fascination with Mr. Whitfield had more to do with his wealth than his conversation, Claire thought wickedly.

After the meal, the ladies retired to the living room for conversation while the men closed the sliding doors into the parlor so that they could enjoy brandy and cigars.

"That was a lovely meal, Diane," Mrs. Whitfield said. "You must have your cook share her broccoli soup recipe with mine."

"I'll certainly ask her, Jennifer," Diane replied graciously. "My, what a lovely gown you're wearing. Is it a Paris label?"

"Of course," the older woman replied, with a smile. "Etienne Dupree. You must know of him."

"Indeed."

"And your gown certainly has the hallmark of Paris," Jennifer added.

"How perceptive of you to notice! It's Charmonne."

They were shutting Claire out, and doing a magnificent job of it. She was made to feel the little country girl supping with her betters.

She stood up.

"Oh, excuse me, Claire. I didn't mean to

exclude you from our conversation," Diane purred.

Claire gave her a level, unblinking look that made her color. "One of my mother's cousins was a Baptist minister," she said quietly. "I remember her telling me that he walked everywhere to preach, and that sometimes his shoes were incredibly muddy. One Sunday, while he was preaching, a young man in the audience kept looking at his dirty shoes with a sort of contempt. My cousin stopped in the middle of his sermon to remind the young man that God was surely more interested in the condition of his soul than in the state of his shoes." She smiled as the message went home to the other two. "Sometimes it behooves us to remember that heaven has no social levels, and that beggars and queens will walk the same streets on that side of life."

Mrs. Whitfield went red. "Well, of course they will. I certainly never meant any offense!"

"Nor I," Diane said uncomfortably.

Claire's eyes didn't waver. "I have no envy of your position and wealth," she said. "And I covet nothing of yours," she added pointedly — and with a smile, despite her anger.

Diane got up from her chair, flushed. "It's rather warm in here, isn't it? I'll have the maid damp down the fire."

Claire was too polite to smirk, but she felt like it. The venomous serpent, playing up to John as if he belonged to her! At first she'd thought that Diane truly loved John and was devastated at losing him. She no longer believed it. Diane played with John like a cruel cat with a mouse. She flirted and teased, but there was no substance to it. John was handsome and a man of position, but Diane probably did not believe him to be her social equal, so he would never have been a true candidate for matrimony. She was certain now that Diane had only been teasing him with their earlier engagement.

John deserved someone better than Diane as an object for his affections. Claire might not have Diane's beauty or her class, but she loved him. One day, that might be enough.

In the meantime, she was going to walk a straight and narrow path, careful not to push her way into John's privacy or make him ashamed of her. But that didn't mean she was going to let people like Diane and Mrs. Whitfield push her around just because she didn't have what they considered a proper background.

The conversation was stilted and rather sparse until it was time to rejoin the men.

John noticed it at once and glared at Claire. Of course, he wouldn't think it was anyone's fault but her own if there were problems, she thought with resignation.

Ted took her arm and led her to the sofa, stalling what John had been about to ask her. He sat down beside her and engaged her in conversation about her motorcar, which he seemed to find fascinating.

"I understand that you can actually work on the beast," Ted said, his eyes lighting up. "I have a friend at Princeton who's pounced on Max Planck's new quantum theory — vaporous stuff, quite incomprehensible to any but physics majors — but he has an interest in motorcars. He built an electric one, which he runs around the town. It's something like that quadricycle that Henry Ford was trying to market in Detroit."

"Henry Ford is a crackpot," Mrs. Whitfield said irritably, still smarting from Claire's earlier rebuke. "These silly machines are only a fad. They'll die out in a year or so."

"I believe that may not be the case," Claire rebutted politely. "They're going to be quite important in the future. They can last longer than horses, and they're impervious to weather and illness."

"You see?" Ted said. "Why, Ford has a factory in Detroit. And Mr. Olds —"

"I have an Oldsmobile." Claire interrupted him demurely. "It has a curved dash and it's quite delightful to drive."

"You must take me for a spin, Claire," Ted said enthusiastically. "I should love to ride in your motorcar!"

Ted's mother was outraged. So was John. Mr. Calverson looked as if he'd like to toss Claire out on her head.

"So should I," Mr. Whitfield said surprisingly. "I agree with Claire. Motorcars are the way of the future. I can even foresee machinery that will replace plow horses in the fields. Yes, mechanization is sure to come. Wise men will seek investments that pertain to this trend, and make fortunes at it."

Mr. Calverson did a hundred-and-eighty-degree about-face. "Just what I've been saying all along," he agreed, grinning. "I'm sure Claire would love to take you both motoring, wouldn't you, Claire?"

"Next time we're in town, we'll make a point of it," Mr. Whitfield said, smiling at Claire. "I'm afraid we have to be on our way back to Charleston in the morning. It's a long journey, even by train. It's been quite an experience to meet you, young woman. Unique." He looked at Calverson evenly. "If this is the sort of executive you employ, then I'll be proud to deposit my funds in your bank when we move our office to Atlanta, Calverson. Your people have amazing foresight. Even their wives," he added.

Claire had to fight back a smug glance at her husband. She only smiled, and ignored the icy looks she was getting from Mrs. Whitfield and Diane.

"Well," John said on the way home, chuckling, "you're full of surprises, aren't you?"

"I like motorcars, and I'm in good company."

"Such as the madcap Ted?"

She glanced at him over the high collar of her cloak. "Ted is like my uncle Will. He looks ahead."

His eyes narrowed. He lounged against the door with his arms folded, staring at her. "What did you say in the living room to get Mrs. Whitfield and Diane so ruffled?"

"I reminded them that it doesn't matter how much money you have when you get to heaven," she said shortly.

"That was hardly politic, in your hostess's home."

"Was it politic for her to be all over you like honey?" she shot back, red-faced with bad temper. "Or cooing up at you with her husband in the next room?"

His eyebrows lifted. "You were playing up to Ted Whitfield."

"I was not," she said, with dignity. "He was playing up to me. I have better taste than to cuckold *my* husband," she added in a pointed reference to Diane.

"Stop right there," he said in a dangerously soft tone.

"If she'd wanted you, she'd have married you before Eli Calverson came along," she continued, unabashed. "But you weren't good enough for her. Now that she's got the golden gander, she can afford to make calf eyes at you behind his back. You're too honorable to take her up on it, after all."

He averted his face. "Diane is none of your affair."

"I know that," she said. "I won't interfere, so long as you remember you're a married man."

"I hardly need reminding," he said shortly. He leaned back against the seat. "The bank's Thanksgiving social is a week from tonight," he added coolly. "I believe the Whitfields are coming down again especially for it."

"How nice." She tucked her handkerchief in her purse. "I don't suppose it would be kind to remind you that you and Mr. Calverson were getting nowhere until Ted mentioned my motorcar."

He glared at her. "No. It wouldn't."

She smiled. He was miffed because she'd maligned his sweetheart. Well, she wasn't going to back down an inch — and the sooner he knew it, the better.

He ignored her for the next week. She thought it was out of pique at the things she'd said about Diane. Actually it was his own confusion that kept him away. His jealousy of Ted Whitfield had shocked and puzzled him. He refused to consider why he'd been jealous of his wife, when he was supposedly in love with Diane.

The night of the bank party, Claire had to go downstairs to find John, because he hadn't waited in their sitting room for her. She was swathed in her black velvet cloak with jet embroidery around the collar. The cloak concealed a dress she'd designed for herself — and had been able to finish in the week since Diane's dinner party. She was certain that it was going to shock her husband, and it would serve him right. She might not have Diane's beauty, but she had a better figure, and this dress was just the thing to show it off. Done in white satin and black organza, it had a tantalizing neckline that rose in swaths of black and white satin to make wide straps across her white shoulders. In her hair she wore a white egret on a black velvet-covered comb. Around her neck she wore a strand of pearls that had been her grandmother's. She looked elegant and sexy, all at once, and the close fit of the gown emphasized her slender young figure. But John hadn't seen it. And he wouldn't, until they were at the party.

He handed her into the carriage with an irritated look. "It isn't a ball," he murmured.

"Good, because this isn't a ball gown," she replied coolly. "I do know what to wear to social events, despite my unfortunate background."

"I haven't said a damned word about your background!"

He was so irritable lately that it was dangerous even to speak to him. Claire clammed up.

Eli Calverson met them at the door of the bank and handed them along to Diane, who raised an eyebrow at the velvet cloak and then dismissed Claire as of no importance whatsoever.

"How lovely you look," John told Diane, approving of the scarlet gown she wore. It was almost too tight, and made her voluptuous figure look frankly vulgar. The color was wrong, too, although it was the newest sensation for fall and winter garments for women. Amazing, Claire thought, how some women were so eager to be in the forefront of fashion that they bought clothes for the fashion and the label alone. She recognized the design, because Evelyn had asked her to improvise on it for a morning dress. She wondered if Diane had any idea just how much she did know about fashion. It would probably shock her if she saw any of the things Claire had made for Atlanta matrons far higher on the social scale than Diane could ever aspire to be. True fashion was the art of knowing what looked good on a woman — and wearing it despite current trends.

Maids had been brought over to the bank to help with coats and cloaks. Claire permitted one of the young women to take her cloak and was delighted when she heard the woman's faint gasp as the cloak fell away.

"Oh, ma'am. That's the prettiest dress I ever saw," the young woman said fervently.

"Thank you," Claire said, and turned to see wide-eyed shock on Diane's face as she saw the contrast between the purity of Claire's gown and the boisterous nature of her own.

John frowned faintly as he studied his wife. The gown didn't appear to be one she could purchase locally. In fact, it looked like a Paris original, but how would Claire find such a garment?

She lifted her chin proudly and walked toward him, but midway there, she was intercepted by three of the firm's young bachelors, and Ted Whitfield.

"Aren't you a pretty picture." Ted sighed, making her a bow. "Milady, you are without doubt the loveliest lady present."

Diane, who heard the remark, bridled visibly. John, watching, could hardly believe his eyes. His bride had suddenly become the most sought-after woman at the bank social, and he didn't know how to handle the feelings that erupted inside him. Nothing in his life had prepared him for the jealousy that roared through him — nor for the raging desire that the sight of Claire in that exquisite gown set ablaze within him.

7

Claire had never felt quite so pretty, or so much in demand. She was drawn from one circle to another, while the women raved about her pretty dress. Everyone wanted to know where she got it. She couldn't tell them that she'd made it herself. She didn't want John to know about her secret career.

She mentioned the name of a boutique whose owner frequently displayed her gowns.

"Yes, dear. But what label is on the dress?" one matron insisted, peering at it hungrily.

"Magnolia," Claire said, improvising.

"Magnolia. Why, how very appropriate for an Atlanta designer!" the woman said.

"Yes," Claire said absently. "Isn't it?"

The one woman present who had no curiosity whatsoever about the garment was Diane.

She moved close to John when Eli momentarily left the room with Mr. Whitfield.

"Isn't her gown just a little revealing for a bank social?" she asked John irritably. "And, really! It's hardly the color for a married woman, all that virginal white!"

John had to bite his tongue to keep from confessing that the color was, in fact, quite appropriate for his untouched bride. He sipped his punch and looked around at the room with its spotless Persian rugs and elegant curtains and crystal chandeliers. He thought privately that his wife's elegant gown fit the setting.

"It isn't even fashionable," she muttered.

John glanced down at her, surprised by the venom in her tone. He'd heard Diane be catty before, of course, but not about Claire. He was surprised to find that he didn't like it. She was glaring at Claire, who was talking with Ted Whitfield and two other young men.

"I don't believe Claire cares much for dictated fashion," he replied.

"Well, it shows," she said shortly. She shifted her pretty shoulders and turned, smiling up at him sweetly. "But what does it matter? You look devastating, John — really devastating. I wish we could be alone."

His heart jumped. Her mouth was soft and sweet, and he wanted it terribly. Abstinence had made him ill just lately, and he was hungry for a woman in his arms. Odd how vividly he remembered the silky softness of Claire's mouth under his.

'You'd like that, wouldn't you, sweet man?" she teased softly, moving closer.

He snapped back to the present with a vengeance and stiffened. "Diane . . ."

She let her body brush his suggestively. "Remember how it was, the night we became engaged?" she whispered. "I let you take off my clothes — and if your silly father hadn't come to visit unexpectedly, I'd have let you make love to me completely."

He scowled. The memory had affected him deeply in the past. Now it was more an annoyance to be reminded of it. "This isn't the time or the place. We're married, Diane — and not to each other."

"Oh, you and your sense of honor," she chided, moving away from him. "It's that military upbringing, of course. You should have gone to Harvard in the beginning."

"I had a better place at Harvard because of my background at the Citadel," he said abruptly.

"The military is necessary, I suppose, but this is so much nicer, John," she said, sighing as she looked around. "Look at all this wealth. Money and power are the truly important things. Anyone can be a soldier."

That wasn't the case at all, but he didn't say so. Diane had never made any secret of her contempt for uniforms. He scowled as he thought how little they really had in common — outside his feverish passion for her body — and that had subsided. She was catty and shrewd, and she liked to play men against each other. She'd sworn that she loved him, but an onlooker would swear that she loved her husband. She played on the winning side, always. When John had refused to go crawling home to his father to regain his inheritance, it hadn't taken her a month to find Eli Calverson and marry him. He remembered stopping for the dog that had been hit by Wolford's carriage, and how Claire had supported his efforts, how she'd comforted the old lady while John worked. She had such a tender heart, and yet she was as fiery as he was.

"What are you thinking?" Diane asked softly.

He looked down at her. "That men are fools," he said carelessly.

She hit his arm lightly. "Silly. You're nobody's fool."

"I wonder." He looked past her at Claire, who was smiling with pure pleasure as those young men made a fuss over her. It looked bad, because it should have been her new husband doing that. Oh, yes. It should be he, not that damned cad, Ted Whitfield, who looked as if he'd have liked to eat Claire with a spoon!

"Excuse me," he said abruptly, and went toward his wife with an expression so fierce that Diane actually gasped.

Claire saw that expression as he came toward her. She was surprised that he'd deserted Diane for her. But she hadn't liked his pointed avoidance of her for Diane.

"Lost for conversation?" she asked pointedly. "Or did Mrs. Calverson . . . upset you?"

He ignored the sarcastic remark and glared at Ted. "There are a number of young single ladies here tonight," he said politely, and suggestively, as he caught Claire's gloved hand in his. "I'd like to spend some time with my wife."

"How odd," Ted said deliberately. "I'd have said that you'd like to spend time with Mrs. Calverson. Of course, I'm an outsider here, so what would I know?" He bowed to Claire quickly, having correctly judged the sudden murderous fury in John Hawthorn's dark eyes. "I'll see you again before we leave, Claire," he added.

John's hand clasping Claire's became bruising as he watched the other man walk away. "By God, he'll challenge me once too often," he said shortly.

Despite the pleasure the contact gave her, she jerked her hand out of his grasp. "He took pity on me because I obviously had no escort," she said furiously. "It hasn't escaped anyone's notice that you've been all over Diane since we arrived, leaving me to the mercy of strangers."

He sucked in a quick breath, stunned by her quiet fury.

"I don't want your company, and you've made it patently obvious that you don't want mine," she continued. "Go back to your fancy peahen, and good luck to you if Mr. Calverson stops courting Mr. Whitfield long enough to see the spectacle you two are making of yourselves. If I'm to spend my time alone, then let it extend to social evenings, as well!"

She turned and walked away from him, right back to the two young men she'd been speaking to when John interrupted them.

To say that he was shocked was an understatement. He gaped at her, totally nonplussed. He hadn't thought that he and Diane had been conspicuous. In fact, tonight he'd felt less drawn to Diane than at any time in the past. He looked around and encountered several pairs of feminine eyes with blatant disapproval in them. He felt vaguely ashamed that he'd embarrassed Claire so publicly. She didn't deserve such treatment from her own husband. But tonight, it really had been Diane making the advances, not himself. Claire, sadly, wouldn't know that.

Diane, also having noticed the looks she and John were getting, cut her losses, went looking for her husband, and stayed by his side.

Claire indulged herself at the punch bowl, especially when Ted Whitfield eased the contents of a flask of straight bourbon whiskey into it to "improve the taste." It improved the taste so much that he helped himself to a second flask in his other hip pocket and became embarrassingly attentive to Claire.

The small band had tuned up and was playing now, so that the couples who wanted to could dance. Claire was pulled onto the floor with Ted, who would have danced very well indeed if he'd been sober. But the way he waltzed was dangerous as he weaved to-and-fro, and Claire finally stopped in the middle of the crowded floor and eased him into a chair.

"Sorry, Claire," he said miserably. "Too much to drink."

"You shouldn't do that," she said. "It's unhealthy."

He shook his head. "You don't understand. It's the only way I can stomach what my old man's doing. He looks so honest, doesn't he, Claire? Honest and intelligent . . . He's a crook, Claire — and he's raised me to be just like him. But since I've met you, I don't want to be one." He caught her hand and held it tightly. "Claire, could you care for me?"

"Ted . . . I'm — I'm married," she said, flustered.

"He doesn't love you," he said irritably. "A blind man could see he's besotted with that Calverson woman. She's trouble, you know. Big trouble. She's not at all what she appears to be; she'll do anything for money. I know what I'm talking about —"

"You must stop, Ted," she said, gently disengaging herself from his grasp. "Let me go now."

"Yes," came a soft, dangerous voice from behind her. "Let her go."

Ted looked up and encountered glittering black eyes. He glared back. "Tore yourself away from the beautiful Diane, did you?" he demanded icily. "You don't want Claire, but you can't stand to see another man appreciate her, is that it?"

"Ted, please don't," she pleaded, because his voice was carrying.

"Let him talk," John said coldly. "When he's finished, I'll help him out the front door, headfirst."

She turned, putting a firm hand on his chest. "No, you will not," she said shortly, keeping her voice low. "You won't risk the merger for Mr. Calverson because of Ted. He's only had too much to drink."

"That's no excuse."

"Think you're some big man because you have a Harvard degree, don't you?" Ted argued.

"One of them is from Harvard," John said quietly. "The other is from the Citadel."

Even through an alcoholic haze, Ted knew what the other man was insinuating. No man got through the Citadel and came out of it a cream puff. For the first time, he noticed the other man's erect posture, the steel in his eyes, the hardness of his face. And he knew at once that he wasn't willing to tangle with years of discipline and conditioning that had produced the man before him.

"I'm in no condition to fight," Ted said, stepping back. "Claire, you won't let him hit me, will you?" he asked in a piteous voice.

"He won't hit you. Will you, John?"

He drew in an angry breath, glaring from the smug, drunken grin on Ted's face to his wife's set features.

"There's your father, Ted," Claire said, and leaning around John, who hadn't budged, she motioned to Mr. Whitfield. "Ted's had a little too much stimulant," she whispered confidentially. "I think you might want to get him home."

Mr. Whitfield nodded. He smiled at Claire. "You're a kind young woman. I'm sorry you're married. You'd have been the making of Ted. Come on, boy," he said wearily, and bent to help his son with an arm around the waist. "Let's get you home."

"Aw, Dad. I was having a good time."

Claire watched them go out. She turned away, but John caught her arm roughly.

"Since it seems to disturb you to see me with Diane, suppose you stay with me for the rest of the evening."

She looked up into his hard face. "Why? Am I being punished?"

He dropped her arm abruptly. "Suit yourself, madam," he said, his voice contemptuous.

She glanced to the door. Mr. Whitfield had just returned, minus his son. He nodded toward her and went back to speak with Mr.

Calverson.

"Sorry to have spoiled your fun," she said to John. "I'm sure you'd have enjoyed punching Ted, but it wouldn't have helped the bank's image, would it?"

She turned around and all but fell into the arms of another young man. This one wasn't inebriated and he didn't know that John was her husband.

"Is this man bothering you, Claire?" he demanded, glaring at John. "Because if he is, I'll be delighted to defend you!"

"Please do," John invited, furious at Claire and still fuming because he hadn't had the opportunity to knock Ted to his knees. This was too tempting. This man was up to his weight, and he wasn't drunk. "Shall we step outside?" he added, without giving the man a chance to learn his identity.

"John!" she said, protesting.

It was too late. The men went quickly to the door. Claire followed and was just in time to watch the younger man throw a punch that was neatly blocked. John hit him so hard that when he went down, he somersaulted and ended up sitting on the ground.

"Come on," John invited, hands loose at his sides, his dark eyes blazing. "You wanted to fight. I'll be glad to oblige you."

The younger man hesitated, and Claire

didn't blame him. John looked like a stranger, his legs apart for balance, his head high, his face hard as he waited for the other man to get up and charge him.

"He's my husband!" Claire said sharply as the younger man got to his feet.

"Your husband?" he exclaimed.

"That's right," John told him. "And you'll be damned lucky if you can walk when I'm through with you."

He moved toward the other man, who backed away with his hands out. "Now, sir. There's no need for that. I'm very sorry to have interfered. I'll apologize right now." He touched his sore jaw. "Please excuse me!"

He turned and headed in the direction of the hired carriages.

Claire's head was spinning, as much from the unfamiliar alcohol she'd consumed in the punch as from John's behavior. She couldn't believe that her reluctant husband had been willing to fight over her. She stared at him speechlessly.

"Would you care to start some more trouble, or are you through for the evening?" he asked, with biting sarcasm. "I've had quite enough. Get your wrap. I'm taking you home."

And he did, despite her arguments. He

shepherded her past the Calversons and out the front door, not stopping until he'd escorted her into their apartment.

"Go to bed," he said shortly. "You've caused enough trouble for one night."

"*I've* caused it?" she asked, fuming. "You could have told him that you were my husband and averted the fight in the first place!"

"What, and spoil my fun?" he returned. He opened the door.

She stared at him. "Where are you going?"

"Back to the party, of course," he replied mockingly. "I was having a good time until you threw yourself at Ted."

"I did not!"

The expression on his face was angry and mocking. "He seemed to think he had grounds for accosting me on your behalf, as your other watchdog did. No man sports with my wife in front of me!"

She put her hands on her hips and glared at him. "But it's all right for you to sport with Mr. Calverson's wife in front of me, is that right?"

She didn't even see him move, but the next minute he had her riveted to him with one arm while the other jerked down the swath of fabric that held up her gown, taking the silk chemise under it, as well. She gazed at him, helpless, with one small, firm breast completely bared to his cold, angry gaze.

"Does this suit you better, my virgin bride?" He pulled her closer. "Are you hungry for my attentions? Then by all means, let me give them to you."

He bent even as he spoke and opened his mouth right on her bare breast.

The sensation went beyond anything she'd ever felt before, even the touch of his hands on her body weeks ago. She arched and shivered, and then went limp from the force of the pleasure as he began to suckle her in a heated fury.

She felt his other hand at work on the bodice, felt him bare her to his hungry mouth. The room whirled around her while his lips devoured her pale, soft flesh, making her burn with a fever she didn't understand.

When he finally was able to drag his mouth from her breasts, she hung there over his arm with her eyes closed, her mouth parted, her body yielding and trembling.

"Dear — dear God," he whispered brokenly.

She barely heard him. He hesitated, but only for a second. She felt him move, felt him swing her violently up into his arms, lift and carry her into his own bedroom and close the door. He stood there, in the darkness, leaning against the closed door, uncertain, shuddering with desire so fierce that he couldn't contain it.

"John," she whispered through tight lips, clinging. "John, you mustn't . . . take me to bed," she pleaded unsteadily. "I'm not Diane! I'm not! Don't take advantage of something . . . I can't help!"

But the words were at variance with the audibly rapid beat of her heart, the longing and curiosity so evident in her eyes.

"Shall I stop, Claire?" He breathed harshly as he put her gently on her feet, bending again to her soft breasts. While he suckled her, he ripped off the white gloves that had covered his hands, and seconds later, she felt their warmth on her skin.

The sensation took the last of her willpower. She wanted him so desperately, loved him so much, that being near him was all of heaven to her. She went limp in his arms, her head falling back as he explored her soft bareness with his mouth and hands. When he picked her up again and carried her to bed, she didn't even have a protest to make.

She yielded completely under the wonder of his ardor. He undressed her with a skill that she was too dazed to recognize. She lay on the cool white damask coverlet like a creamy sacrifice, open to his eyes in what little light filtered in through the wispy curtains, while he worked deftly at removing his own clothes.

When he finally came to her, warm and strong and very alien against her soft skin, she had recovered just enough to allow the return of her earlier apprehension. She was stiff in his arms, nervous and withdrawing when he touched her intimately for the first time.

"Shh," he whispered, calming her, and his fingers moved again, this time finding a secret that she didn't want to give him.

He heard her shocked gasp even as he felt her body coil and lift. "There?" he whispered huskily, and touched her more firmly.

She sobbed. The pleasure was indescribable. She grabbed at his shoulders and dug her nails in, writhing as he made her feel the most sinfully delicious sensations.

He heard her gasp rhythmically. He moved, inserting his knee between her legs, coaxing her to open them, to permit him even greater freedom with her body. She was beyond fighting him now, her legs falling open, her hips lifting in a quick, searching rhythm.

"Oh . . . please!" she cried on her last jerky

breath before the heavens opened and she exploded up into them.

There was an odd sensation of tearing, a flash of pain with the pleasure. Somewhere in the back of her mind, she realized that he had moved over her, that his body was between her splayed legs. She felt a part of him that she only dimly recognized as it penetrated slowly inside . . . inside her body!

"John!" she cried out.

But he didn't stop. His movement grew longer, deeper. He pushed down against her, over her, his hands under her back, under her hips, pulling, pulling, pulling . . .

He was tearing her inside. She felt the sensation grow, of being filled up, overfilled. She whispered something, frantically pushing at his hair-roughened, sweaty chest. He made a sound. His hand went between their bodies and touched her, where he'd touched her before. The pleasure came back, sharper now, intense, painfully intense. And suddenly she couldn't be filled enough, not deeply enough to satisfy the emptiness that became her whole being.

She pushed up into him, her hips arched and pleading as his rhythm grew violent, reckless. One of the slats hit the floor, and even the sharp sound wasn't enough to break her concentration. She held on, gasping, sobbing, reaching toward that hot, sweet, blinding pleasure that was somehow just beyond, just above, just . . .

She went over the edge of the world with him. She fell into heat and throbbing softness, into aching completion that made her whole body feel as if it had tensed beyond relaxation.

As she trembled into exhaustion, she felt his body go rigid, heard the rough sound that was dragged from his throat as he began to shake. His hot face burrowed into her damp throat, and his hands on her hips made bruises as he shivered and shivered against her.

The windows were closed, but she heard the baying of a dog beyond the curtains, far away in the night. She heard the sound of the clock on the mantel. She heard the ragged sound of his breathing and the hard, rhythmic beat of his heart.

He moved. She felt the sweat on his long, powerful legs moisten her own as he shifted restlessly, without withdrawing from her. He groaned softly, and his mouth slid up her throat to her cheek, and, finally, into the cushion of her parted lips.

His hands slid along her body, savoring its perfection, teasing her soft breasts, easing down to caress the inside of her white legs.

She felt him swell. The sensation was exquisite. Little skirls of renewed pleasure traveled along her nerves, arousing her all over again. She moved under him, sensuously now, her hands sliding along his back and down over his firm buttocks.

"Yes," she whispered recklessly against his mouth. "Yes, again . . . again!"

He groaned loudly as his mouth opened on her lips and his body began the rhythmic movements that were now familiar and pleasurable. She slid closer, clung, moved as he moved. She laughed deep in her throat as she felt the rise of heat, the beginning of the long, sharp spiral of ecstasy.

He heard the sound she made and it drove him to madness. He forgot everything but the silkiness of her beneath his demanding body. It seemed such a short time later when she cried out and scarred him with her nails . . .

She didn't hear him leave her. The sunlight on the pillow, slashing across her eyes, was the first indication she had of morning. Her eyelids opened and she stared blankly at the ceiling until it occurred to her that this wasn't her room.

With blinding suddenness, the events of

the evening before came flooding into her mind.

Shocked, embarrassed, she sat up, hugging the sheet to her nakedness. John wasn't there. There was no sign of him, no sound of him, in their apartments. Her clothes had been picked up from the floor where he'd thrown them. They were draped across the rosewood chair next to the bed, with her undergarments discreetly placed beneath the evening gown she'd worn. Her shoes were there, too, toes pointed away from the chair.

She glanced toward the other pillow and saw the imprint of John's dark head there. But there was no note, no communication. He'd simply dressed and left her, apparently unconcerned — as if such nights were commonplace.

Cautiously she eased out of bed like a thief about to be caught. As she pushed back the bedclothes, a dark stain lay vivid against the once-spotless white of the sheet. She flushed, knowing that the laundress would remark on it. If it had only been on her own bed, she could have made some excuse about her monthly. But this was John's bed!

She grabbed up her things and rushed barefoot across the sitting room and into her own room, quickly closing the door behind her. She saw herself in the full-length mirror. She looked flushed and guilty, and there were marks on her white skin.

Curious, she put her things on the bed and moved closer to the mirror. Yes, there was a bruise on one breast, and several on her upper thighs where his hands had gripped her so tightly when she'd satisfied him the second time. She half turned, and saw more faint bruises on her buttocks. Her eyes were no longer those of an innocent. They had dark circles from her initiation into passion. Her lips were swollen, red. Her nipples had gone tight and dark as she looked at herself, as if they remembered the heat of John's insistent mouth as he'd suckled her.

"Oh!" she cried out, embarrassed at the memory.

She poured water into the basin and got out a flannel and soap and bathed a little. She felt less besmirched afterward, dressed and perfumed, but later she must have a tub bath to wash away the feeling of tarnish. John had admitted that he loved Diane. How could she have permitted him to make love to her? Was she no better than a woman of the streets?

She was so ashamed that she couldn't face

him that evening. She pleaded a headache to Mrs. Dobbs, forgoing supper. She went into her room and locked the door.

It was a wasted effort. John didn't come home for supper. In fact, it was after midnight when she heard him unlock the door to their apartment. And his footsteps didn't even hesitate as he went directly into his room and closed the door firmly behind him.

8

In fact, John was just as ill at ease as Claire was. His desire for his pretty, innocent wife had finally overcome his self-control. Like a drunken fool, he'd gone at Claire with all the finesse of a rutting stag, like some sensual animal. He hadn't even taken special care about her virginity. His need of her had been so great that her innocence had been the last thing on his mind. And the second time, her own sensuality had dragged him under. Imagine Claire wrapping her soft body around him like a robe, he recalled with faint surprise — actually entreating the hard, deep thrust of his body . . .

He groaned out loud. Her sweet response had humbled him. He'd made love to her out of anger and confusion and jealousy and frustration. But no man alive could have asked for a sweeter fulfillment than Claire had given him so generously. He remembered the faint taste of whiskey on her mouth, probably from the punch. But it was love that had made her yield so sweetly to him, not alcohol. She loved him, and she had proved it again and again through the long, sensuous night, curling into his body with absolute trust, whispering encouragement, praise, soft endearments. He could still taste her on his mouth, that rose-scented skin so white and soft and responsive . . .

He had to force his attention back to the business at hand, and stifle the disturbing thoughts. His military upbringing had helped him learn to do that, even with the most disturbing memories of his life. He had no idea what he was going to do. But he knew one thing: his feelings for Diane weren't nearly as strong as he'd thought they were. Otherwise, he couldn't have been so ardent with Claire.

Claire had thought long and hard about the lie she'd told the woman who asked the name of her dress designer. It wouldn't do to be caught in such a falsehood. She decided that her best course of action was to sew some evening gowns under the "Magnolia" label, and toward that end, she visited the owner of the small boutique that sometimes displayed a gown for her. The owner was delighted to have original designs of such quality as the dress Claire showed her. Secrecy was assured, because Claire told her that she didn't want her husband to know that she was working. And, as the older woman agreed, anonymity would give an air of mystery to her creative name and her designs, as well.

She was off to a running start, with all the work she'd already been commissioned to do for the governor's Christmas ball. She worked diligently to meet deadlines, all the while making sure that she would have a special gown of her own for the occasion.

For a week, she and John avoided each other with varying degrees of clumsiness and embarrassment, especially on her part. She couldn't even look him in the eye, and he seemed to understand her shyness and indulge it without anger. But when Thanksgiving rolled around, they had to eat at the table together and suppress their feelings so that Mrs. Dobbs wouldn't think anything was wrong with their relationship. To do anything to cause more gossip was unthinkable.

"You really should take Claire out more, John," Mrs. Dobbs said pleasantly. "Honestly, she seems to spend all her time upstairs, sewing and sewing."

John glanced at his wife. "Sewing what?"

She almost dropped her fork. She hadn't realized that the treadle machine made enough noise that Mrs. Dobbs could hear it all the way downstairs.

"I've been trying to remake some of my things," she confided after a minute.

John felt himself bristle. "I'm not a poor man," he said curtly. "There's no need to alter old clothes. Buy new ones. I've told you before to use your account at Rich's."

Her fingers tightened on the fork. "Very well, John."

Mrs. Dobbs went to bring in the cake she'd sliced. While she was away, John leaned back in his chair and stared levelly at Claire until she flushed. "I've been meaning to speak to you," he began softly, and her heart beat erratically as she recalled their long, sweet night together. "But I couldn't find the right words."

"Oh?" she asked.

He sighed. She wasn't helping him at all. He glanced at his plate, changing his mind. It was too soon to speak of what had happened, so he mentioned something else entirely. "I've been asked to organize a charity dinner next Saturday to benefit the local Presbyterian orphanage. You know that it was devastated by fire, and the children have to be kept together, all ages, in one common room. There is an urgent need for rebuilding." He paused deliberately before he added, calculatingly, "I thought of asking Diane to do it for me . . ."

To his utter delight, her eyes came up flashing gray fire. "I am perfectly capable of organizing a dinner!"

Even anger was better than her painful shyness. He smiled gently. She was so pretty in a temper. "Of course you are. But I need monied people to attend this one, to make pledges to fund renovations for the home."

"I told you, I can organize it."

He was smiling. He must think of her as helpless and useless. It was another thorn in her heart.

"I won't let you down, John," she said proudly. "At least give me the benefit of the doubt."

"Do you think you can solicit the presence of so many members of Atlanta society, people whom you don't know?" he added softly, trying with all his might not to offend her.

She smiled wistfully. "You don't think much of me, do you, John?" she asked quietly. "Your opinion of me was of great importance once," she added, with a desperate grasp at her pride. "How fortunate that

I no longer care what you think."

His expression was so strange and unfamiliar that she couldn't quite explain it. She put down her napkin and got to her feet, forcing him to his. "I'll organize your dinner if you'll let me have the details."

"I'll list them on paper for you," he said, struggling to keep his inner turmoil hidden, "along with the names of the people I'd like you to invite. If you have any difficulties . . ."

"I won't, thank you just the same. If you'll excuse me, I don't want dessert. Please make my apologies to Mrs. Dobbs." She turned and went quickly up the staircase, the sad holiday behind her.

John watched her until she was out of sight, feeling alternately miserable and angry. So she didn't care, did she? It hadn't seemed that way in his bed, when she was holding him so tight he had marks all over his shoulders the next day! But if that was the way she wanted to play it, let her save her pride. He could forget that his body ached day and night for the comfort of her own. Idly he wondered what Diane would have thought of his lapse.

But he was surprised to realize that Diane's opinion of him mattered less than Claire's. Claire was pretty, he thought.

178

Pretty and loving and generous and spirited. She should have a husband who spoiled her, adored her, treated her like a princess. Someone like Ted would have loved taking care of her . . .

Ted! He was furious as he realized how much attention the other man had paid her, and how it had angered him. Convenient marriage or not, she was still his wife; Ted had no right to be familiar with her. There had better not be any further trouble in that direction, he decided firmly. No man was going to touch his Claire. When he realized what he was thinking, he laughed aloud, surprised. Only Mrs. Dobbs's return kept him from talking to himself.

He'd wanted his charity dinner arranged in only a week, and Claire had found it easy to comply, despite the fact that she'd had to hire a messenger boy to hand deliver the invitations. Most social engagements required notice of three weeks, and John surely knew that. But she explained in her invitation that there was some urgency — since there had been a fire at the orphanage recently and the children were suffering. She'd hired a good local restaurant for the evening, where the meal would be catered, and she'd invited all the society women whom she knew from her charitable works. She even knew some who weren't on John's list, and she'd invited them, too.

The evening of the dinner arrived, and she wore another of her new creations, a black-and-white gown that was dramatic enough to bring a gasp of envy from Mrs. Dobbs even as it caused John to stare.

"I don't remember seeing that dress," he remarked.

"And you haven't," she replied coolly. "It's an original, by a local designer."

"How beautiful," Mrs. Dobbs said, with a sigh. "Oh, my dear . . . if only I were young enough and pretty enough to carry it off. You shall be the envy of every woman present."

Claire smiled warmly. "Thank you, Mrs. Dobbs."

She drew her long black velvet cloak with its white satin lining closer around her. "We should be going, so that we won't be late," she told her husband.

He took her arm and escorted her out to the waiting carriage, signaling to the driver when they were securely inside.

He turned, staring at her through the lantern-lit interior. "You do look charming," he said, his eyes going to her upswept hair. Around her neck she wore her grandmother's pearls and no other jewelry, except her small wedding band under the long white gloves that accessorized her gown. "Who is this designer?" he added curiously.

"The label is Magnolia," she replied.

"How appropriate. She's very good," he murmured, eyes narrowed. "It's almost too formal for such a setting."

She lifted her chin. "I recall that you said the same thing about the dress I wore to the bank's social evening," she said, without thinking, and then went scarlet as she recalled what had happened when John took her home.

He remembered, too. His dark eyes glanced over her face quietly. "I remember less of the dress than what was under it, Claire."

She clenched her evening bag tightly and averted her face.

"You shouldn't need reminding that we're legally married," he continued. "It's perfectly permissible for you to spend the night in my arms."

She cleared her throat. "It was a mistake."

"Was it?" He shifted as the carriage turned. "Has it been long enough for you to know?"

She didn't understand him for a moment. When she did, she stiffened. "Of course it's not been long enough to know if there would be a — a child. But I hardly think . . . I don't expect . . . that is . . ."

"Let us hope for the best," he said after a minute, thinking privately that he would like a child, a little boy or a little girl with soft gray eyes like Claire's. He smiled.

She didn't see the smile and misunderstood the comment. "As you say, let us hope for the best," she agreed, almost choking on the words. She loved him. But he was telling her quite coldly that he wanted no children with her, and also that he had no intention of risking it a second time. Presumably, he was hoping that Diane would someday be free and he would have his children with her. It was a sobering thought.

"Here we are," he said as they arrived at the restaurant. He helped her out of the carriage, instructed the driver, and escorted her inside.

Diane and her husband were early, already waiting for their host and hostess. Diane turned just as John helped Claire out of her cloak, and the blonde woman's eyes flashed angrily. Claire was wearing an outrageously beautiful gown.

"Why, how . . . extravagantly formal, Claire." Diane laughed. "Are we attending a ball or a simple dinner?"

Claire refused to be intimidated. She looked pointedly at the plain black silk of the other woman's gown. "*Simple* would seem to describe it, I suppose," she said, and smiled deliberately.

Diane glared at her, but before she could reply, John's hand tightened on Claire's arm. He was about to speak, to defend his wife against the catty remark. Claire prevented it with her comment.

"I understand," she whispered to her husband as Diane and Mr. Calverson were interrupted by two arriving couples. "She's allowed to insult me, but I can't retaliate, is that so?"

He frowned. "Claire . . ."

She pulled angrily away from him and went to greet Evelyn, who had just arrived with her husband. John sighed. She didn't understand at all.

If John was surprised to see how warmly Claire's greeting was received by one of the premier socialites of the city, he hid it well. He joined Claire and was introduced to Evelyn and her husband. This introduction was followed by a number of others, and as the company was seated, John began to realize that his young wife actually knew these women.

Diane seemed equally taken aback — not

only by Claire's knowledge of the women, but by their friendliness toward her. Despite all Diane's efforts, Evelyn had never graced the halls of Diane's home. Neither had at least three of the other women, even richer than Evelyn and apparently on the best of terms with Claire.

"You seem to know our little Claire, Mrs. Paine," Diane remarked halfway through the meal.

"Know her? I certainly do," Evelyn said, with faint hauteur, and Claire held her breath, waiting to be unmasked as a designer. But Evelyn exchanged a secretive smile with her and she relaxed. "Claire has been invaluable to us, you know," she told Diane. "She's a tireless volunteer, baking things for our bazaars, donating handiwork, making lace . . . Why, she's priceless. None of us would reap half the benefits from our charities without Claire's participation. I'm sure her husband is quite proud of the time she devotes to our causes, even though they do rob her of time with him. We felt that we couldn't refuse her invitation to this dinner to benefit the orphanage, not after all she's done for us."

John was shocked. He started to admit that he'd had no idea she was involved in such projects, but he realized that this would be a mistake — with Calverson staring at him and already jealous of the earlier gossip about John and Diane.

"Yes," he said, recovering his poise. "I'm quite proud of Claire. She's good with her hands, isn't she?"

"Indeed," Evelyn replied.

"Are you going to the governor's ball, Mrs. Paine?" Diane broke in, addressing Evelyn.

"Certainly. I'm having a gown designed especially for it by Magnolia. Really, my dear. You should avail yourself of her services. She does concoct the most delightful gowns."

Diane sat taller in her chair, offended and not daring to admit or show it. "I must make her acquaintance. Does she live in Atlanta, then?"

Claire stiffened once more until the older woman spoke. "She lives hereabouts," Evelyn said vaguely. "And you, Mr. Hawthorn — are you and Claire going to the governor's ball?"

"I'm afraid not," John replied blandly, shocking Claire, who'd worked feverishly to get her special gown ready in time. "We're expecting visitors from out of town on that weekend, and they're the sort of people who don't approve of dancing. Very religious, you see," he added, and looked so convincing that Claire almost believed him. But he'd said nothing about guests. And she'd so wanted to go to the ball. She was disappointed, but she tried not to show it.

"There will be other years," she said absently.

"What a pity," Diane said, glancing at John with disappointment in her soft eyes.

John didn't react to her look at all. He was deep in his own thoughts. He couldn't admit that he didn't dare go for fear of confronting his own family. He wanted nothing to do with his father. The thought of running into the old man at the ball made him angry and uneasy.

And Claire knew nothing about the feud. She would have loved to know all about her taciturn husband, but he shared nothing about his past life with her.

"Will your parents attend the ball, John?" Diane asked innocently, setting the cat among the pigeons with a smug smile in Claire's direction.

Claire didn't know much about John's parents, as Diane had guessed. She sat stiffly, trying to adjust to this new information, while Diane toyed delicately with her crystal glass.

"I don't know," he said abruptly, and gave

her a glare that actually made her eyebrows fly upward.

The servers began to bring in the first course, saving him from any more complicated reply than that. But Diane had successfully ruined the evening for Claire, who felt like an utter fool.

John knew it, and was sorry. He stared at her all through the delicious meal, but she talked to Evelyn and refused even to look at him.

By the end of the tedious evening, John had pledges for more than enough money to make all the necessary repairs to the orphanage and pay for new toys for Christmas.

"Your wife is quite an organizer, I must say, John," Mr. Calverson said when all the guests had gone and he was standing outside the restaurant with Claire and Diane and John. "My dear, you've done the bank proud tonight. I shall have to find other projects for you. I had no idea you were on such a friendly basis with so many socially prominent matrons!"

"Yes, she is a dark horse, isn't she?" Diane asked, with pure bile. "Shouldn't we go, Eli? It's very cold out here."

"Certainly, my dear. Good night, John, Claire."

He tipped his hat, put Diane in the carriage, and they drove away.

Claire got into their own carriage without John's assistance and sat as far away from him as possible, refusing to respond when he commented on the night, the party, and the weather.

She was on her way upstairs before he came into the house, but he was only two steps behind when she reached their apartment.

"Claire!" he called shortly when she started into her bedroom.

She stopped, turning elegantly. "Yes?" she asked, her voice as cold as her heart.

"There are several questions I'd like to ask —" he began.

"And several I'd like to ask, as well," she shot back. "But I realize that I'm unlikely to obtain answers, since you obviously feel that I have no importance in your life whatsoever. You made that abundantly clear tonight. Diane knows all about your background, I gather," she added coldly.

"We were engaged," he said heavily.

"Yes, and we are married," she replied, gray eyes sparking with fury. She tossed her purse and her cloak onto the arm of a chair beside the door and turned to confront him. "Yet I know more about Mrs. Dobbs downstairs than I know about you!"

He took a cigar from his pocket and clipped off the end with a cutter. "What do you want to know about me, Claire?" he asked suddenly — and with a softness in his dark eyes that confounded her. She didn't know how it pleased him that she was curious about him. In recent days, he'd almost convinced himself that she'd fallen completely out of love with him.

"Are you going to smoke that in here?" she demanded. "Because if you are, I shall sleep in my automobile in the shed!"

He cocked an eyebrow and chuckled at her vehemence. "I hadn't planned to smoke it inside. I usually have it on the veranda before I retire. Outside, my dear . . . where the smoke troubles no one."

"No one except God," she said coolly.

He ignored that. "What do you want to know about me?"

It was an opening that she almost took advantage of. He was offering to tell her, presumably, anything she wanted to know. But as relaxed as he appeared to be, she sensed a tension in him. She didn't want to provoke a scene such as had happened on one other evening, to have him throw up to her that she'd tempted him.

"What use is it?" she asked, and sounded

unutterably weary of the whole thing. She started to turn when his voice stopped her.

"My parents live in Savannah," he said, volunteering something that she would never have asked him. "My father and I have been estranged for a number of years. I never go home, nor do they come here. He has forbidden my mother, my brother, and my sister to speak to me."

She moved to the velvet-covered chair and held on to its carved rosewood frame for support. Her heart beat madly. "Why?"

He shoved a hand into his pocket with a rough sigh. "I was in the fighting in Cuba. I joined the service after I graduated from the Citadel in '89 because I was tired of books and education, and I loved the very thought of soldiering and war." He laughed coldly. "You see how romanticism warps the mind? I thought the military glorious and exciting and adventurous." His gaze fell to the Persian rug on the floor and traced its swirls and lines. "But my father convinced me that the military was no life, so I mustered out to go to Harvard. Then, as you know, I came here in '96 and began to work for Eli. But in '97 there were rumors of an impending war with Spain, so I reenlisted. The talk of fighting invigorated me. I went home to my family on leave, raving about the mistreatment of Cuban nationals at the hands of the Spanish, which I had heard from a newspaperman passing through town. My young twin brothers, Robert and Andrew, were incensed by the plight of the Cuban people and impressed by my tales of military life. They went right out and joined the navy." He paused briefly. "They were on the USS *Maine* when it blew up in Havana Harbor in February of '98, two months before the United States declared war on Spain and sent armed forces to fight in Cuba."

She hardly dared breathe. "I see."

He looked up. "My father blamed me for their deaths. No explanation I could make would satisfy him. After war was declared, I was in the thick of the fighting outside Havana." He shrugged powerful shoulders and fingered the unlit cigar with the hand that wasn't in his pocket. "I was wounded. They contacted my father and he sent a telegram back. It read that he had no son in the army." He laughed coldly. "So you see, I really had nothing to come back to."

"You were engaged to Diane before you went to war."

"I had been," he corrected. "I was keeping company with her when I enlisted. I proposed while I was on leave, the Thanksgiving before my unit shipped out for Cuba, while my brothers were raw recruits looking forward to their hitch on a ship," he said. "She wanted me to ask my father for . . . something." He refused to mention his family's wealth or his inheritance, since it was lost anyway. "My father refused, which created the first rift between us, and she married Calverson when I shipped out to go to war."

"While you were in Cuba," she said, infuriated.

He sighed. "She was alone and in financial trouble," he said, absently defending her even now. "I'm certain that Calverson persuaded her that I might not come back at all. He was here and I wasn't, and her family was in desperate need."

Claire was thinking that if her family had been in desperate need, she'd have worked herself to death trying to save them, but she wouldn't have forsaken a fiancé in a war to do it. She didn't say that. She was sure that he wouldn't hear criticism of Diane.

"It was a sad homecoming for you," was all she said.

He spoke briefly about the cold, lonely dock on the eastern tip of Long Island where his regiment had been sent from Cuba. Coming from the tropics to the icy cold of Long Island had been responsible for making many of the men sick. It had taken a petition signed by Teddy Roosevelt and the regimental officers to get the U.S. government even to rotate the troops out of Cuba, where they were literally starving to death. And instead of sending them back to Florida to muster out, they were sent to New York State. John had arrived in America, wounded and disillusioned, with only the companionship of fellow soldiers to make it less stark.

The experience had hardened him. His memories of Cuba would always be bitter-sweet as he recalled fallen comrades and yellow fever and the Cuban resistance. He also remembered Teddy Roosevelt's deep, booming voice praising his Rough Riders for their sacrifices and their valor, and wishing that he'd been part of that volunteer force, under Teddy's command. He respected the man. Obviously, so did those fire-eating recruits of his, many of whom had been lawmen in the West, some even outlaws. A Texas outlaw had, in fact, been given a pardon thanks to Teddy's intervention after the man served so valiantly in Cuba.

The experience of meeting Roosevelt had colored his memories. Roosevelt became governor of New York State, and later ran on the ticket with Republican incumbent presidential candidate William McKinley, as his vice president. McKinley won on November 6, 1900.

"It was quiet, at least," he said. He searched her eyes. "Did I ever tell you what a difference you made by coming to see me in the hospital?"

She beamed shyly. "Did I, really?"

"You kept me alive, I think. You were always smiling, always happy. It was one of the best times of my life." Amazing, he thought as he spoke, that he hadn't realized at the time how important Claire was to him.

Claire felt her heart swell. "I hoped you didn't mind that I came with Uncle Will. I enjoyed doing what little I could for you. I suppose Mr. Calverson had no qualms about giving your job back to you when you returned. People thought it a little strange, you know, because you'd once been engaged to his wife and he'd taken her from you."

"Yes." He'd wondered about that himself from time to time. "But I suppose it didn't hurt that I had a degree in business and that I was a wizard with numbers. In fact, I also worked in a bank up North while I was in school at Harvard."

194

She watched him trace a path along the unlit cigar, as if he were remembering.

"You never spoke about Cuba, even on those long evenings when you and my uncle Will played chess in our parlor."

His gaze lifted to hers. "I try to forget. Most of the memories are not pleasant ones."

"Uncle Will said that you were given a medal for what you did in Cuba."

"I had a Silver Star," he said, without telling what he'd won it for. "And a Purple Heart for that wound in the lung."

She remembered seeing a rough scar on his chest, just below the nipple. She averted her face, to hide her own memories.

"I know that your parents died of cholera when you were ten," he said.

She looked at him, surprised. "Uncle Will told you?"

He nodded. "Did you finish school?"

"Yes. I wanted to go on to college at Agnes Scott and read history, but there was no money."

"Because Will spent it all on his passion for machines," he said, guessing.

She flushed. "I didn't want it so badly after all, I suppose," she said, hedging. "And it was fun learning about my uncle's motorcar."

His eyes were all over her, like hands, tracing and appraising. They narrowed, smoldered. He wanted her. Just like that. She was his wife. He had a hunch that she wouldn't deny him. All he would have to do was kiss her. One kiss, and he could have her; it was in her eyes. She, like him, remembered the ecstasy they'd shared.

She bit her lower lip hard, trying to restore sanity to a mind crazy to have him. She lifted her face. "I must go to bed," she said firmly.

His dark eyes glittered. "Whose?" he asked quietly.

The flush got worse. "My own, unless you don't mind increasing the risk of a child," she said deliberately.

His jaw tightened. "It would be worth any risk," he said huskily. "I want you."

Such plain speaking embarrassed her. She lowered her head. "I am not Diane," she said through her teeth.

The sound of her name on his wife's lips went through him like a knife. His intake of breath was audible. As if he could ever have confused the two of them! Did she realize what an insult she'd just offered him? His fist clenched in his pocket, and the fingers holding the expensive cigar all but crushed it.

"Perhaps it would be better not to take the risk," he said stiffly. "Good night, Claire."

"Good night, John."

She went slowly into her room and closed the door. Once inside, her heart raced wildly. If only he had said *Damn the risk!* But here was proof that his hunger for Claire was only physical. All she had to do was mention Diane, and all his ardor died a quick death. It was something she must remember, she told herself firmly, and she refused to think of what might have happened.

9

The next day, Claire was surprised by a visit from Evelyn Paine, who had a special request.

"I know it's short notice, and you're working so hard to make gowns for Jane and Emma and me. But I have a friend visiting from Savannah with her daughter, and she'd dearly adore having you sew a special gown for her daughter's coming-out party."

"I'd be delighted. But why did you come in person instead of just sending a note?" Claire asked curiously.

Evelyn looked around. "Is Mrs. Dobbs at home?"

"Why, no. She's gone shopping."

"Thank goodness. Claire, this is rather a sensitive issue, and I have no wish to broadcast it. I had to come myself." She leaned forward, elegant in a burgundy suit with a white ruffled blouse and a broad-brimmed hat to match the suit. "The matron visiting me is your husband's mother. Her own husband has forbidden her to contact him, and she gave her word. But she did not promise that she wouldn't contact his wife."

Claire almost gasped. "I don't know what to say!"

"Say yes. She is staying at my home. She and Emily, her daughter. They're wonderful people. They want very much to meet you. Come home with me now."

Claire hesitated. John would be livid if he found out. And how would she explain her absence?

She looked up and sighed. She and John were already so far apart that one more thing wouldn't really make much difference. "I'll come," she told Evelyn.

She wasn't sure what she expected to see. John was tall and dark and elegant, so she had a picture of his kinfolk in mind that was nothing like the people she met. His mother was small and fair and fragile-looking. His sister Emily was tall and elegant, and also fair but with dark eyes. They stared at Claire for so long that she felt uncomfortable.

"You are John's wife?" Maude Hawthorn asked hesitantly.

"I'm afraid so," Claire said. "I suppose

you were expecting someone beautiful . . ."

"Nonsense," Maude said, and smiled as she came forward to take Claire's hands. Her blue eyes were as warm as her fingers. "If I'm surprised, it's at my son's good taste. Evelyn has shown me a sample of your talent at needlework, my dear. It was more than just an excuse to bring you here. We really would like you to sew Emily's coming-out gown."

"Indeed so," Emily said, coming forward with an enthusiastic smile of her own. "I've never seen such intricate embroidery and beadwork. You're so talented!" She chuckled, her dark eyes twinkling. "Imagine my big brother being so wise in his choice of brides!"

"It wasn't wisdom, I'm afraid . . . it was pity," Claire said, with more bitterness than she realized. "My uncle had died and I had no means of support. Because of his friendship with Uncle Will, John was concerned for my welfare."

Maude, who knew her son very well, had never known him to do anything drastic out of pity alone. From what Evelyn had told her, this young woman had character and integrity — and she wasn't mercenary. Not like that other woman whose scandalous behavior with John Hawthorn had reached his mother's ears even far away in Savannah.

"You know something about us from John, I imagine?" Maude said hopefully.

Claire hesitated, waiting for inspiration.

Evelyn mistook her silence and smiled. "If you'll excuse me, I'll see about getting us some tea and cakes." She closed the sliding doors of the living room behind her.

Claire turned her attention back to Maude Hawthorn. "I know almost nothing about you," she said painfully. "John doesn't speak of his family to me. At least, not much."

Maude looked crushed. "I . . . see."

"Oh, please. Don't look like that," Claire entreated. "John and I spend very little time together," she added honestly. "Our marriage is one of appearances, you see." She sat down heavily on the velvet-covered couch. "The truth is that he married me to spare himself, the bank, and Mrs. Calverson any more poisonous gossip. He had been somewhat indiscreet, and tongues were wagging. Marrying me gave me a roof over my head and protection for him."

Maude sat down beside her. So much for her hopes that this was a marriage of love! "Then he still can't stay away from her," she said heavily. "I had hoped, so much, that he was finally finished with that ill-starred attraction."

"So had we all," Emily added, taking the rosewood chair across from the sofa.

Maude spread her hands in silent appeal. "As you may already have noticed, Mrs. Calverson is not a favorite subject at our home. It was she who caused the first rift between John and his father, demanding that John be given his inheritance at once. There was no way my husband could comply, and John knew it. The nineties were, as you know, extremely unfavorable years for the banking industry. We are only just now finding our feet."

Claire was entranced. "Are you . . . your family . . . bankers?" she asked, with eager curiosity.

Maude smiled. "Yes. My father was president of the largest bank in Savannah, and my husband is now chairman of its board of directors. He also sits on the board of three other prominent banks, one here in Atlanta. My son Jason owns a huge shipping business in Savannah and a fleet of fishing boats. He is the only son we have left at home now. We are very close to him, although we miss John so much."

Clearly deciding to change the melancholy subject, Emily said, "I have my coming out at the spring charity ball in Savannah. You would have plenty of time to sew a gown for me."

"Would you?" Maude pleaded. "We've seen Evelyn's gowns. You're very talented."

"What if John finds out?" Claire asked. "He'll think I've gone behind his back, and I have."

Maude's blue eyes were piercing. "You love him, don't you?"

"With all my heart," Claire said miserably, "for all the good it's done me. He'd walk over my dying body to get to the beautiful Mrs. Calverson. I have no illusions whatsoever about his feelings for me; he has none."

Maude's indrawn breath was audible.

"I've shocked you," Claire said. "I'm sorry."

Maude's face grew strained. "You say John said little about our family. Did he tell you about Robert and Andrew?"

Claire frowned. "Robert and Andrew?" she murmured. "Oh. His brothers."

"Yes, my dear," Maude said, and her face began to show its age. She folded her hands in her lap. "Robert and Andrew were our youngest sons. They joined the navy shortly after John came home in his uniform, so dignified and enthusiastic about saving the Cuban people from Spanish domination."

She traced the fingers of one hand over the back of the other. "They were aboard the USS *Maine* when it went down. Both were killed."

"John told me what happened. It must be a painful memory for him. He could hardly bear to speak of it to me."

"It is equally painful to us. But my husband blamed John. He cursed him and disinherited him, and vowed never to speak to him again. Sadly, he forced that same silence on Emily and Jason and me. I have obeyed him in all things in the past. But he is very ill with his heart, and I know that he regrets this situation. He is too proud to approach John." She looked up at Claire. "I had hoped that you might find a way to coax John into coming home to visit."

Claire's thin shoulders lifted and fell. "You must see now that I could coax my husband to do nothing," she said, with a bittersweet smile. "John and I are strangers, in almost every way."

"I had hoped to find a totally different situation."

"I'm sorry," Claire said helplessly. "Is your husband very bad?"

"His heart is weak," Maude said. "Although I think it is his alienation from John that has made it so. We often say things in the heat of anger that we later regret. He was grief-stricken for his sons, and he refused to believe that their passing was an act of God. He had to blame someone. John was the easiest to blame. It wasn't John's fault, Claire," she added sadly. "They'd planned to join the service since they were boys. It was unfortunate that it should happen quite so soon after John's visit, and that they should serve on a doomed ship."

Claire's eyes widened. "Why, that is why John refused to discuss attending the governor's ball at Christmas!" she exclaimed involuntarily. "It was because he expected his father to be there."

"He will not," Maude said. "Because he can't travel this far. Neither Emily nor I will come without him."

"Yes, but I can't tell John that without his realizing how I know."

"I see." Maude smiled wistfully. "I think you would have liked the ball."

"I know I would have," Claire replied. "But we never get everything we want, do we? Now, what about this gown for Emily?"

They spoke enthusiastically of Emily's coming-out gown, and Claire sketched some possibilities. She settled on one with a keyhole neckline and short puffy sleeves with an empire waist.

"It's very unconventional," Emily said, with a grin. "I shall love it!"

"*Unconventional* is part of my name," Claire informed her. "You should hear the comments from the local men when I drive my uncle's motorcar! In fact, I had to leave it parked because two of John's friends made such a fuss."

"You have a motorcar?" Maude asked. "Claire, I must see it! Can we go for a drive?"

"I wish it were possible," Claire said wholeheartedly. "But if you come home with me . . ." She frowned. "On the other hand, how would Mrs. Dobbs know who you are? And John won't be at home. Yes, of course you can!"

Maude and Emily were both excited at the prospect of a ride in Claire's automobile. Maude confided that she would love to have one of her own — and would persuade her husband to buy her one.

"Then you will truly have an excuse to visit, Claire," Maude told the younger woman. "To help me learn how to work on it."

"First I will have to join the local women's suffrage movement to keep the men out of my hair," Claire said jokingly.

206

"Of course you will," Maude said easily. "I belong to the Savannah chapter, and so does Emily. We are not content to sit by and let men make all the rules for us."

Claire was intrigued by her husband's family. What a pity that she couldn't tell him so.

She managed to get the motorcar out of the shed without rousing the entire neighborhood. Mrs. Dobbs was at home, but Claire made sure that no introductions were made. She kept her guests outside, near Evelyn's carriage, which waited for them half a block away. It was a tight squeeze to get herself and Maude and Emily all into the little two-seater, but they managed it. Claire cranked the machine and they went down the road and back again with squeals of delight. Fortunately they didn't meet a horse — and old Mr. Fleming, who lived on the corner, wasn't outside to yell threats of police action.

It wasn't until she'd parked the car again and surveyed the faintly greasy clothing of her guests that she realized she should have provided dusters.

"It's a messy business just now," Claire said, apologizing.

"Yes, well, our clothing is dark and our

faces will wash," Maude assured her, with twinkling eyes. "Claire, what a marvelous invention! I must say, it's invigorating."

"I think so, too," Emily seconded.

Maude looked back at the rooming house where John and Claire lived. "I wish I could have seen John," she said as she made her way to the waiting carriage.

"I wish you could have, too," Claire said, embracing her and then Emily. "But at least we've met."

"And we'll keep in touch, through Evelyn," Maude said doggedly.

"Meanwhile, I'll work very hard on your dress, Emily," Claire added, with a smile.

"Come and see us, if you ever can," Maude said gently. "You would always be welcome, even without John."

"I'll remember that. Have a safe journey home."

"You take care, Claire."

Maude signaled to the driver to take them back to Evelyn's house, and Claire went slowly inside after the carriage was out of sight. She was smudged with grease and dirt again, and it was a blessing that John would be working late.

She never questioned if he was seeing Diane somewhere in these long evenings when he didn't come home. She wasn't sure she could bear the answer.

It was inevitable that Mrs. Dobbs would mention Claire's guests over the evening meal.

"I had hoped that you might bring them inside, Claire," Mrs. Dobbs said, with faint reprimand. "I had a cake nicely sliced and tea ready to pour."

"They were already late for an engagement," Claire said on a laugh. "I'm sorry, but there was no time. Evelyn had told them about my motorcar and they just had to see it for themselves."

"Evelyn Paine?" John asked, frowning.

"Why, yes. She's frequently a guest here," Mrs. Dobbs said smugly. "She comes with some of her friends to visit Claire."

John eyed his wife with open curiosity. "So that was how you became so well acquainted with the cream of Atlanta society. You have them over for tea."

"And they have me over for tea, as well," Claire replied, stung by his faint sarcasm.

"Quite often," Mrs. Dobbs seconded. "They're charming company."

John put down his fork. "What a pity that you never thought to mention these visits to me," he said calculatingly.

Her eyebrows rose. "When would you have been available for me to tell?" she asked. Mindful of Mrs. Dobbs's curious glance, she amended, "I mean, you work such long and late hours, John. And at night you're much too tired to speak of your day."

"I expect those social evenings wear you out, don't they, Mr. Hawthorn?" Mrs. Dobbs asked pointedly. "My sister-in-law accompanied her husband to that gathering at the Calversons' the night before last. I believe you were there alone. She thought it rather odd that a newly married man would attend any evening affair without his bride."

She got up with an apologetic glance at Claire and swept off to the kitchen.

Claire felt her temper begin to rise. She stared at John with cold eyes, noting his sudden tension.

"Obviously you didn't feel inclined to take me with you," she said bluntly.

"It was a business meeting."

"Mrs. Calverson wasn't there?" she persisted.

He threw his napkin down. "Yes, she was there!"

"And Mrs. Dobbs's sister-in-law was there, also."

He got to his feet. He felt guilty — and because of it, he sought refuge in bad temper. "The Whitfields were also in attendance, and judging by past events, I thought it diplomatic to keep you and Ted Whitfield separated," he said, with some heat.

"Are you accusing me again of encouraging Ted?"

"Didn't you?" he asked, his smile as mocking as his tone. "I do recall almost coming to blows with him over you the last time you were together. That couldn't have happened if you hadn't encouraged his advances. And those of other bank officers."

She stood up, too, very slowly. "And naturally, your feelings for the elegant Mrs. Calverson are nothing more than those of a banker for his business partner's wife?"

His eyes darkened. Beside his powerful thigh, one lean hand clenched. "Be careful, Claire," he cautioned softly.

"Why?" she demanded. "You obviously believe that you have every right to spend your time ogling Mrs. Calverson and making sure that I don't do anything to spoil your fun. But I mustn't be seen near Ted, is that right?"

"I don't ogle Mrs. Calverson!"

"That isn't what it looks like!" she snapped. "Our marriage will do very little to stop the gossip if you continue to feed it in such a manner."

Mrs. Dobbs came back before he could

reply, looking worried and nervous.

"Shall we continue this discussion upstairs?" John asked curtly.

"No, we shall not," Claire replied, shocking him. "I have no wish whatsoever to speak with you about such a distasteful subject. My opinion is of no consequence to you, anyway — since you don't care what I think of your philandering."

He was outraged. "I have never philandered!"

"Ha!"

He turned and left the room, pausing just long enough to retrieve his coat, hat, and cane from the rack in the hall before he went slamming out the front door.

Mrs. Dobbs hesitated. "The first days of any marriage can be very difficult," she said encouragingly.

"This marriage has been nothing short of difficult since its beginning," Claire replied shortly. "I should never have married him. It's my own fault for thinking I could change the way he feels. He can't really help finding Mrs. Calverson attractive. And I have neither the beauty nor the charm to compete with hers."

Mrs. Dobbs came forward and took her hands. "Claire, you have so many wonderful qualities," she said earnestly. "Please don't let that woman break up your marriage."

"How can I fight her influence?" Claire asked wearily. "I had no idea that he was going to socials without me."

Mrs. Dobbs looked guilty. "I shouldn't have said anything. It just rankled to have him keep quiet about it. You had a right to know."

"Yes, I did," Claire replied firmly. "Thank you for telling me. I should have hated to hear gossip about it."

"Gossip," Mrs. Dobbs said, shaking her head. "How terrible it can be."

"As I have learned. Good night, Mrs. Dobbs. Thank you for sticking up for me."

"You won't do anything rash, Claire?" she asked worriedly.

"I've already done something rash," came the reply. "I married him."

The next day, Claire had a message from her friend Kenny Blake; he wanted to see her. She took a carriage into the city and went to find out what he wanted.

She was surprised to find Kenny with a tall, elegant white-haired man who was looking at one of Claire's gowns.

"I borrowed this from the boutique to show Mr. Stillwell," Kenny told her, with a grin.

Stillwell nodded politely. "Mrs. Hawthorn, I'm delighted to make your acquaintance. This," he said, gesturing toward the gown, a white-and-black silk one with jet bead details, "is the most beautiful creation I've seen in many a long year. I would like to display it in my store."

"His store," Kenny informed her, "is Macy's department store in New York City."

She gasped. "You can't be serious!"

"I assure you that I am," he replied solemnly. "And I think you'll find that your asking price is far too low for such an original." He named a price that left her speechless.

"Sit down," Kenny said quickly, providing her with a chair. "I told you she wasn't going to believe it," he added to Mr. Stillwell.

The older man chuckled. "So I see. But you are very talented, Mrs. Hawthorn, and I believe we can do a great deal of business. Your designs can be sewn by a local concern for us, and we will market them. I assure you of the highest quality, your own personal label, and strictly a couture trade. All you would invest is the time to sketch your ideas and sew a model for us."

"I can't believe it! I just can't!" Claire said, tears of pure joy streaming down her cheeks. "I never dreamed of such a thing!"

"I did," Kenny said smugly.

She was beside herself. "I will be finan-
cially independent," she said almost to herself.

"Wealthy," Mr. Stillwell corrected. "Very
wealthy, if these designs do as well as I
expect them to."

"There's just one thing," she interjected.
"My husband must not know."

"I have no reason to tell him," Stillwell assured her.

"And I'm quiet as a clam," Kenny added.
"No one will know. You'll be known simply
as Magnolia."

"Quite."

"In that case, Mr. Stillwell, I'm your girl."

He grinned from ear to ear.

Claire was bursting to tell someone, anyone,
about her good fortune, but she didn't dare.
If she told Mrs. Dobbs or Evelyn, as trust-
worthy as they normally were, they wouldn't
be able to keep a secret of such magnitude.
So Claire had to keep her tidings to herself.

"Oh, Kenny! I'll never be able to thank
you enough!" she said enthusiastically after
Mr. Stillwell had exchanged addresses with
her and was on his way to another meeting.

"It was my pleasure," Kenny said. He
smiled ruefully. "I've missed you since your

marriage, Claire. I called once or twice, but your husband told me that you weren't available to speak to me."

That came as a surprise. "When was this?" she asked.

"One morning just after your marriage — and then again two weeks ago."

She grimaced. "He didn't tell me."

He shrugged. "A husband is entitled to be jealous of a new wife, I suppose," he said charitably. "But I would have liked to congratulate you, at least." He eyed her. "Didn't you know about the wedding gift I sent, either?"

"What wedding gift?"

"A set of thimbles," he said. "Porcelain ones. I know how much you enjoy your needlework."

"No, I didn't get them," she said, smoldering inside.

"Of course not. He sent them back," he told her, shaking his head. "He's a very possessive man, your husband."

"Apparently," she agreed. He could see Diane Calverson whenever he liked, but she wasn't allowed to have a wedding present from an old friend! It was outrageous.

"Would you like a soda before you go home?" Kenny asked.

"Yes, I would," she said, smiling.

He grinned. They went to a soda parlor about a block away, where she indulged in a sticky, delicious hot fudge sundae. It was like old times to sit and talk with Kenny, who had been a frequent visitor to her uncle's home. Even though they were no more than friends, she'd missed him since her marriage. She could talk to Kenny — something she was rarely able to do with her husband.

"I'm delighted that you're going to do this designing job," Kenny said. "I hope it won't get you into any trouble at home."

"As long as John doesn't know, it won't," she said honestly. "And you've promised me that you won't tell him."

"Indeed I have," he assured her.

She sighed. "It's like a dream," she said, smiling at him. "It's something I've always wanted to do — and here it is, falling right into my lap. I can hardly wait to get started. I have all sorts of ideas!"

"You can send them to me by messenger. Or bring them by when you're in town. I'll get them to Mr. Stillwell," he said. "That way, there won't be anything to connect you to him."

"You're a good friend, Kenny. I'm lucky to have you."

"That works both ways." He smiled back

and touched her hand lightly.

It was unfortunate that Diane Calverson happened to be passing the window at that moment and witnessed the innocent touch.

10

That evening, Claire was shocked to discover — at the last minute — that John had invited the Calversons for dinner. Mrs. Dobbs had prepared a scrumptious meal for them, but a maid employed by John for the evening had served it, because Mrs. Dobbs was going out to the theater with friends.

Eli Calverson seemed worried and a little preoccupied, while Diane was making an obvious effort to be especially nice to John.

Over after-dinner coffee, Claire noticed that John was staring at her with the coldest, angriest dark eyes she'd ever seen. Diane, on the other hand, was sweetness itself.

"What a lovely apartment house," she said to Claire, looking around. "Of course, it's not quite the same as having a place of your own, but I suppose it's the next best thing."

Claire studied the other woman, hesitating so long to make a reply that the artificial smile on Diane's face began to waver.

"Under other circumstances, I should have enjoyed having a home of my own," she replied finally, with a smile as cool as her tone.

"Other circumstances?" Diane echoed.

"Why, yes," Claire told her, aware that the men were too involved in talking business to overhear. "If I had a husband who loved *me*."

The bitter emphasis on the last word made Diane's eyes widen, but before she could reply, Claire turned away to direct the maid clearing the table.

"That was a lovely meal, Claire," Mr. Calverson said graciously.

"Thank you, but it was Mrs. Dobbs who prepared it."

"Oh. I assumed . . ." he began, unsettled.

Claire's hands folded together at her waist. "I would never presume to invade another woman's kitchen, even if I'd known that we were expecting guests for dinner," she said, dropping a bombshell right in her husband's lap.

"John!" Eli Calverson exclaimed. "You invited us to a meal and your wife wasn't told?"

"My wife likes her little jokes," John said, eyes slicing into Claire.

"Oh. Oh!" Eli chuckled. "Yes, I see. Well, we must be on our way, my dear," he told Diane.

"I'll have the maid fetch our coats," Diane volunteered. "Where did she go, John?"

"Through here." He escorted Diane into the kitchen.

But the maid wasn't there. Claire had glimpsed her going out the back door with a bucket of ashes to empty from the wood-stove.

"Excuse me. I'll take these dishes off the table for her," Claire told Mr. Calverson.

She gathered the plates, stacked them, and carried them down the hall to the kitchen — arriving just in time to see Diane in John's arms, with her lips pulling away from his.

Claire stood stock-still. Diane was flushed and laughing nervously. As he moved back, John had an intense expression on his face that defied description.

"I don't have to ask you to leave, do I, Mrs. Calverson?" Claire asked pleasantly. "I'm sure you realize that all I have to do is go back into the parlor and tell your husband what you've been doing with *my* husband in *my* home."

Diane nibbled her lower lip. "Now, Claire . . ."

221

"Get out!" Claire said, with smoldering fury and flashing gray eyes. "Right this minute!"

"Claire —" John began, moving toward her.

She jerked away from him, rattling the dishes in her hands. Her breasts heaved with the effort of her breathing. She was milk-white, but angry enough to overcome her numbness.

"You scoundrel," she said harshly. "You utter scoundrel!"

He looked shocked. Diane brushed past him with a muttered apology and ran into the hall. The maid was there and she ordered her to bring their coats.

"Yes, ma'am," the maid replied, and ran to do as she was bidden.

There was a faint murmur of voices as Diane went back into the parlor, but Claire scarcely heard. She was glaring at her husband as if she'd like to hit him with the plates, shaking with temper and reaction.

"Kindly make an effort to control yourself until our guests are gone," John said, with icy formality.

"Your guests, not mine," she returned. Her voice shook; her face burned. "If you ever bring that slut into my home again, I'll tell your fancy bank president the truth about the two of you, and to the devil with gossip!"

"Claire!" he said sharply.

She took a calming breath, put the plates down, and swept past him out the door and back to the parlor.

"Thank you for a lovely evening, Claire," Diane said, with a forced smile. She looked at John through her lashes. "Good night, John."

"Good night. Thank you both for coming," he replied, smiling easily as he and Claire escorted them to the door.

"Nice to see you again, Claire," Eli said, with a distant smile, apparently unaware of any undercurrents. "Now don't trouble yourself about this merger with Whitfield. Just because a few people are disgruntled, there's no need to worry."

John was scrambling to get his thoughts organized. He was reeling from Diane's behavior and Claire's reaction to it. "I've heard some gossip, and this morning one of our investors actually asked me if we were solvent," John told his boss, and found it odd that Calverson's cheeks seemed a bit flushed.

Calverson patted him on the arm. "How ridiculous." He chuckled. "Why should Whitfield want to merge with us if there was any shadow on the bank's reputation? And I don't have to remind you, dear boy, of our new assets — thanks to your calculated act of kindness toward the general's widow!"

John frowned. "It wasn't a calculated act," he said.

"Bad choice of words," the older man said. "Come, Diane. We must be away. Good night, dear friends."

John said the appropriate things, but he was worried. He'd heard more than one comment about the bank's assets. He made a mental note to have a conversation with the bank's head bookkeeper, without Calverson's knowledge.

Claire seethed. Her attention was far from Calverson and remarks about the bank.

She stood quietly by while John said all the socially correct things. Diane and Eli got into their waiting carriage and went off down the cold lamplit street.

Claire went back inside, shivering with the cold and her feelings of betrayal. She couldn't manage to look at John. Seeing Diane in his arms had shattered her last hope of any sort of life with him. She wouldn't be set aside for his mistress. She had too much pride.

"I'll pack my things this evening and leave in the morning," she said.

"The hell you will."

She whirled to face him, just as the maid poked her head into the parlor.

"I've finished, Mr. Hawthorn," she said, with wary looks from husband to wife. "May I go now?"

"Certainly you may — and thank you for your help."

"Thank you for the work, sir. The money will come in right handy with Todd out of his job," she replied, with a smile. "Good night, sir, madam."

"Thank you," Claire added, almost choking on the words.

The maid let herself out. She lived two doors down, and it was a safe neighborhood. All the same, John went to the front porch and watched her until she had entered her own small apartment behind the main house of her landlord.

As he closed the door again and locked it, Claire started up the stairs. "I'm sure you'll understand that I have nothing to say to you," she said over her shoulder. "I'm leaving you."

"We're newly married," he said shortly. "I won't let you walk out on me."

She turned, her slender hand resting on the banister. "How do you propose to stop me? If you chain me to the floor, I'm sure

Mrs. Dobbs will ask why. Short of that, you won't be able to keep me here. I will not be used as a cover for your shameful affair with that woman anymore. The idea of it! Kissing her like that in my own house! I must have been out of my mind to marry you in the first place!"

He took a deep breath. "It wasn't as bad as it looked," he replied. "And I'm not having an affair with her. I give you my word."

She searched his lean face. The things his mother had told her came back to her — and she saw the pain and grief that must have shaped him into this taciturn man. He'd loved Diane. He still loved her. Could she really blame him? Diane might not be her idea of the perfect woman, but people were rarely loved for their flaws. Diane must have qualities that he admired, even if Claire couldn't see them.

Her shoulders rose and fell. "Your conduct is none of my business anymore," she said, with quiet defeat in her tone. "Do what you please, John."

"Where do you plan to go?" he asked curtly. "To your friend Kenny?"

Her eyebrows arched. "I beg your pardon?"

"You accuse me of having an affair, but I can assure you that I haven't been seen holding hands in public. In a soda parlor, of all the damned places! In broad daylight!"

Dimly, she wondered how he'd known that — if he'd actually seen her with Kenny. "It was totally innocent!" she snapped. "And while we're on the subject, where is the wedding present he sent to me? And why was I never told that he called to congratulate us?"

His chin lifted. "I don't share. You're my wife. As long as you are my wife, you won't accept presents from other men . . . and that includes sundaes!"

"How did you know?"

"Because Diane saw you and told me," he replied.

"How very convenient!" She snapped her skirts with an angry hand. "So I can't have a sundae with a man in a public place, but you can kiss another woman in my kitchen, is that right?"

"She kissed me, if you must know!"

"And you couldn't defend yourself," she drawled sarcastically.

He came away from the door and up the staircase so quickly that she didn't have time to get out of his way. He caught her around the waist with one arm, while his free hand tangled in her high coiffure.

"Perhaps if you kissed me more often, I

wouldn't have to go to other women for it."

She fought him like a tigress, furious with herself for being jealous, furious with him for his behavior. He'd kissed that horrible woman, and she hated him!

But, oh, his mouth was so warm and passionate, his arms so strong and comforting around her slender body. She felt her lips parting involuntarily as the slow, deep kiss went on and on and on.

He murmured something against her lips and bent to lift her into his arms. He was breathing roughly as he mounted the rest of the stairs and carried her into their apartment, kicking the door closed behind them.

He didn't put her down. He carried her into his bedroom, as he had once before. This time he didn't bother with putting out the lights or even closing the bedroom door. He fell onto the bed with Claire under his lean, tense body; his hands went under her long skirt, against the soft, warm skin of her thighs.

"John," she said in a choked, halfhearted protest.

"Shh," he whispered into her mouth. He was trembling, as she was. His hands moved urgently between them, removing barriers, gently, coaxingly.

She felt him go into her with a sense of

shock. They weren't even undressed. But as she tried to protest, his tongue went deep into her mouth, echoing that other fierce, slow, deep movement of his body that brought no pain at all. Tides rose and fell inside her body, inside her mind. She heard their mingled erratic breathing, heard the slide of cloth against cloth, skin against skin. His hands were bruising where he held her as his body began to move fiercely. She hadn't dreamed that such pleasure could exist. It should have hurt, because he was so demanding. But it didn't hurt. The pleasure came upon her in wave after wave of sensuous heat. She tasted him, breathed him, as his body buffeted hers in the utter silence of the cold room. She heard him begin to groan even as his control slipped and he gave in to the damning urgency of his body. She moved to accommodate him, lifted into him, arched under him. He cried out and so did she as the pleasure exploded in a sinful, shameful tide of ecstasy so great that she thought her body would never be able to bear it . . .

She felt the trembling of her own body echoed in his. Her arms were tightly around him; her legs had curled around his. They lay intimately joined, fully clothed, with his heart beating madly against her bound breasts.

Her mouth was so dry that she could hardly manage speech. "Was it . . . because you wanted her?" she whispered.

His intake of breath brushed his chest over her sensitized breasts. "No, it was because I wanted you." He pulled away from her and looked down into her wide, silvery eyes. Slowly his hand went to the buttons of her lacy black dress and he began to unfasten them. He was still joined to her, and the movements were stimulating, erotic.

"I'm going to strip you," he whispered huskily. "Right down to your silky skin. And then I'm going to take my own clothes off, and enjoy you all night long. When morning comes, there won't be an inch of you that I don't know, that I haven't touched or kissed or nibbled with my teeth." As if to emphasize the words, his mouth went down hard over her soft breasts, right through the fabric, and she felt his teeth bite softly into a hard nipple. She gasped.

He moved, laughing deeply when she shivered; her eyes widened as he looked into them. "Yes, you're still ready for me, Claire." He moved again, catching his breath as the movement brought him totally back to life. "And I'm more than ready for you!"

■ ■ ■ ■

Claire lay awake in the darkness, sick at her own shameless response to the ways John had touched her, the places his mouth had invaded.

She lay under a single white sheet, completely nude, thankful that the light was finally out so that she didn't have to see, again, the cold triumph in her husband's face. He'd used her, she thought furiously. He'd used her like a woman of the night — and she'd not only let him, she'd wrapped herself around him like a snake and whimpered with pleasure. She'd whispered things to him that she couldn't bear to remember.

Gingerly she moved the sheet and started to sit up. A steely hand caught her arm and jerked her down onto a warm, still-aroused male body.

"No, you don't." He breathed roughly. "I'm not finished."

"John, please. I can't!"

"Are you sore inside?" he whispered against her mouth.

She flushed. "No, but — oh!"

His fingers had found her, touched her, eliciting again that mindless delight that stiffened her softness against his hair-

231

roughened nudity.

"You are the sweetest taste of heaven I have ever had," he whispered as his touch grew bolder. "The sweetest honey on earth. I could die trying to get enough of you. I want you more than I want to breathe, little one." He drew her mouth down to his and, while he kissed her, he moved her slowly, exquisitely impaling her. "Yes," he whispered tenderly. "Yes, take me inside you and caress me, hold me, make me mad with pleasure. Forget the things old women have told you about this and be a woman with me."

"I don't . . . understand," she whimpered as he moved her.

"Yes, you do. Sit up and take me, Claire."

He threw off the covers and half lifted her until she was above him, over him. His hands supported her hips, and his lifted up to meet hers, teaching her the rhythm. Her breasts rose sharply with the vicious pleasure he kindled in her.

"Yes," he said ardently. "Yes, Claire. Now, darling. Now, darling. Yes, move on me. Move on my body. Claire. Move, move —" He gasped as her slow, sinuous motions made him shiver. He laughed, deep in his throat, and then groaned. His hands contracted, demanding as he brought her to him and lifted her away in a rhythm that brought the ecstasy flying back.

Her fingers were on his, holding them to her thighs; her body seemed no longer to be under her control. She laughed, too, fiercely, as the pleasure bit deep into her body. She looked down at him in the moonlit room, her breath rasping as she saw him helpless, powerless, totally at the mercy of her body and his need of it.

She moved again, deliberately this time, teasing, her eyes glittering with the fever of what she was doing to him. He cried out as she quickened the darting motions of her hips; she held his hands, pulling them into closer intimacy as the spiral began.

The springs were loud. The slats moved. She didn't care.

"Darling, take me." He groaned. "Take me!"

"Yes." She shuddered, pushing. "Yes, all of you. All . . . of . . . you!"

She felt the explosions to the very tips of her toes. She wept harshly, groaning, as her body riveted itself to his and convulsed. Under her, he arched up high, a ragged sob tearing out of his throat. She saw his face contort even through her own heated delirium, and she thought, He is mine!

She wept because it was so brief and so

beautiful, and so quickly gone. She lay against the damp vibration of his chest and wept bitterly.

"Why can't it last?" she bit off. "Oh, why?"

His hand smoothed her long, tangled hair; he held her hips to his, where they were still joined. "I don't know," he whispered unsteadily. His mouth searched for hers and kissed it languorously, tenderly. "I've never let a woman mount me," he breathed into her mouth. "I love the way it feels."

She buried her face in his throat. "Don't!" she whispered, embarrassed.

His hands swept down her back and up again slowly. "Can you still feel me?" he whispered, pressing down on her hips. He shivered. "I can feel you . . . all around me, like a soft, warm sheath."

"It is shameful . . . to speak of it," she whispered.

"You are my wife," he replied gently. "Nothing I do to you is shameful. No way I touch you or kiss you should be embarrassing. I am part of you, and you are part of me. We are one person when we love like this, Claire. One flesh, one heart, one soul." He took an unsteady breath and held her closer. "Dear God, I never knew such pleasure as you gave me tonight! I can barely get my breath — and still I want to bury myself in you and have, again, that fierce, mad completion."

She clung to him, shocked and yet sympathetic. "I am . . . a little sore," she confessed.

"That is hardly surprising," he said. "Forgive me. I was far too demanding."

"No. I . . . wanted it."

His hand smoothed her hot cheek. "A madness we shared." He drew in a slow breath. "Go to sleep now, little one."

She opened her eyes and stared across his chest. "Like . . . this?"

"Yes. Like this. Joined as intimately as man and woman can join." His arms wrapped around her. "I can't bear to pull away from you. Unless it hurts too much . . . ?" he asked quickly.

"It doesn't hurt," she whispered back, as profoundly moved as he sounded. She relaxed against him, feeling again the wonder of the intimacy they were sharing. Her breasts sank against the warm hardness of his chest and she laughed secretly, because even that faint movement aroused her.

He seemed to understand, because he laughed, too. "Yes," he whispered above her head, "we find all too much pleasure in each other's nakedness. But we must sleep now."

"I suppose so."

She forced her body to relax again and

closed her eyes. Amazingly she fell asleep.

She felt cool air on her body. It was uncomfortable and she was sore. Light streamed in the curtained windows, touching her swollen eyelids.

She opened her eyes and found a pair of dark, intent eyes staring down at her. She blinked and came awake. She was lying nude on the sheets. John had lifted the cover away; he was looking at her nudity as if he'd never seen a woman without her clothing.

It should have embarrassed her, but it didn't. Not at all.

Her nipples went hard under that intent stare and she shivered.

"Your body is exquisite," he said quietly. "Even after the long night, I can look at you and become aroused all over again."

She did flush, then, at the desire that darkened his lean face. She was ashamed of what she'd given away in the darkness, and desperate not to let him see how enslaved she was, physically as well as emotionally. "I hope you enjoyed yourself," she said icily. "Did you have fun pretending that I was Diane?"

The insult hit him right between the eyes. "Is that what you thought?" He laughed coldly. "Or is that what you'd like to be-

236

lieve?" He didn't understand how the passionate lover of last night had become this mocking stranger.

"Of course. You were kissing her in the kitchen — and as soon as she left, you carried me in here. I'm sure it wasn't overpowering love that motivated you," she said, with mangled pride. "You said yourself that you only married me to spare Diane's reputation. Why pretend that last night was anything other than misplaced lust?"

His temper flashed fire. He glared at her with his hand in his pocket. "Lust is an appropriate description. We went at each other like animals in heat. Although," he drawled, "I have to admit that I've never had such a night, not even with a sporting woman. You're hot, Claire. Hot and ripe and even more sensuous than Diane," he added, with deliberate cruelty, because her words had hurt him.

She sat up, holding the cover to her breasts. "You can say that with certainty?"

"Of course I can. I've seen Diane without her clothes. You aren't that naive, surely?"

The color drained out of her face. "You've . . . made love?"

"We were engaged," he replied, with glittering eyes, avoiding a direct answer.

Her heart was beating furiously. She

couldn't see the faint apprehension in his dark eyes for her own pain. It didn't occur to her that her harsh words had wounded him, or that his realization that he cared for her had left him defenseless and that he was trying to retain his pride on the heels of her insulting accusations. As if he could pretend that she was Diane!

"I have to go to work. I assume that you'll invent an appropriate excuse to stay with me after last night?" He taunted her softly. "You can have me as often as you want me, Claire. I'll make love to you every night, if that makes you happy. And eventually, I may even be able to stop pretending that you're Diane, in the dark," he added, hating himself as he said it.

There couldn't have been a greater insult. She stared at him with ice in her heart. She was numb. Without feeling. Without hope.

He watched her, waiting, hoping that the wall might come down and that she'd admit she still cared for him, that she'd loved him the night before. But she didn't.

"That was a despicable thing to say," she said finally.

"No more despicable than your accusation to me. As if I could use you to alleviate what I feel for Diane. The two emotions are as different as night and day."

"You did use me," she said huskily.

"And you loved it. You wrapped your legs around me and threw your head back and screamed with pleasure when I drove deep into you!"

She went scarlet.

He leaned forward, one hand propped over her head on the brass railing of the bed. "I didn't force you last night. You wanted me. You still want me, even now. Look, Claire." He jerked the cover away and traced a hard nipple before she squirmed her way beneath the sheet.

He stood erect, his narrowed eyes watching the expressions play across her face. "You went running to your childhood friend the minute my back was turned," he said coldly. "Well, run to him now, my dear, and see if he can make you claw his back in the darkness."

"I did not —"

He unfastened the collar of his shirt and drew it away from his shoulder to show her the deep red scratches she had made.

She gasped as he refastened it.

"There are more," he informed her. "Several are . . . lower down. You were quite demanding, at the last."

She put her face in her hands and shivered with embarrassment.

"Oh, good God! Stop looking like you've been damned!" he bit off. "Women scratch in the throes of passion. Sometimes they even bite. It's nothing to be ashamed of. Passion is violent. Lovemaking can bring pain as well as pleasure, especially when two people feel that kind of desire for each other."

"How could you?" she moaned.

"How could I *what?* Make love to you or make you face how you acted with me?" he asked. He tilted her face up to his. "Sex is fun. I enjoyed you and you enjoyed me. We're married. There's no reason we can't enjoy each other for as long as we're together."

"You don't want to be married to me."

He chuckled. "There are times when I love being married to you. Last night was one of them."

She glared at him.

He lifted an eyebrow. "When you have your bath, you might take a look at your hips," he said. "I imagine you'll find bruises, if not a few scratches that match those on my back. You weren't the only one who completely lost control."

She swallowed, a little less ashamed. He seemed to find it easy to talk about. Of course, he was experienced.

"It will all work out," he said as he turned toward the door. "I'll stay away from Diane and you'll stay away from your friend Kenny, and every night I'll give you ecstasy. Eventually, maybe I'll even give you a baby. That should be enough for both of us."

Lust, she thought. Mindless desire. Two bodies in a bed while he thought of Diane, wanted Diane, lived for Diane. And a baby . . . what sort of life would it have with such parents as they would become?

"Nothing to say?" he asked mockingly.

"Nothing at all."

His eyes went over her bare shoulders above the sheet. "Then I'll see you tonight, Mrs. Hawthorn," he said huskily. "And even if I can't make love to you, I'll strip you out of your gown and feast my eyes on you until I'm mad with desire."

"The devil you will!" she snapped.

He cocked an eyebrow and chuckled at her high color. "Oh, you'll let me," he said confidently.

He smiled smugly and went out, closing the bedroom door behind him.

"Just you wait and see what I'll let you do," she muttered. She got out of bed with a furious thud and started to pick up her gown when she saw her body in the oval full-length mirror.

Her breasts were faintly red from the hunger of his mouth. There were more marks on her belly and her white thighs. She colored as she saw the bruises he'd alluded to on her slender hips.

She looked . . . sensual. She lifted her hands and put them under her breasts, supporting them.

The door opened; he looked at her, all her secrets revealed as her smoky eyes met his.

His jaw clenched. "If I thought you could take me, I'd have you right there in front of the mirror, and we could both watch."

She flushed. Her wide, sensuous eyes searched his as he looked at her.

"God, Claire!" He breathed roughly. "God!"

He moved forward and pulled her against him, bending to find her mouth in a frenzy of desire.

"I can't," she whimpered. "I want to, so badly —"

"Here!" He caught her hands and pulled them to his body, moved them, taught them while he kissed her. But a few seconds were enough to make the hunger unbearable. He put her away from him with one helpless shudder and swallowed down his need.

"No," he said unsteadily. "We can't." He was barely able to speak. Her eyes were wide, curious, almost frightened. He held her by the shoulders fiercely, thinking he might scream from frustrated desire. Bit by bit, he let go of her, and, without a single glance, he went out the door.

He'd never known such desire. He didn't know if he could live with it on a daily basis, without ravishing his wife nightly.

And what of Diane, who loved him, whom he loved? He felt unfaithful, dirty, ashamed — of his behavior with Diane, not with Claire.

He felt the lowest of the low, sick with himself and furious at Claire for being indifferent to him except in bed. She could have repulsed him if she no longer cared for his opinion of her. Why hadn't she?

The answer was the most painful realization of all. It was because she wanted him, of course. She couldn't deny him anything, because she was as much a slave to her desire as he was to his own. That didn't mean that she loved him. Never once, during the long, exquisite night, had she whispered words of love. He hadn't realized how desperately he wanted to hear them, from her. His pure, innocent wife had suffered for so long, loved him unselfishly, and all she'd had for her pains was his indifference. He remembered when she'd offered her love with both hands and he'd rebuffed her because of Diane. He couldn't recall now how he'd felt about Diane in the first place, because his hunger and need and deep affection for Claire had completely overshadowed it.

It was a pity, he thought, that he never drank spirits. Right now, he could have used something to numb his mind.

He sat at his desk at the bank, weary of the emotional turmoil that seemed to be the hallmark of his life of late. Absently he thought about what Calverson had said last night about the bank, and he got up and started toward the office of the head bookkeeper.

But on his way, a loud voice arrested his movement.

"I heard there was money missing from the bank," an old man was saying to Eli Calverson. "My friend has a hundred thousand dollars here. He tried to draw it out and he was told there were insufficient funds!"

Eli was flustered and nervous. He was actually wringing his hands. "Sir, we lend money as well as take it in," he explained. "At times, we have to depend on our deposits to make up the difference. We have just added a huge sum to our assets —"

"You're lying!" the old man said accusingly, his cane lifted as he flared at the bank president. "You can't cover your deposits. This bank isn't solvent. I want my money! I want it all! Right now!"

Other people in the bank were looking at the elderly man, whom John recognized as one of their major depositors. He moved toward the man, just as more loud murmurs were heard and the crowd began to line up at the clerks' windows.

"I want my money, too," a woman said firmly.

"So do I," a younger man said. "I won't risk my life savings here!"

"Wait!" John said, holding up his hands. "You can't start a run on the bank. If you withdraw your funds, there will be an imbalance and nobody's money will be safe."

"Did you hear him? He said it himself — there's not enough money to cover our deposits! Give us our money!" the younger man raged.

"Clear the lobby!" Calverson said harshly. "Guard, get everyone out of the bank right now!"

The guard, hired by the bank to keep watch over the lobby for potential troublemakers, pushed his coat aside to show his badge and the pistol tucked in his belt.

"Go home now, ladies and gentlemen. The

bank is closed," the guard said, motioning toward the door. "Let's go. Let's go, please. Move along now."

They went along complacently at first. Then just as they reached the door, the old man with the cane turned on the guard and struck him across the head. The guard went down.

"Lock the door, quick!" Eli called frantically. "Good God! What do we do now? They'll break the door down! John, go out there and assure them that the bank is solvent!"

John paused by Calverson, his voice low so that it didn't carry. "I want your word that I'll be telling the truth."

Calverson's eyes fell. That black gaze of Hawthorn's was intimidating. The man had been a soldier, used to giving orders, and he was frightening. "Of course . . . of course, it's solvent. I'd never lie about that," he said, with a placating smile. He touched John's shoulder hesitantly. "Go on, now, my boy, and calm them down. Reassure them."

John was uneasy, but he had little choice. First he'd stop the run on the bank. Then, at his first opportunity, he was going to get some answers. He didn't understand Calverson's eagerness to merge the bank with Whitfield's enterprise. But it would mean a huge injection of capital almost at once, if the merger went through, and for the first time John had to ask himself if Calverson *needed* that huge injection of capital. The only possible reason for that would be . . . if money really was missing from the bank! He went to the front door with a feeling of apprehension. And it wasn't because of any fear of the crowd howling outside on the sidewalk.

11

John would have been even more uneasy if he'd known that Claire was already acting on her plans to leave him. His harsh words that morning had rubbed her pride raw, left her with nothing to look forward to but their physical hunger for each other and their indulgence of it.

John's mother and sister had issued her an invitation to visit them, and she was going to take them up on it. In the back of her mind she knew that it would be the very last place John would think to look for her, because he didn't know they were acquainted.

In defiance of John's dictum that she not drive Uncle Will's little car, she took it to town, planning to go to the train depot and buy a ticket to Savannah. But first she had to talk to Kenny and give him her designs for the buyer from Macy's. The sketches would mean a little more private income, and she would need it now. Then she wanted to go to the bank to see John one last time.

She didn't know what she could say to him. He'd made his feelings so plain that she had little doubt of his contempt. All he could offer was lust, and it wasn't enough.

She drove up to Kenny's store and he came out, grinning, to meet her.

"I like your mode of transportation! You still can get it to run, can't you?"

"Of course I can," she agreed, smiling as she removed her goggles, aware of stares from passersby.

"Do come in," he invited, helping her down from the little car. "Have you something with you for Mr. Stillwell?"

"In fact I do," she said, drawing the big portfolio from the other side of the seat. "I thought you might like to send these on to him. I can have the others done in three weeks. Well, just after Christmas, anyway."

"I'll make sure he knows."

She followed him in, nodding at a customer as he led her to his office in the back of the shop.

"This is Mrs. Kenner, my secretary," he said, introducing a middle-aged woman with a kind smile. "Mrs. Kenner, this is Mrs. Hawthorn. She and her late uncle have been friends of mine for quite some years.

She's the designer I told you about: Magnolia."

"Oh, my goodness!" Mrs. Kenner exclaimed. "How glad I am to meet you at last. I've so admired your gowns in the shop window down the street. How very talented you are!"

"Thank you," Claire said modestly, with a smile.

"Sit down, Claire, and let's go over your work. Sorry, Mrs. Kenner, but they're very confidential. These are the designs for Macy's. So could you . . . ?"

"I'll go and make a nice pot of coffee for us. How would that be?" Mrs. Kenner asked, with a conspiratorial smile as she rose from her desk.

"That would be fine," Kenny said. "We'll only need five minutes."

"Very well, sir."

Kenny looked at the elegant drawings one by one, shaking his head at their innovation and style. "Claire, you really are talented."

She smiled. "Thank you, but do you think they'll do?"

"They're very, very good. Thank you for letting me see them. I'll make sure they're on the next train to New York, carefully packaged."

"I appreciate all your help, Kenny — more

than you know. I may need to be independent very soon," she said miserably.

He winced. "Claire, can't you tell me what's wrong? Is there any way I can help?"

She shook her head. "I wish you could. But it's my own problem. I have to solve it. You're a dear, Kenny." She got up. "I won't wait for the coffee. I must fly. I'm leaving town for a little while. I'll contact you as soon as I'm sure where I'll be. I won't tell you where I'm going. That way if you're asked, you won't have to lie."

"You're worrying me," he said.

"I'm sorry. But I did need to give you those sketches. I don't know exactly when I'll be back."

He came forward and took her hands. "Can't you tell me where you're going? I'd never let anyone know."

He was such a sweet man. She shook her head. "I know that. But I'm afraid I can't, Kenny, dear."

"If you ever need me, I'll be right here," he said firmly. He glanced over her head and frowned at what he noticed. "That's odd. There's not usually such a crowd in front of the bank at this hour."

She turned and followed his stare, then caught her breath. That was her husband's bank. And it wasn't a crowd outside the

251

doors so much as it was a mob.

She could see John just in front of the door. There were loud cries from the mob and a surge forward. Something was thrown.

Suddenly, flames erupted in a vacant building across the street and jumped to a wagon parked at the edge of the wooden sidewalk — and from there across to the haberdashery shop behind the bank. The mules that were hitched to the wagon panicked, broke their traces, and turned the wagon over in the middle of the street in their run to safety. The burning wagon effectively blocked the only road that led past the bank and clothing store off Peachtree Street.

"Oh, dear," Kenny said. "If the fire brigade isn't called, there'll be a disaster."

"Yes, but the fire is blocking the road, see? The horses won't go through that wall of flame," she exclaimed, watching as a man in a buggy used all his strength to control his horse. "And the telephone wire has just burned through! There will be no way for them to call all the way across town to the fire station for help."

"Someone will have to go for help," Kenny replied.

"I will," Claire said, with determination. "I can drive right through the flames — fast enough so that the rubber of the tires doesn't melt — and go right to the fire station down Peachtree Street."

"It's too dangerous!" he said, protesting.

She glanced back toward the bank where the crowd was surging forward right toward her husband. "I must! John could be killed — if not by the mob, by the fire!"

While Kenny was still protesting, she cranked the little car, jumped in under the wheel, and rattled the gears, getting it to go in her hurry. Then she pulled away from the sidewalk and aimed it at the wall of flame.

Somewhere she heard a loud, shocked exclamation, but she put her foot down and kept right on going, right into the heat, the flames. She shot through on the other side, sweating and half afraid that she'd caught the tires on fire. But aside from a faint smell of smoke, there was nothing to alarm her.

"Good boy, Chester!" she exclaimed.

She drove as quickly as she could down the street, but it seemed to take forever to get to the fire station. Finally, she reached it. She ran up the steps with her duster catching on the heel of her shoe in her haste, recovered her balance, and darted into the fire station.

"There's a fire and a riot at the Peachtree City Bank!" she exclaimed to the first man

253

in uniform she saw. "Oh, please! Come quickly!"

"A fire, ma'am? Where did you say?"

She told him. He thanked her and started to race toward the back of the station.

"I'll also inform the police about the mob, ma'am," he called over his shoulder.

She nodded and went back out to her car. She cranked it and turned it back in the direction of the bank, her heart pounding as she hoped against hope that help would arrive in time to save her husband. Despite their disagreements and his lack of feeling for her, she loved him too much to turn her back on him when he was in need.

As she reached the side street where the bank was located, she saw that the flames were still shooting up from the top of the building. But the wagon had burned up, and the street was passable now. She gave a thought to the owner of the lost merchandise as she passed through the smoldering ashes and stopped beyond the bank building.

The crowd was being pushed back by uniformed policemen, who had apparently been summoned by someone else in her absence.

She moved forward, dusty and grimy, her goggles in her hand, as she pushed through

254

the crowd far enough to see her husband.

Her heart jumped when she spotted him. His face was bruised and his immaculate jacket was torn. One sleeve was unbuttoned, the cuff link torn from it by an angry hand. He looked intimidating just the same, and no one was trying to lay a finger on him now. A groaning man was sitting up on the sidewalk, holding his bleeding face in his hands.

"Good enough for you!" a woman said loudly. "That's what you get for trying to hit a man who can fight back, you low coward!"

"They've lost all my money!" the man replied.

"No one has lost anything!" John shouted. "The bank is only going to merge with an investment firm. This will immediately double the assets of the bank, and increase interest and pay dividends! No one will lose a penny!" He wasn't telling the whole truth; he couldn't guarantee that the merger would actually go through — especially if Whitfield suspected there was a shortfall in funds. But it might stop a riot to say so.

There were still murmurs, but not so angry now.

"Go home," John said shortly. "This is no way for civilized people to behave. Your money is safe. You have my word on it."

The crowd began to disperse.

"Mr. Hawthorn wouldn't lie," one man said as he and his wife passed Claire. "His word's good enough for me."

"Me, too," said another.

Claire, so proud that she could have burst, moved forward, toward her husband. But before she could work her way through the crowd, Diane Calverson came up on the sidewalk and ran to John with her handkerchief out.

"Oh, my dear!" she exclaimed. "Are you all right?"

She touched his face with quick, worried hands, and Claire watched him smile gently at her. If she'd had any last-minute doubts about their feelings for each other, that settled them. Her heart fell in her chest. Those two people loved each other. The kiss she'd witnessed in the kitchen of their apartment house had only reinforced her certainty of their feelings for each other. They couldn't help feeling as they did. And no matter how hungrily John might reach for her in the darkness, this was the woman he loved.

She went back to her car. She cranked it, got in under the wheel, and turned it toward home.

As it went noisily away, it caught John's attention. He stared after it, shocked. He hadn't noticed Claire. What was she doing driving in that thing?

Several firemen had arrived on their engine while John was settling things with that irate customer; they were already pumping water onto the blaze across the street.

One fireman passed John. "Brave woman, your wife, Mr. Hawthorn," he said, with a grin. "The chief said she came roaring up to the fire station in that contraption to summon help. Drove right through the flames, too. You must be very proud of her. What a lady!"

He went on to do his job, leaving John quiet and worried — with Diane hanging on his arm.

"Did you see Claire as you came up?" he asked her.

She shrugged. "Darling, I never see Claire unless I have to," she replied. "Honestly, such a plain and drab woman —"

He jerked away from Diane, but before he could speak Eli came up beside them, rubbing his damp forehead with his handkerchief. "That was damned close. Thank you, John. I can't imagine what got into those crazy people!"

John knew something was wrong. Eli looked guilty and he wouldn't meet John's eyes. And Diane's sudden affection, the way she looked at him, as if she were turning all her allegiance from Eli to John . . . he wished he knew how to explain these events.

"It's all right now. The police have dispersed the crowd and it looks as though the fire is all but out," Eli said, with a quick smile. "Go home and clean up, John, and then come back. I'll reassure our employees that they aren't going to be lynched."

"Don't even joke about such things," Diane said harshly. "John, shall I go with you?"

"To his home?" Eli asked angrily. "Diane!"

She glared at her husband. "If he needs me, I shall go with him."

Eli didn't say a word. White-faced, he turned and went back into the bank.

"Never mind him," Diane said. "He is a fool, and soon he will be in such trouble that no one can help him. My darling John," she said sweetly. "You love me, not Claire. You always have. And I love you." She glanced around, making sure that there was no one close enough to hear her. She moved closer. "I want you, John. I will give you anything you ask. Anything at all. Eli was a mistake; I know that now. I will leave him

258

very soon."

John moved away from her. "I haven't time to discuss this right now," he said stiffly.

He hailed a passing carriage and got in, leaving Diane speechless on the sidewalk.

Claire was in the parlor with Mrs. Dobbs, having cleaned up since her brush with the fire. She looked defeated. His Claire, defeated; it was painful to see her so.

John glanced at her as he paused in the doorway.

"Why, Mr. Hawthorn! Are you all right?" Mrs. Dobbs asked worriedly. "Claire was just telling me what happened."

"I'm fine," he replied. "I came home to change clothes." He hesitated, because he didn't know how to approach her. "Claire, I should like to speak with you."

She didn't know how to refuse. She had to go with him, or make Mrs. Dobbs even more suspicious. She got up and preceded him up the staircase.

He closed the door. "The fireman said you drove through the flames to get help."

She lifted her chin. "Chester is a fine little automobile. I had no doubt that he'd make it through. It was only a small fire at the time."

259

"It was a great risk — and required great courage, just the same." He moved forward. "Are you all right?"

The tender concern in his deep voice made her weak. She couldn't permit that. She forced a smile. "Right as rain," she said primly. "I trust that you weren't badly hurt?"

"A few cuts. Nothing worth mentioning." He scowled, searching for the right words. "You didn't come to see about me . . . after you brought the firemen."

"Mrs. Calverson was ministering to you," she said calmly. "I hesitated to intrude."

"You're my wife," he said shortly. "You had every right to intrude."

The nerve of him! she thought furiously. "You have a convenient memory about that! Whenever Mrs. Calverson comes near, you seem to forget you have a wife!"

"Claire . . ." He took a long breath. "I realize that my recent behavior has been less than admirable. I've been confused, you see. Our marriage has had its — shall we say . . . interesting moments just recently."

She stared at him, though embarrassed. "You mean we have slept together. I believe you remarked that it was compensation for not having Diane."

"I said no such damned thing!" he

260

snapped. "I would never use one woman to forget another."

She straightened. "You intimated that the marriage bed was our only common ground."

He winced inwardly at the calm, cold accusation. How could he defend himself — when he'd said so many harsh things to give her that idea? He'd made so many mistakes, and he couldn't seem to rectify even one of them!

"I said a lot of things," he replied. "We know so little about each other, Claire. We married for all the wrong reasons, and we've — *I've*," he amended, "done nothing to try and smooth it out between us. Perhaps when this latest disaster is dealt with, we can begin to find new ways of living together."

"Such as?" she asked belligerently.

"We could go out more often," he said. "To the opera or the theater, if you like. We could have all our meals together." He studied her drawn, wan face. "We could be husband and wife in every sense, Claire."

Her chest rose and fell roughly as she fought to breathe normally. How she longed for what he was suggesting. She loved him so. Life was uncertain at best. He could have been killed this morning. The terror of it made her face go pale. But despite her love and her fears, he wasn't hers. She might have saved him, but it was for Diane. How often had he said so?

"You kissed her," she said.

He exhaled impatiently. "I explained to you that she did the kissing!"

"Yes, you explained it. I didn't believe you then and I don't believe you now. You told me that you loved her, and that she loved you, on the day we were married," she said, with painful bitterness. "Has that changed, John?"

He hesitated, trying to find the right words to undo the damage. He was hungry for Claire, and Diane had actually become a nuisance. He wanted nothing more in the world right now than to clasp Claire tight to him and hold her, comfort her, reassure her. But when he stepped forward, she immediately stepped back. He must go slowly with her, woo her, pamper her. She'd had so little from him. He daren't rush her.

He smiled gently. "Many things have changed, Claire," he said quietly. "We must talk about them. But for now, I have to get cleaned up and go back to the bank to help sort out the mess. The fire never reached us, but it came very close. We can talk tonight."

"Talk," she echoed softly, thinking that their situation had gone far beyond conversation. "Yes. Well, I'll leave you to tidy yourself." She started to turn away.

"Claire, what were you doing in town, in the automobile?" he asked abruptly, just having remembered that she had apparently driven near the bank at the time of the riot and fire.

She turned. "I had come to town to visit Kenny Blake," she said, with pure malice, remembering Diane's soft fingers on his face.

His eyes glittered. "I've told you to have nothing to do with him!"

"You invited Diane to my home — and let her make the cattiest sort of remarks to and about me," she replied belligerently. "During our entire marriage, you've treated her like your sweetheart and me like an interloper. Well, at least I've had the decency to visit Kenny in town. And I was not alone with him," she added, stretching the truth just a little. "I was in his shop."

"For what purpose?"

She couldn't admit that she was using Kenny as an intermediary for the Macy's buyer. She lifted her chin. "Think what you like, John."

He could have raged at her. He would

have, but he knew that he was standing on shaky ground. She was correct to say that he'd done nothing to discourage Diane, and he *had* told Claire that he loved the other woman. Suddenly he felt guilty, and low and ashamed. This woman loved him. What had he ever offered her except pain and humiliation?

She turned back toward her doorway. "Whatever you think of me, I'm glad that you're all right, John," she added dispiritedly, thinking that she might not see him again for a very long time and trying valiantly not to show her feelings for him.

Her tone was defeated, lost. He knew that she wasn't having an affair with Kenny, but he was jealous of the man just the same. He wanted to take her in his arms and comfort her. He wanted to talk to her, to discuss their marriage. He called to her, but she went out the door without even looking back, then closed it with unusual firmness.

He cursed under his breath. What could he have said, anyway? She'd seen Diane with him. He remembered having smiled at Diane, as well. She'd only think it was more of the same, more of what she'd seen in the kitchen when Diane had kissed him. He didn't have the words to explain how drastically his feelings had changed for his reluctant wife. Perhaps by tonight, he thought. He just needed a little time to think it all through, to decide how to say it. It was his own fault. If he hadn't been so disparaging about the exquisite night they'd shared, if he hadn't let his fears rule his harsh tongue, how different it all might have been. Her response had been glorious. Many men went all their lives with women whose very coldness shattered their dreams of love. Claire had been magnificent. And what had he said to her? He'd managed to imply that sex was all he wanted from her, that he felt nothing more than lust. He groaned at his own stupidity. Leave it to a man, he thought bitterly, not to know what he felt until it was too late.

He changed his clothes, called a quiet goodbye to Claire through the door, and went back to work. If Mrs. Dobbs thought their behavior unusual for a couple who'd just risked being killed by a mob or burned up in a fire, she kept her thoughts to herself. Even a blind woman could tell that there were problems with this marriage. She only hoped they'd be able to solve them.

12

Claire had her bags packed and ready to go in no time at all. She would never forget that it had been Diane who'd rushed to John's side when he'd been hurt at the fire, Diane whose comfort he'd craved. Well, he could have his precious Diane. She was through fighting for a man who wanted someone else. She was going to leave, just as she'd threatened to. He was all right, and if he loved Diane so much, there was nothing else she could do except leave him to it. He'd said they would talk. Talk, ha! And about what? About a divorce? She didn't doubt that he would ask her for one now.

For just a moment she thought of driving Chester to Savannah, but that would be far too great a folly. Driving a couple of blocks in Atlanta was one thing; driving across the state was something else. The little car barely made it between Colbyville and Atlanta without mishap. On the long, rutted, dangerous road to Savannah, she could throw a band, have four flat tires, break an axle, or have engine failure. And without parts, or enough space to carry the amount of gas she would need to make the trip, it would be foolhardy. She couldn't even be certain that she could find gas at drugstores along the route. The roads were far more suited to wagon travel than automobile. She would have to take the train and hope for the best.

She went to see Chester one last time, hoping against hope that John wouldn't do away with it in her absence. Things seemed so hopeless.

She patted the little car's door gently. "You were very brave this morning, Chester. I'm proud of you. And I'll be back for you, old dear," she told it. "Someday."

The carriage driver took her bags out for her. Before she got into the carriage she'd hired to take her to the train depot downtown, she stopped long enough to tell Mrs. Dobbs goodbye.

"Oh, dear. Oh, dear," Mrs. Dobbs said worriedly. "And after this morning, too . . . But whatever shall I tell Mr. Hawthorn when he comes home and finds you gone?"

"I've left him a note," Claire said, pretending to be casual about the whole affair. "Everything will be all right, Mrs. Dobbs. We had a slight misunderstanding and I need to get away for a while. I'm only going to visit my cousin for a few days. I'll be back soon."

"For a few days?" She brightened. "Oh, thank goodness it was nothing serious between you and your husband!"

"Yes," Claire lied, feeling guilty. "Now, you go on about your business. I'll be back before you know it."

She swept out the door. Perhaps she should have left John a note. Truly, she hadn't thought about it. She couldn't think of anything to tell him that she hadn't already said. He'd know why she'd left. There was no need to elaborate.

John Hawthorn came home that afternoon to an empty apartment. There was no sign of Claire, and her best cloak was missing from her chifforobe. He leaned against the doorjamb and stared blankly at the room she'd occupied. He'd half expected this, but it still came as a shock. He'd waited far too long to act like a husband, and when he had, he'd lied about his motives. Then this morning he hadn't been able to find the right words to explain that he'd much rather have had Claire's hands than Diane's doctoring his cuts. He'd been confused, especially after the passionate night he'd shared with his wife. And her confession that she'd visited Kenny Blake had sparked a spurt of jealousy that had diverted him.

Mrs. Dobbs stuck her head around the door.

"There you are!" she gushed. "I know it must be lonely for you while your wife's away visiting her cousin, so I've invited my sisters over to dine with us. I thought you might like some company this evening."

So that was what she'd told Mrs. Dobbs, that she was going to visit a cousin. Did she have a cousin? She'd never spoken of one.

"She was going by train, I believe," he said, fishing.

"Was she? She didn't say, but I'm certain she would have taken the train if it's any distance. Her little automobile is still in the shed. I'll have the evening meal ready at the usual time. If you want anything special for dessert, Mr. Hawthorn, you only have to say so."

"Thank you, Mrs. Dobbs," he replied courteously. "But I'm not terribly hungry. I have to go to the depot." He didn't add that he was going there to try to trace his wife. He hoped he could find her.

■ ■ ■ ■

Inquiries at the depot proved fruitless. The depot ticket agent had been taken sick quite suddenly and had been transported to St. Joseph's Infirmary. The relief agent had no idea which young woman this earnest, dark-eyed man was seeking so urgently. John went to the bank the next morning with a heavy heart, no closer to an answer than he had been the whole sleepless night. Where was Claire?

On an impulse, he had the carriage drive past Kenny's shop, just to check that the man was still in town. Sure enough, the little weasel was clearly visible through the window. John leaned back in his seat, vaguely ashamed of his suspicions. Claire wasn't the sort of woman to run off with another man unless she told John about it first. She was too honest. He only wished that she'd stayed and talked to him before she set off for God alone knew where. She had no relatives, and no close friends. He sighed heavily. It hurt him to think of Claire alone in the world, without even a little cash to tide her over, unless she'd taken the housekeeping money with her. If she had, she'd be able to afford a decent place to stay.

The thought worried him, so when he got to the apartment, he went immediately to the small pot on the bookshelf where she kept the housekeeping money. It was a relief to find it empty — as empty as the apartment. He'd never minded being alone before his marriage. Now, he found he minded it very much. Where, he wondered miserably, had Claire gone?

Claire arrived in Savannah weary and dispirited. She checked into a hotel downtown and a porter carried her luggage for her. As a precaution, she used her maiden name when she signed the register.

"Miss Lang," the clerk echoed, and gave her a suspicious look. Young ladies of quality rarely traveled in the South without an escort of some sort, generally an older aunt or cousin. His eyes narrowed. "Will you be staying long?"

"Hopefully not very. I have relatives here," she said, and smiled at him. "I've come from Atlanta to see them."

"I see. And they are . . . ?"

She looked him steadily in the eye. "You're very inquisitive for a hotel clerk," she said evenly. "Would you make the same demands of a male guest?"

His cheeks burned. He coughed and cleared his throat. "Do excuse me. It is, of course, your business."

She lifted her chin and smiled haughtily. "I can see that the suffragette movement needs more stimulus in this community."

His eyes widened. Now he knew who she was — she was one of those worshipers of Susan B. Anthony and Margaret Sanger, one of those "modern" women who thought and behaved with the freedom of men. He found them all distasteful, but it wouldn't do to antagonize one of them. God forbid that they should invade this hotel to protest any bad treatment of one of their own.

He gave her a conciliatory smile. "I've put you in Room 202. It's a very nice room, overlooking the bay. There's a —" he hesitated, searching for the word "— a ladies' room just down the hall from you."

"Is there a telephone?" she asked.

He nodded. "Certainly. You may use the telephone in the office, at your leisure. You have only to ask."

"Thank you," she said politely, and followed the porter with her luggage up the staircase.

When she was alone, she drew the curtains and looked out at the bay. Savannah was a

272

beautiful city. She opened the window and breathed in the fresh sea air. There were other places on the Georgia coast, farther outside the city, where mills spewed smoke into the air and there was an unpleasant odor from them. Here, the air was salty and brisk and clean.

She gave a thought to John and how it must have felt for him to come home to an empty apartment. She knew that he'd worry, even though he didn't love her, and she was sorry. But she couldn't go back. There were too many problems; she needed breathing space. Perhaps he, too, would have time to make the decisions he needed to make. If he still loved Diane, he should give up Claire. Both of them would be better off apart, regardless of the gossip it caused. She had her work now, and she could support herself nicely without his help.

She closed the curtain and walked back to the single chair by the bed, running her hand over the carved walnut back. She must decide what to do. The hotel was pleasant enough, but she was nervous about staying here on her own.

She hoped that Maude would want her to stay at the Hawthorn home, but her unexpected arrival might cause problems with

273

Maude's husband. It was best to have a place to stay, just in case. But she must call Maude Hawthorn and tell her that she was in town. She allowed herself to think of nothing more than that, and went downstairs to do it.

The clerk escorted her to the telephone switchboard, where the hotel operator sat. Claire didn't know the number, but the operator did. She put Claire right through to the Hawthorn home, and gave Claire a curious, interested glance as she waited for the connection.

"Here, I have it for you," she said after a minute.

Claire picked up the receiver of the telephone nearby.

"Hello, is this Mrs. Maude Hawthorn?" Claire asked. "This is Claire . . ."

"Claire!" Maude exclaimed. "My dear, where are you? Is John with you? Is he all right?"

"He's fine," Claire said. "I've come to see you. I'm staying at the Mariner Hotel on —"

"A hotel? Oh, Claire! How could you? I'll have our man get the carriage hitched up and I'll be right there to pick you up. Don't argue, dear. I really can't allow you to stay at a hotel! I should be no more than thirty

274

minutes. I'm so glad you've come."

The connection was cut. Claire smiled self-consciously. Well, it seemed that the nervous desk clerk would be relieved that she wasn't to be a guest in this hotel after all. She thanked the operator, nodded at the puzzled clerk, and went back up to her room.

The porter brought her bags back down again and she paid the small amount due on the room.

It was, in fact, less than thirty minutes before Maude swept into the hotel like some grande dame in her long, elegant black suit and feathered big hat. "My dear!" she exclaimed, and came forward to hug Claire warmly. "Harrison," she called to her liveried driver, "do get Claire's bags and put them in the carriage, please."

"Yes, ma'am," the driver said, tipping his hat.

"Harrison is part of the family," Maude confided. "He's been with us forever." She glared at the clerk, who was staring. He quickly occupied himself with his books. "Come, dear. Let us go."

"I annoyed him," Claire told Maude when they were outside. "He was very nosy, so I made mention of the women's movement and he became quite friendly."

Maude chuckled. "It's quite active here. One day we'll have the vote, Claire — and then we'll show these men how to build a proper government!"

"Yes, we will," Claire agreed. "I have thought about joining our Atlanta chapter, but I hesitated because I didn't want to do anything to endanger John's position."

"My dear, how thoughtful of you. And how silly." She grinned as they got into the carriage with Harrison's help and the door closed. "John is less conventional than you think. I'm sure he would be shocked that you hesitated to do anything for fear of embarrassing him. Take it from me, child. John can't be embarrassed. I know. He's my son."

"I suppose you're right."

"Why are you here, Claire?"

Claire grimaced. "I felt like a change of scenery," she murmured evasively.

"And you don't want to talk about it. All right. I won't pressure you. But you know you're very welcome in my home, Claire — for as long as you would like to stay."

"How kind you are," Claire said, with genuine feeling. "I would like to get to know John's family. Thank you for giving me the opportunity."

"And we should like to get to know his

wife. It has been a very long two years for me, Claire . . . with no contact at all between our son and us. I think Clayton feels just the same, but is too proud and stubborn to admit it. Your visit may prove more productive than either of us dream. I pray that it will."

"Will it cause trouble for you, though, with your husband?" Claire asked worriedly. "You said that he was in bad health . . ."

"He will be happy to welcome John's wife," Maude said bracingly. "Believe me when I tell you that he would do anything to mend the rift between himself and John. He will see your presence as a step in that direction, and welcome you with open arms. You wait and see!"

Heartened, Claire let the last of her worries go.

Minutes later, Claire was walking up the steps of an elegant colonial-style Savannah house beside Maude. It sat on the corner of one of the many squares that made up the quaint city on the Atlantic, and like most of the houses in this section, it had a walled garden stretching around the back. Because the Christmas season was in full swing, there was a gay wreath on the front door done in familiar Victorian pale pink and blue ribbons, and there were garlands of holly and fir limbs on the gate.

She noticed the brass lion-head door knocker as Harrison opened the door to admit the two ladies, then brought her suitcases in behind them. A young maid hovered until Maude waved her away with a smile.

"Make yourself right at home," Maude said. She stuck her head around the living room door. "Emily, you'll never guess who's here!" she called.

Emily came out into the hall, her face lighting up when she saw Claire. Emily hugged her, then all three women went into the parlor, where they plied her with tea and tea cakes.

"Just imagine! She'd checked into a hotel. A hotel!" Maude muttered. "I shanghaied her and brought her here."

"As you should have," Emily said firmly. "Claire, it's so good to see you again!"

"It's good to see the two of you, too."

"Does John know that you're here?" Maude asked after their first cup of tea was poured.

"No," Claire had to admit.

This was news, indeed. Maude leaned forward. "Something happened, didn't it?"

Claire's lips compressed. "I really can't

speak of it." She decided that it would be best not to mention the run on the bank. That would only serve to upset everyone. "Suffice it to say that he has put our marriage in great jeopardy, and I had to get away, to think things out."

"You can't mean to divorce him?" Emily asked plaintively.

"Certainly not," Claire replied. "I won't stain his reputation with a second scandal in as many months. It may be that we must live apart, but I won't ever besmirch his name or that of his family."

"You're very kind, Claire," Maude told her.

"Besides, he may come to his senses one day," Claire added, with a wan smile. "He might even miss me."

"Absence affects the heart, they say," Emily agreed, smiling encouragement.

"Then I still have hope. Emily, I packed the fabric for your gown and brought it with me. I thought, as I was coming, we might as well have a fitting."

Emily was enthusiastic. "What a wonderful surprise!"

"You're sure I won't be in the way here?" Claire asked hesitantly.

Maude took her hands warmly. "My dear, you're most welcome. Believe me, I wouldn't hesitate to shoo you right out the door if you weren't. In fact, you'd never have left the hotel if I hadn't wanted you here."

Claire felt relief wash over her. "Thank you. I hope that one day I can return your hospitality."

"So do I," Maude said, and the look in her blue eyes was far away as she thought of her eldest son.

Working on Emily's dress would keep Claire busy. She was only thankful that she'd already finished — and had delivered — the gowns for the governor's ball she'd been making for Evelyn Paine and the others. That was one worry she no longer had.

It wasn't until after the evening meal that Claire met her host. Col. Clayton Hawthorn was a tall, thin, gray-headed, and very dignified man. Claire was taken to see him in his bedroom facing the sea. The old man looked pale and lackluster there on the spotless white sheets. The bay window was open a few inches so that the cool sea breeze could blow in on this pleasant December day.

He wore a mustache and goatee, and his dark eyes studied Claire carefully.

"Maude, you didn't mention that we had a guest." He scolded his wife gently.

"No, I didn't want to wake you, Clayton," she replied, with a smile. "This is Claire Hawthorn," she announced.

The old man scowled. He didn't speak. He only stared.

Claire went right up to the old man's bedside, staring down into his drawn, pale face. "I am married to your son John."

His dark eyes narrowed. "Why are you here?" he asked bluntly.

Claire's chin jutted. "Because he doesn't appreciate his good fortune in having had the sense to marry me!" she replied pertly.

The old man's eyes began to twinkle. He chuckled weakly. "Is that so?"

"I hope that my absence will show him the error of his ways," she continued. "Although I have another purpose in coming here. I'm making your daughter's gown for the spring ball."

"You sew?" he asked.

"She's a designer, my dear," Maude said. "The 'Magnolia' of whom the recent society page spoke so eloquently."

"What?" Claire asked, pleasantly surprised at the news.

"Our society page described the gown you made for Mrs. Evelyn Paine to wear to the governor's ball, Claire," she explained. "And raved about its unique design. There was quite a good drawing of Evelyn wearing it, and an added comment that the designer would soon be doing work for Macy's in New York. Is that true?"

"Well, yes," Claire admitted, smiling at the enthusiastic comments that followed. "A buyer has commissioned me to design evening gowns for a special collection at his store in New York City. I was very excited that he thought so much of my work." She grinned. "It really is quite an honor."

"Indeed it is!" Maude said. "Does John know?"

Her face fell. "I didn't have the opportunity to — to tell him." Remembering what she'd learned about John's father, she regretted saying even this about her husband. The old man hadn't spoken to his son in two years. He was frail and obviously ill, and here Claire was making things worse. She decided then and there not to mention the bank riot at all, or anything about Diane.

She went to sit on the edge of the chair by Clayton Hawthorn's bed. "John helped me when no one else would, after my uncle's death. Our marriage hasn't made him happy, but he's a good man. He's always involved in charities that benefit the underprivileged, and he lends money sometimes when he probably shouldn't. He has a kind heart."

Clayton stared intently at his son's young wife and saw the hopelessness in her gray eyes. He reached out and patted her hand gently. "He must have some sense. He married you, after all." He smiled sadly. "I'm an old man, Claire. I've lived to regret some of the things I said to my son when my twin boys were buried. Grief does strange things to the mind. It certainly wasn't John's fault, any of it. I was still upset over his infatuation with that gold-digging woman, and his determination to make a career of the service. At least he changed his mind about that."

"He's a very good banker," she assured him.

"He was a very good army officer, too," Maude interjected, with a long sigh. "I think he'd have been happy to stay in the service and go where he was sent. We still get mail for him from men he served with in Cuba."

Clayton Hawthorn had the grace to admit that this was so. He grimaced. "I wanted him to follow in my footsteps, to have one son who was willing to keep the family tradition of banking. I shouldn't have been so unyielding. John has to live his own life, the way he sees fit."

"It would please him if you were to tell him so," Claire remarked gently.

Clayton's eyes had a wistful look. "It's not so easy to admit fault," he confessed. "Perhaps, one day, I can meet him halfway. But he doesn't even correspond with us."

"Because you forbade him to," Maude said haughtily. "And refused to let me write to him, as well."

"I was wrong," the old man had the grace to admit. He glanced plaintively at his wife. "You never used to heed what I told you to do."

Maude smiled. "You were ill. I didn't have the heart to go against you, even though I disagreed."

"I'm feeling a little better now," he said, drawing in a long breath. "This sea air is good for me. Write to John if you wish." He averted his eyes. "You might even invite him down for Christmas dinner."

"Oh, Daddy! You're wonderful!" Emily said enthusiastically, and bent to hug her father warmly.

"Jason will think so, too," Maude assured him. "He misses John. They're so much alike."

"Don't forget, Jason is a shipbuilder," Emily told Claire. "He's very enterprising."

"You'll meet him one day soon," Maude

volunteered. "He doesn't live at home, but he visits us frequently. We're all very close. I'm sure he'll want to meet his new sister-in-law."

"Does he look like John?" she asked.

Clayton chuckled. "No. He looks like me."

"He's as tall as John, but he's huskier," Emily said. "And his hair is blond, although he has dark eyes like Daddy and John."

"He has the same temper, of course," Maude said demurely.

Clayton glared at her.

"And the same scowl," she added deliberately.

Her husband made an irritated sound. But when Maude reached out and slid her hand into his, his fingers curled around it warmly. They looked at each other in a way that Claire had hoped she and John would, one day. Sadly, that day seemed as if it would never come.

Jason was very different from his brother. John was quiet and stoic, but Jason was outgoing and entertaining. He seemed to know every fish story from Maine to Florida, and he told them all to a delighted and enthusiastic audience in the parlor. If his smile was any indication, he liked Claire on sight. She liked him, too. In looks, he did resemble his older brother, even with their differences in coloring.

"Why didn't John come with you, Claire?" Jason asked. "It's about time we healed some wounds here," he added.

"John doesn't know where she is," Maude said softly. "There's been . . . a misunderstanding."

"About his ex-fiancée?" Jason asked tersely.

Claire's eyes widened. "How did you . . . ?"

"I met her when they were engaged," he replied, and said no more. "You didn't tell him where you were going?"

She shrugged. "It seemed rather pointless at the time."

"What happened?"

She told him, but left a great deal out.

Jason shook his head. "My brother hasn't so much as sent a card home in two years."

"Nor have we corresponded with him," Maude said sharply. "Clayton was so very sick at first that I didn't dare go against him. He's better now, in some ways, but he won't get out of bed. He just lies there, as if he's waiting to die. Why, he won't even read a book, and he used to enjoy the classics so much."

"Perhaps Claire's presence will rejuvenate

him," Jason remarked.

"He did perk up when they were introduced," Maude had to admit.

"It was the first real interest he's shown in anything for months," Emily added. "It was nice to see Papa smile again."

"There's a sewing machine in my sitting room," Maude told Claire. "You're welcome to use it any time. I hope you'll stay for a while. Christmas is only a little over two weeks away."

"I know. I was looking forward to spending it with John. It would have been our first one together," she said sadly. It broke her heart to think of all the plans she'd made, of her dreams. Now she'd be here, and John would be . . . where? At the Calversons', probably, she thought bitterly. Where else?

"You can spend it with us," Maude said. "We'll have guests in, and perhaps it will even persuade Clayton to show some interest in life again. Just take one day at a time, Claire — and trust in God to help things work out as they're meant to."

"I'll do that," she promised.

As the days passed, Claire found herself fitting very nicely into the Hawthorn circle. She missed John, of course, and she still felt guilty about worrying him, now of all times — when he had such problems at the bank. But that couldn't be helped.

To keep herself occupied, she began to take little snacks in to Clayton, then coaxed him to eat them. His appetite improved and so did his color. And she discovered why he didn't read his beloved books anymore.

"I can't see," he confessed, embarrassed. "There's a sort of film over my eyes. I can see people well enough, but I can't read."

"Suppose I read to you?" she suggested.

His whole face brightened. "You could find the time?"

"Of course I could." She smiled. "Just tell me what you'd like to hear."

He did. There were novels like Herman Melville's *Billy Budd* and nonfiction classics like the histories of Flavius Josephus, Tacitus, and Herodotus. Claire sat and read to him every afternoon while the sea breeze brought its salty flavor into the room. She'd questioned the wisdom of all that fresh air at one time, but it did seem to be helping him. He improved daily.

"Have you always been a banker?" Claire asked him one afternoon after she'd finished reading him a chapter of Herodotus about the Egyptians.

"Not always," he replied. "In my younger

days, I was a sailor. I loved the sea. Still do. Jason inherited the sea fever from me — and even though he owns the fishing fleet, he still goes out with the boats sometimes." He sighed wistfully. "I wish I could go out with him. I miss a deck under my feet. I had a yacht until I became too ill to sail her," he added. "I miss her as much as I'd miss Maude if, God forbid, I ever lost her."

"Can't you go out with Jason?"

He pondered that. "I don't know. I've improved since you've been here," he said, glancing at her amusedly. "Perhaps in a few more months, when spring comes, I might try it."

"Does John like the sea?" she asked, with her eyes demurely downcast.

He sighed. "You don't know him at all, do you, girl?"

Her slender body moved restively in the chair. "Not really," she confessed. "We don't speak of personal things."

"What a loss. Maude and I have always been good friends, since we were children. We've known each other all our lives." He drew the covers tighter around him. "John liked the sea, yes — but not enough to join the navy," he continued. "He sailed with me when he was younger. He can handle a boat as well as Jason. But I made it impossible

289

for him to come home. You know about the boys?"

"Yes," Claire said sadly. "I'm so sorry."

"I'm sorry, too — sorry especially that I blamed John for something that was not his fault. The boys were keen to go to war, and all my ranting and raving wouldn't change their minds. I had to let them go. It was my own guilt that I took out on John."

"God has plans for us that don't always coincide with our own," she said firmly. "He had need of your boys, and He took them. You have to realize that we have no power over life and death. And death is a thing that all of us will experience, a certainty. One cannot blame other human beings for a divine call."

"I know that now," he said sheepishly. "But at the time, I was rather out of sorts with God. I've come to realize that His will is stronger than mine. I hope I've made my peace with Him. Now I want to make it with my son before it's too late." He looked at her intently. "Is it too late, Claire? Does he speak of me?"

She swallowed. "He doesn't speak of any of you, except that once, when he told me why you didn't speak to each other. I'm sorry. But then," she added helpfully, "we don't speak of personal things as a rule, as I mentioned."

"Yes, yes. I remember." He closed his eyes and then opened them again. "Life is so hard, Claire. Harder than ever for us older ones, once we stop walking in step with the younger folk. I remember when convention was everything, when men treated women like fairies and idolized them. Now women have so many causes, so many complaints. A man hardly knows how to treat them." He grimaced. "And all these modern things, telephones and electricity and motorcars. Where will it all end?"

"Progress cannot be stopped," she commented. "And motorcars are very exciting. I have one, you know. It was my uncle's. I drive it — and I can even repair it!"

He sat up in bed. His eyes almost popped. "You can repair it? Heavens, aren't you afraid of it?"

"Not at all," she assured him.

"I never heard such a thing. And you a woman." He winced. "There I go again. You see? I will never reconcile myself to the changes, to the modern life. I fought in the Civil War, Claire. I've seen men blown to bits. I've seen children starve to death. But I've also seen the closeness of families and the joy of community life without any newfangled improvements. I live in a horse-

and-buggy world that is ever so quickly giving way to motors and machines." He shook his head. "I have no desire to live in a world that has left me so far behind. Even my attitudes are outdated."

She reached over and patted his hand. "Your outdated attitudes suit me very well. You just go right on having them, and let these modern people rush about as they like. There will always be a portion of society that clings to the old ways and considers them sacred."

"You're a tonic," he said after a minute. "You give silver linings to all my dark clouds."

She chuckled. "I'm very glad. Now, as a reward, will you tell me some more about my husband?"

He smiled. "Indeed I will. What do you want to know?"

"What was he like as a small boy?"

"That may take days and days," he said.

She settled back into her chair. "Then you'd better start right now," she said merrily.

She learned a lot about John from his father, about his quick temper and his kindness. She learned that he'd given all his pocket money once to a small boy whose lunch had been taken away by bullies. John apparently did a lot for the poor without telling anyone, and he never refused a cry for help, even when it put him in danger. She learned that he could swim, but hated it, and that he'd been champion tennis player of his local group. He'd been a keen horseman until Cuba, and he could sail even if he didn't love the sea. She learned things that she might never need to know again. Because John didn't know where to find her — and she didn't want to go home to find him with Diane.

All the while, though, she missed John and wondered how he was. She also wondered about her sketches for Macy's that Kenny had sent to New York. She telegraphed Kenny and had a reply back in no time. He said that everything was all right, the designs were in New York, and he would have payment for her soon. He would send the money by Western Union. That relieved her mind a lot. She'd have money to support herself — and whatever happened, she wouldn't have to depend on John for her living.

Meanwhile, she'd put aside a simple crepe gown, which she'd brought in case there were any social evenings, because it no longer seemed to fit her in the waist. Maude had seized it and carried it into Savannah, where it was displayed in a local clothing store. She'd come home beaming one day, with the news that the design had attracted such incredible attention that there had been women actually fighting over it. The owner wanted more.

"If you want work, Claire, here it is." Maude chuckled.

"I may very well need it, if my Macy's designs don't sell," Claire confided. She frowned. "It's so odd that the crepe dress won't fit. I must have gained more weight than I realized. I eat when I'm nervous and upset, you see."

"You don't look overweight to me, my dear," she said kindly, and smiled.

Claire's hands rested on her flat stomach. She had a nagging suspicion about the weight gain that she wasn't about to share with anyone. She'd lost her appetite and felt sick a morning or two, as well, but she also kept that to herself. She wouldn't think about it, she decided, until she had to.

13

John felt his life had gone sadly awry. He missed Claire. He worried about her. And he worried, too, about the bank.

Rumors that something was wrong at the bank persisted after Claire's abrupt departure. Eli Calverson had shown up that next morning after the riot only long enough to unlock the front door, then he'd left like a shot, mumbling something about feeling unwell. He looked unwell, all right — pale and drawn and worried. That only intensified John's feeling of apprehension.

As John had already decided to have a talk with Dawes, the firm's chief bookkeeper, he went straight in to see him. The little man was very nervous, and John's mere presence seemed to intimidate him.

"I assure you, Mr. Hawthorn, that Mr. Calverson keeps a very careful eye on my books, and he hasn't said a word to me," Dawes said. He cleared his throat, red in the face and all but blabbering. "I suggest that you take up any problems you may have with Mr. Calverson and not me."

"I'll do that, Mr. Dawes," John said evenly. "But you realize, I hope, that if auditors have to be called in, your name will be the first one under suspicion if any faults are found. And it won't be Mr. Calverson who will face a judge and jury."

Dawes's eye grew huge behind his spectacles. "Of all the outrageous things to say!" he blustered, almost upsetting his inkstand. "How dare you speak to me in such a manner!"

John's eyebrows lifted eloquently. "I have every intention of pursuing this, Mr. Dawes," he replied calmly. "If I were you," he added, his dark eyes narrowing, "I'd think very carefully about cooperating with the authorities."

"What . . . authorities?"

"The Pinkertons, Mr. Dawes."

The little man followed him all the way out into the lobby of the bank, stuttering and pleading in frantic whispers. John turned as he reached his own office.

"If you have anything to say," John told him, "this is your last chance."

Dawes gnawed his lower lip until he tasted blood. For a banker, Hawthorn had a very intimidating demeanor. He meant what he said. And with Calverson gone, there was no one left to face the blame except the bookkeeper.

"Calverson . . . made some . . . withdrawals and then falsified entries to explain them," Dawes said in a whisper. "He threatened to . . . that is, he threatened *me* . . . if I didn't cooperate. It's something to do with the reason he wanted to merge the bank with Whitfield's investment firm so quickly. I don't know why. He didn't trust me enough to say."

John had seen men blackmailed while he was in the service. Dawes looked like a person with dark secrets. The threat of exposure had forced better men than Dawes into a life of crime.

"I'll do what I can for you, when the time comes. If you cooperate," John added meaningfully.

Dawes let out the breath he'd been holding. "I'll do whatever you say, Mr. Hawthorn."

John nodded. "Go back to work, for now."

"Yes, sir."

Dawes ambled back the way he'd come; John stood with his hands in his pockets, scowling. He hadn't seen the president of the bank again this morning — not even a glimpse of him — after Calverson had unlocked the doors promptly at nine.

His first stop was Calverson's office, where his secretary, Henderson, was sorting mail.

"Has Eli come in?"

Henderson looked up and blinked. "No, sir. He went back home right after he unlocked the doors. You remember . . . ? I believe he was unwell."

"Yes, he said so. I think I'll go over to his home and check on him," John said, so as not to arouse suspicion. "I'll be there if I'm needed urgently."

"Yes, sir."

He got his hat and overcoat and cane, went out into the nippy air, and hailed a carriage. All the way to Eli Calverson's palatial home, he was thinking about Whitfield and this merger. Eli hadn't been honest with him about a lot of things. Something was going on, and he meant to find out what.

He only wished he knew where Claire was. No one had heard from her or seen her since she left on the train. He'd even been to see Evelyn Paine, but Evelyn was as worried as he was — and equally in the dark as to Claire's destination.

When he got to the Calverson home, he

was still brooding about Claire. He tapped on the front door and waited for the maid to admit him.

"I want to see Eli Calverson," John told her.

"Mr. Calverson isn't . . . available, sir. Shall I ask Mrs. Calverson to come down?"

He was surprised. "Yes, please."

He waited until Diane appeared from a room in the back of the house. Her eyes were red, but she forced a wide smile at the sight of him. "John! How wonderful to see you!" She held out her hands for him to take and pulled him with her. "Do come into the parlor."

She led him out of the hall and closed the sliding doors behind them.

"I'm so glad you've come," she said worriedly. "I'm so upset. I don't really know what I should do." She tugged a handkerchief from her pocket and dabbed at her eyes. "Oh, John. It's such a frightful mess."

He'd never seen her quite so genuinely upset. "What's wrong?"

"Eli's . . . very ill," she said. "I've just had the doctor. He's in . . . what is it called? Oh, yes. Quarantine." She dabbed at her eyes and nose and peered up at John over the lacy handkerchief with faint calculation. "He's ever so sick. I'm quite sure that he won't be able to come back to work at all this week . . ." Her voice trailed off.

"Diane, do you know about any unusual activity at the bank?" he asked.

"Why, no, John," she said, with wide eyes. "I do know about the riot, of course, because I was there. Eli was very upset." She made a gesture. "That's what caused him to be sick, all the worry about those investors making such silly accusations. As if anyone would embezzle money at our bank! The very idea! You don't think Eli would steal from the bank, do you, John?"

And John thought, You little schemer. Something was afoot — and Diane was up to her pretty neck in it. She couldn't know about the bookkeeper's accusations, thank God. He'd make sure she didn't find out. Whatever Eli was up to, he wasn't going to get away with it. John wasn't about to be left holding the bag.

Diane moved close to him, smiling sweetly. "How I've missed you, John," she said. "I should never have married him, you know."

How sugary sweet she sounded. But she looked nervous. She looked frightened, as well.

"Won't you stay for a little while?" she said, wringing her handkerchief. "I'm so lonely and upset — and we haven't had a chance to talk alone together in such a long time. I do so badly need to talk to you, John."

Once, her nearness would have driven him mad with desire. Now it only irritated him.

Diane's wan face lifted to his. "Claire has left you, hasn't she, John? It's all over town. Now you can divorce her and have me. You can make peace with your people and get your inheritance. We can live very well . . ."

"What about your sick husband?"

She hesitated. She looked frightened and her eyes didn't quite meet his. "I can't think about him now. You do still want me, don't you, John? Darling, you remember how good it was between us when we were engaged." She brushed her body against his lightly, almost frantically. "We must meet again. At my sister's perhaps, and very soon. We must be very discreet, of course, but we must make plans very quickly, my darling. Before Eli . . . uh, that is, before Eli . . . recovers completely," she added quickly.

John thought how he would have hated to be married to such a woman, who had no qualms about running away from a sick husband — *if* Eli was really sick, which he doubted very much. Diane was ready to cut and run, just as Eli was, but she seemed to prefer a different direction altogether.

Perhaps she had no stomach for dodging the law.

She was making crazy plans, and he wanted no part of them. He was sorry for her, because Eli Calverson would inevitably be proved guilty of embezzlement and serve time in prison. She would lose everything. But right now the most important matter was to find out how much Eli had taken and recover the bank's money. It made him sick to think of all the people who had trusted the bank with their life savings — and who now stood to lose.

Eli must have been squirreling money away for a long time. Whitfield probably wasn't in on this, but did he know what Eli had planned? That was a worrying thought, especially if there was an overdraft that Eli was counting on Whitfield to cover.

"I really need to speak to Eli," he said. "Couldn't I do it through the door?"

She flushed and mopped at her brow. "That would be . . . unwise. No, John. The doctor said no one could see him, or — or talk to him. You — you must go away."

"Very well, then," he told Diane, removing her clinging hands. "I'll come again, when Eli is stronger."

She smiled nervously. "Yes, well . . . that might be best." She bit her lower lip. "Yes, it might," she said, seeming to speak to herself. "For now, at least." She glanced up at him. "I'll send word to you when we can meet. I'll try to make it very soon. You will come to me, John?"

"Certainly." He strung her along, thinking that it would be just as well to keep tabs on her until Eli reappeared. But he had no interest in pursuing their old relationship. He thought only of Claire now. Looking at Diane, he wondered how on earth he'd managed to fall under her spell. She was lovely, but Claire was superior to her in every way. Especially in the ways of kindness and love. Diane's only concern was solvency, with whomever she could attain it. Why hadn't he realized that in the past? Or was it only that he'd lost her — and her very elusiveness made her desirable?

He dismissed the thought. His mind was on Calverson now, and how to stop him from getting away. If only he could get up those stairs undetected and see for himself if Eli was at home. But he didn't dare risk it. He might spook the man into running too soon.

He left Diane and went directly to the police station. He told an inspector everything he knew, begged him to use the utmost discretion, and encouraged him to alert the Pinkerton detective agency.

"By a stroke of good fortune, several of them are due in town this weekend for a convention," the officer told him. "You'll have a good group to help sort this out. Mr. Hawthorn, you're certain of what you've told me?"

John's expression was grim. "Utterly certain. But I don't think the bookkeeper will speak freely until the money is found and an arrest made. He's a frightened fellow."

"We'll keep that in mind, sir. Thank you for coming to see me. We'll be in touch. As I hope you will, should you receive further information that might be of help to us."

"Certainly, I will," John promised.

He walked outside the police station with a worried scowl. He couldn't be absolutely certain that any funds had been embezzled. Only the bookkeeper's forced confession was evidence of it — coupled, of course, with Eli's strange behavior. The books would have to be audited by the bank examiners to find any real evidence of fraud. That would take time. Meanwhile, Eli Calverson would certainly try to get away. And if that happened, guess who would be left to take the blame!

■ ■ ■ ■

The next week was a nightmare of comforting frightened stockholders, watching the bookkeeper, and keeping a close eye on Diane to see what he could learn from her. He gave the excuse of checking on Eli's health to stop by her house daily, just for a few minutes at a time. Diane ate it up, thinking she had him dazzled. But each time, John listened and watched carefully for any sign of Eli. He found none.

In between he missed Claire and worried about her. She could be anywhere. What if something happened to her? He'd never even know. It infuriated him that she'd left, just as his life was falling apart. She believed that he loved Diane, but he didn't. He only wanted Claire back, with all his heart.

At the end of the week, things seemed to be getting better. The Pinkertons arrived in town a day early, and one of them turned out to be a very old friend of John's named Matt Davis. The man was Sioux, very evidently so, and easterners who had never seen a real live Indian found him alternately fascinating and intimidating. It amused John, who knew Matt's background.

He took Matt out to dinner the very

evening he arrived and laid the case out for him.

"Leave this to me," Matt told him. "I'll have it out of your bookkeeper in five minutes."

John's eyebrows rose. "You don't still carry that bowie knife?"

Matt grinned. "I don't need to. I've picked up a lot of new methods over the past ten years. You'd be surprised at how easily I get information these days with minimum force."

"I'd be surprised at the minimum-force bit, certainly," John replied, tongue in cheek.

Matt sipped his sherry. "You're wearing a wedding ring," he remarked.

"That's right. I've been married a little over two months — and my wife has already left me," he stated dryly.

"Is that a joke?"

"Not really." He sighed. "Claire actually is missing. I hurt her badly with my attention to my ex-fiancée. I was at fault. I hurt her, and she ran. I can't really blame her. Now I can't even discover where she is." He looked up. "When you get through with Dawes, you might take on my case and help me track down my wife."

Matt pursed his lips. "Does she have friends in the city?"

"Legion," John replied. His dark eyes went even darker. "Including a clothier named Kenny Blake . . . with whom she seems to spend a lot of time lately."

Matt put down his glass. "Interesting," he said neutrally.

"Don't get the idea that I haven't put a foot wrong," John had to add. "I've not treated her well. She had every reason to leave me."

"But you want her back?"

John was surprised — not only by the question but by his abrupt answer. "With all my heart."

"All right. But first things first. I came here on business, and I've got to give a lecture during the conference. But I'll see your bookkeeper and we'll take it from there. Don't worry. I'm on the case."

"So modest."

"Glad you noticed," Matt said, without a pause.

Matt did what he considered the most necessary thing first.

He went to Kenny Blake's men's emporium to buy a vest. Claire had poor taste, he decided, if she could prefer this little dandy to John.

"Something I can do for you, sir?" Blake

asked, approaching the man warily because he was tall and lean and had an untamed look, despite his expensive clothing.

Matt wanted to intimidate Blake, so he looked down at him without smiling, then hesitated for just a heartbeat before he answered. "I'm with the Pinkerton detective agency. I believe you know a woman named Claire Hawthorn?"

Kenny's face went white. He swallowed the lump in his throat. "Yes."

"She's missing. I'm searching for clues as to her whereabouts before we pursue the foul play aspect of the case." He looked as if he thought Kenny had murdered her.

"She's fine," Kenny blurted out at once. "She's in Savannah."

Matt scowled. "Savannah?"

"Yes, with the Hawthorn family. I'm not supposed to tell her husband. She doesn't want him to know."

"Are you having an affair with her?" Matt asked bluntly.

"No! How dare you!"

"You've been seen with her lately."

"Yes, on business!" Kenny blustered. "She's just contracted with Macy's department store in New York City to design a line of exclusive evening gowns for them. Her husband doesn't know that she has a separate income, doing business as the designer 'Magnolia.' She's already quite famous locally."

Matt stared at him.

"I swear it's just business! Look!" He rushed into his office, leaving the man to follow. Kenny's secretary looked up, startled, and then couldn't look away. Matt Davis was a striking man, even if his nose was a little large. He was an Indian. She'd never seen one, except on a buffalo nickel. He fascinated her.

Matt recognized her expression and gave her a cold stare. She swallowed, touched her hair expressively, and went quickly back to work. Matt was careful to hide his grin.

Kenny came back. "Yes, here it is. There was one sketch that didn't get in the package. I saved it for her."

He showed it to Matt, who had more than a passing knowledge of exclusive clothing. He nodded as he studied the fine, neat lines of the unique gown. "She's very good."

"Isn't she?" Kenny beamed. "I've known her for years, ever since she came to live with her uncle. She's a sweet, gentle girl. Much too good for her husband — and him running around with that married woman."

Matt's eyebrows lifted. "What married woman?"

"That Mrs. Calverson. Her husband's president of the bank. She and John were engaged once. Some people think he's still carrying on with her. Mr. Calverson's very ill now, though, they say — confined to bed and quarantined. I daresay she'll stay close to home for a while. Pity Claire went away."

"Yes." Matt handed the sketch back with a lean, immaculate dark hand. "Thank you for your cooperation."

"Don't tell her husband where she is, if you've an ounce of decency," Kenny pleaded, with genuine concern. "She only needs a little time to decide what to do. Perhaps it will make him appreciate her more. She loves him so much. It's all but broken her spirit to have him ignore her and pay court to that wicked Mrs. Calverson."

Matt had learned more than he really wanted to. He understood more about John's troubled marriage than he'd been told, too. "I won't tell him where she is unless I have to."

"That will do nicely. Thank you. When I give my word to keep a confidence, I don't like to break it."

Matt's opinion of the man went up a notch. "Neither do I."

"Now, can I help you with anything else?"

Matt smiled. "As a matter of fact, you can.

I fancy a new vest."

Kenny grinned. "I have some good silk ones, just in from New York City. Let me show them to you."

The next morning, very early, Matt went to see Mr. Dawes at the bank. It took him less than two minutes to get every single thing he needed out of the little man and propel him forcibly to the nearest precinct to spill his guts to a police stenographer.

Dawes immediately gave up Eli Calverson to save himself. Two police officers were sent around to the Calverson residence with orders to arrest the man, no matter how sick he was. But to their surprise, when they forced their way in with a search warrant and went up to his quarantined bedroom, it was empty.

"Why, the doctor said he was too ill to move!" Diane gasped theatrically when they saw the neatly made bed and the empty room. "Wherever could he have gone?" she added ingenuously.

"Perhaps he died and was removed without your realizing it," an older policeman said sarcastically.

She glared at him. "I am not shielding my husband! He asked me not to risk myself by coming in here. And he gave me this in case anything really terrible happened to him. He said I was to show it to the police." She took a sealed envelope from her pocket and handed it to the man, looking up at him with guileless blue eyes and a sweet smile. "I can't imagine what it says."

I'll bet you can't, the veteran officer thought, but he only nodded. He tore the envelope open and scanned the handwritten lines. His lips made a thin line.

He turned, motioning to the other officer. They bade Mrs. Calverson a good day and went quickly out the door.

The letter, in Calverson's own hand, accused John of embezzling thousands of dollars from the bank. His wife, Diane, had had nothing to do with the theft and didn't know his plans, so she shouldn't be questioned. He would make himself available to the police the minute John was safely in custody. The bookkeeper, he wrote, would verify his story. John was trying to steal his wife, Eli wrote plaintively and because, he charged, "Hawthorn knew he would need huge sums of money to keep her — money that he didn't have — he stole that, too." Dawes would never testify against John, he alleged, because John had threatened the little man, who led a secret life that included evil sexual practices. And now, he, Calverson, was going to go into seclusion at a friend's house in town until John was apprehended. He added in a postscript that he feared for his life.

The letter, with a signature and handwriting that was confirmed by Eli Calverson's own secretary, was evidence enough for the police to arrest John.

John was demoralized and furious to be led out of the bank in handcuffs. He vehemently denied any knowledge of the embezzled money, but Calverson's story sounded very logical. And to clinch it, Calverson had sent the same letter via his lawyer to the newspapers to be opened and published in the case of John Hawthorn's arrest. The next morning, the front pages of every Atlanta paper carried the story that the young vice president of the Peachtree City Bank was under arrest for embezzling the bank's money.

John sat in his jail cell in a brown fury of impotence. He'd lost his wife and he was the prime suspect in a bank theft. If his life had seemed hopeless before, it was certainly hopeless now.

Eli Calverson, as he'd promised, had immediately reappeared on the doorstep of his home, apparently completely recovered from his "illness" the minute he knew John was safely in jail. He invited reporters to his home so that he could give them his sad tale of intimidation by his vicious, embezzling vice president, while his beautiful wife charmed the male visitors. Everyone believed him, with the exception of one hawkeyed reporter who wanted to know, quite loudly, where the bookkeeper Dawes was.

"Oh, he's in hiding, too," Calverson said quickly. "But I know where he is, and he'll come forward at the appropriate time to testify. I've told the police so."

"Wasn't there a case of suspected embezzlement filed against you some years ago?" the reporter said persistently.

"I really feel too weak to continue," Eli said, pretending to swoon. "I've been ill. Thank you all for coming. I'm sure you'll do the proper thing with this story. Investors must be protected from such charlatans. To think he was my own protégé, and my friend!"

The reporters ate it up, glaring at the man who'd asked such harsh questions that he had poor, dear Mrs. Calverson in tears. When they left, Calverson gave his wife a hard look.

"You did very well, my dear," he said, with

cold menace. "Continue to do as I tell you, and we'll pull this off."

Diane was unusually pale. "I do not want to run —"

He caught her arm roughly. "But you will," he said firmly, twisting it until she cried out. "This was as much your fault as mine, with your incessant demands for pretty trinkets and clothes. Now you'll pay the piper with me! Do you understand?"

She choked. "Yes, Eli. Of course. I'll do whatever you say!"

He scoffed, but he let her go. She'd do as she was told or face the consequences. His only real concern now was escape. He had to do it while attention was focused on John Hawthorn. His revenge on the man who'd attempted to cuckold him was sweet, indeed — and made even more so by the thought of the money he'd squirreled away. All he had to do was get to Charleston and take a ship to the West Indies. There, he could live like a king. He'd use Diane as a blind until then. But afterward . . . well, a rich man could get any woman he wanted. Diane's coldness had wearied him. He was ready to ditch her and look for a woman with beauty and a kind heart. She could go back to Hawthorn, with his blessing. And the fool was welcome to her!

John, sitting alone in his cold cell, wondered if Claire ever thought of him. She probably believed he still loved Diane. That was a joke. Diane was surely in league with Eli. What a pity, he thought bitterly, that he'd been too blinded by his obsession with her to see clearly why Eli Calverson had hired him in the first place. The old man had surely been planning this for years, taking little bits of money out of the bank and letting Dawes cover up for him. If he wasn't lynched, the absence of Dawes, and Calverson's continued attacks in the press, would surely convict him. His future was sorely in doubt — and he hadn't a friend in the world to come to his rescue. Not even his wife was likely to come to his aid, if, wherever she was, she knew of his ill fortune.

It was inevitable that the Savannah papers should pick up the story about a young bank executive arrested for embezzlement in Atlanta. But it wasn't the story in the newspaper that alerted Claire to her husband's predicament. It was a telegram from Kenny Blake.

"Your husband arrested for bank fraud

and in grave danger," the telegram read. "Come at once. Kenny."

"Oh, heavens!" Claire exclaimed, falling back in her chair as if she'd been struck.

Maude and Emily rushed to her side. Maude read the telegram with no thought for courtesy. "It must be in the newspapers, too," she added, and rushed to the front door. She came back with the paper in her trembling hands. "Yes, it's in here, too. Oh, Claire! They say he's stolen thousands of dollars and that there's talk of lynching!"

"But this is ridiculous. John is the most honest man I know. He would never steal from investors."

Maude looked at the younger woman with love and gratitude. "I know that. I'm so glad that you know it, too. But what shall we do, Claire? If I tell Clayton, the shock may finish him."

"I don't think so," Claire replied. "I think it will provide the challenge he needs to bring him to his feet again."

"It's a terrible gamble," the older woman said worriedly.

"Yes. But think of the reward if it succeeds."

And the tragedy if it fails, Maude was thinking. But she kept her worries to herself. She studied Claire for a long moment.

"Very well. But let's break it to him gently."

And they did, as gently as it was possible to tell someone that his eldest son had been arrested for theft. They showed him the newspaper, the headlines of which he could barely make out.

"Of all the damned outrages," he exploded, and then begged the women's pardon for his language. He shook the paper at his wife. "If I catch the scalawag who did this — and blamed my son for it — I'll cane him bloody!"

"John's in jail," Maude said gently. "What do you want us to do?"

"I'll do what needs doing," he muttered, easing himself off the bed. "By heaven, I'll see about these charges myself. Maude, send for a carriage to take me into town. I want to stop and get our attorney to go with me on the next train to Atlanta."

"Are you sure you're fit to travel so far, Clayton?" she asked, hesitating.

"Do I look it?"

She smiled. "I suppose you do, my dear. Very well. I'll do what you say."

Claire insisted on going along, and Maude wouldn't stay behind with her husband on a long journey. She went, as well, leaving Emily — although she had wanted to go with them — in the care of Jason.

The family attorney, Harland Dennison, a thin man with a firm demeanor, wasn't averse to the trip. They all got tickets for Atlanta and set out with the barest minimum of clothing and toiletries.

Rather than check into a hotel first, they went straight to the Atlanta jail nearest the bank. There was a small crowd outside with placards denouncing John. Clayton gave them angry glares as he pushed his way through, ahead of Maude and Claire, then led the way into the precinct.

"Send that thief out here, Chief Stanton, and we'll lynch him for you!" an angry man called.

As Clayton and Maude went into the police station, Claire turned and moved back to the top step. She glared straight at the man who'd yelled the threat.

"My husband would not steal a nickel if he were starving," she said firmly. "And anyone who really knew him would be aware of that! If he was the guilty party, why didn't he run?"

There were murmurs. That hadn't occurred to anyone, apparently.

"Would a man who stole so much money stay here?" she continued. "Would an innocent man stay in town and wait for a lynch mob? And if Mr. Calverson, who accused my husband, is so innocent himself, why is he still hiding in his house? The newspaper says he won't even go to work at his own bank. He makes his foul accusations from hiding! Would a brave man do that? And where was he during the run on the bank, when my husband was forced to go out and defend the reputation of it? Was Mr. Calverson risking his own neck? He was not! Only my husband had the courage to face the mob. Is such courage the hallmark of a thief?"

There were more murmurs.

Claire lifted her chin and glared down at the milling crowd. "My husband has been falsely accused. And if you will be patient for just a few days, I will prove it to you."

There was a long pause and some loud murmuring. Finally the man in front spoke for the rest. "I guess we won't lose any more money if we wait," he said sullenly.

"Guess he would have run, if he'd done it," another added. "And he never ran from that mob."

"In this country a man is supposed to be considered innocent until he is proven guilty," Claire continued. "My husband will be exonerated, and every penny of your money will be recovered. I promise you so!"

There was another pause and loud murmurs. After a minute one man stepped forward. "We'll see, then," the mob leader conceded. He let his placard fall and motioned to the other men, leading them away from the jail.

When she got inside, it was to find John being brought out from the back of the building. He stopped when he saw his parents and Claire. He was so shocked he couldn't speak.

"There you are, my boy," Clayton said heartily, as if they'd parted in harmony only the day before. He moved forward, extending a hand. "I've brought Dennison. He's going to get you out of this place. We'll post bail. Then we'll set about proving you innocent, whatever it takes."

John's eyes narrowed as he dragged them away from the joyous sight of Claire and looked at the father he hadn't seen in two years. Clayton Hawthorn was thinner, and he looked frail, but his eyes were as determined and fiery as ever. "You're certain that I am innocent?" he asked, with a mocking smile.

"Don't be absurd," his father said stiffly. "You're my son — even if I have been an old fool of a father. I know you're innocent."

John met the extended hand and shook it

with warmth and respect. "It's good to see you again, sir," he said formally, although there was sincere feeling in his deep tone.

Clayton smiled faintly. "Yes. It's good to see you, too."

"Such formality! Men!" Maude grumbled, pushing past her husband to hug her son fiercely. "Oh, my dear! What a mess you've landed yourself in this time!" she said heavily. "But we'll get you out somehow, even if we have to bribe a judge or threaten him at gunpoint."

"Mother!" John chuckled, hugging her close.

"I do know a judge," she added thoughtfully as she extricated herself. "We were sweethearts in grammar school. But he sits on the bench in Florida, so he would hardly be any help to us."

"The truth will be help enough," Clayton said. "And you can stop flaunting your old boyfriends at me, you hussy!"

Maude giggled, and John looked past his parents to Claire. His heart jumped at the mere sight of her, and he realized how much he'd missed her in his life. He'd never had such a sensation of joy in his life before, but even as his dark eyes glittered with emotion, she lifted her chin and stared at him with frank resentment. He scowled as he saw her belligerent expression. She hadn't forgotten a thing, apparently. He knew then that her resentments would have to be overcome, and it would take time. That was all right. He had plenty of time — if he wasn't lynched in the interim, he thought darkly.

"What are you doing with my parents?" he demanded.

"She's been staying with us," Clayton offered.

"I decided that it would be the last place you'd look for me," she told him.

"So it was." He appeared angry now. "I'd no idea where to find you!"

"You were occupied with Mrs. Calverson just before I left, as you recall," she said in a near whisper. "I didn't think you'd miss me."

Maude stepped between them. "This isn't the place," she said gently.

"You're right," John agreed reluctantly, still angry at Claire's jibe. "But thank you all for coming, just the same."

"Families must stick together in times of strife," Maude told him.

"I've paid the bail," old Dennison said, rejoining them. "You're free, for the moment," he added to John. "Let's go."

John went out the door with them and

down to the waiting carriage. It was a tight squeeze, but they managed to fit. The carriage took them to the biggest hotel in town.

"Do you still have the suite at Mrs. Dobbs's house?" Claire asked John. "And is Chester all right?"

"Yes. Mrs. Dobbs refused to throw me out — even in the face of sour public opinion. Quite a woman, Mrs. Dobbs."

"We'll get rooms here," Clayton said as the carriage stopped at the Aragon Hotel. "Claire, go home with John and get him cleaned up. Then you can meet us here at the hotel for the evening meal."

"I don't . . ." she began, embarrassed.

"Yes, that would be best," John said before she could talk her way out of going home with him. "We have a lot to say to each other."

"Do we?" she asked coldly.

The elder Hawthorns waved at them as the carriage pulled off down the street toward Mrs. Dobbs's house.

John leaned back and stared at Claire. She looked fine-drawn and remote, elegant in her dark suit and perfectly coiffed. He sighed as he thought how good it was to have her home again, even reluctantly. He'd wasted so much of their time together. Now, when the chips were down, she stood by him. Diane, he knew now, would have already run for the hills.

"I'm indebted to you for coming back," he told her, "and most especially for bringing my parents with you. We've been alienated for some time."

"I remember."

"Did my father talk to you about it?" he asked persistently.

She turned in her seat to look at him. "Yes, he told me everything, just as you had. Your father will tell you himself that he deeply regrets blaming you for something that was, after all, an act of God. He has reconciled himself with God and now wishes to do the same with you. He has been very ill. But just lately, he seems to have rallied."

He smiled. "Because of you, no doubt," he said, and without sarcasm. "You have a kind heart, Claire. It would take a statue not to warm to you."

"You're very kind," she said formally, and looked out the window at the lighted houses.

"I had asked one of the Pinkertons to find you for me," he remarked.

"Why?" she asked, with honest surprise.

He frowned. "Because I was worried about you. I had no idea where you were, even if you were all right." He shrugged, glancing away. "And I missed you," he added stiffly.

"If you'd asked Kenny, I imagine he'd have told you, even though I asked him not to."

His eyes glittered with suppressed anger. "You think I would go to that prissy little bounder to ask the whereabouts of my wife?" he asked tersely.

"He may be prissy, but he's my friend," she returned. "He's been a better friend to me than you ever were!"

"Indeed?"

He sounded arrogant again, and jealous. That was a laugh. She sighed, studying him. "There's no need to pretend that you have any feeling for me," she told him. "I came back out of loyalty, nothing more. I could hardly desert you in your time of need. I had no idea, no idea whatsoever, that you would be accused of embezzling money from your own bank. What an absurd idea! I had to come home and help defend you. It is my duty as your wife."

He felt the words as if they'd been a blow aimed at his heart. Now he had her real reason for coming back, and it stung. He'd hoped that she might have come back because she still loved him. "I see," he said dully.

She must have convinced him. Good. She

couldn't bear him to know how deeply she loved him, when he was still pining for Diane. "Your parents very kindly gave me a place to stay — and made me welcome while I decided what I was going to do. You needn't worry about me. I can make my own way in the world now."

"With help from your friend Kenny?" he asked icily.

She searched his hard face. "Actually, yes . . . in a way," she said. She lifted her chin. "My friend Kenny introduced me to a man from New York who has an interest in the evening gowns I design. I will have an income of my own. So my welfare really is no longer your concern," she said amiably. "You can worry about Diane instead."

He stared at her without comprehension. As if any mystery man from New York would buy dress designs from an unknown Georgia woman! And what evening gowns? He'd never seen her work on anything like that at her sewing machine, although he did know that she could sew. Most women could, even if ready-wear clothing made it largely unnecessary for women of Claire's class. But he didn't believe her elaborate lie. She was obviously making it up to save her pride and convince him to let her go. "Diane is married," he reminded her.

"Probably not for much longer, if her husband is indeed the culprit who stole the money. Can you really see Diane following Mr. Calverson to the ends of the earth, guilty or not? She isn't the sort to live on the run, regardless of the amount of money he's embezzled. Her family name means too much to her."

He was amazed that she knew that. He'd only just learned it the hard way.

"Eli accused me of embezzling the money — and Dawes of being my accomplice."

"Mr. Dawes will certainly clear you —"

"Mr. Dawes has conveniently vanished." He interrupted her gruffly. "He was out on bond and apparently left town. No one has any idea where he is, although Calverson has promised to produce him in time to testify against me."

"You said the Pinkertons have been called in?"

"Indeed they have, at my insistence," he said. "And one of their men who served in the war with me just happened to be in town for their convention. He's the best investigator I know. He took Dawes to the police and was working to find evidence against Calverson when I was arrested. Last night he came to see me in jail."

"He isn't from Atlanta?"

"No, he's from Chicago. He'll work with the local detectives. His name is Matt Davis." He smiled. "You'll like him. He's quite unusual."

"Unusual how?"

"Wait and see."

Mrs. Dobbs opened the front door when the carriage pulled up at the house and came out to meet them.

"I'm so glad that you're both back," she said warmly. "I know you're innocent, Mr. Hawthorn, and I've told everyone so. Are you acquainted with a man named Davis?" she added worriedly. "Because he's inside waiting for you." She leaned forward. "He looks like that picture on the Indianhead nickel! I think he's an Indian!"

"He is. He's Sioux."

"Sioux?" Claire exclaimed.

"Yes. Come and meet him."

"He won't . . . ? That is, he — he doesn't . . . ?"

"Mrs. Dobbs, universal brotherhood . . . ? Forgive and forget . . ." John prompted, teasing her. "We're all friends now."

She flushed. "Of course!" She gathered up her skirts. "I hope he knows we are."

A tall, very dark man in an expensive suit waited for them in the hall.

"Good to see you out again, John," he said.

John shook the extended hand. "Good to be out, Matt."

He glanced at Claire with studied indifference, and she noticed that he had very long, straight black hair, tied in a neat ponytail. "The missing Mrs. Hawthorn, I presume."

"Yes. How do you do, Mr. Davis?"

"Very well, thank you." He studied her for a minute longer and decided that he need never tell John that he'd discovered her whereabouts. She was back. That was all that mattered. He turned to John. "I heard from the police that your father had arranged for you to be freed on bail. I came by to tell you that I've been checking our files, looking at Calverson's background for anything that might help point a finger toward him. So far I've turned up only one thing that might give us an advantage, and I got that from a reporter who wrote the only story questioning Calverson's accusations. It seems that Calverson was once under suspicion at a bank in Maryland for embezzling. The case was dropped for lack of evidence, although a young clerk was blamed for the theft and spent some time in jail before he was cleared of the charges.

That was just before Calverson opened the Peachtree City Bank in Atlanta."

John whistled. "Apparently he learned through the experience to have someone standing by to be blamed while he got off."

"Some would say that he was falsely accused," Matt replied. "But it sounds like a method of operation to me. And a very successful one. He could get away with it here unless we can catch him with the money somehow."

"Do you have anyone watching his house?" Claire asked abruptly.

Davis's eyebrows went up. "I beg your pardon?"

"He can't be planning to stay in town if he's guilty, can he?" she continued. "He probably knows the case against you won't stand up. Either he has the money with him or he's stashed it somewhere. It wouldn't surprise me one bit if he tried to sneak away in the middle of the night. Now that he's got John on the line, he's very likely to consider it safe to get away. After all, everyone knows that he's been at his house. He's entertained the press there twice."

"He has relatives in Charleston who would hide him, help him get onto a ship and get clean away," John added. "Claire's got a point. I think he'll run. His house should be watched."

Matt grimaced. "I'd love to have a man watch it, but in a small community like this, all the neighbors know who belongs and who doesn't. A stranger would stick out like a sore thumb. He'd be spotted immediately, no matter how careful he was. And while I can have a man watch the depot, I can't keep him there indefinitely."

"Leave that to me," Claire said, with a slow smile. "I think I know a way to keep Mr. Calverson's home under close scrutiny, and he'll never know."

"What do you mean to do?" John asked her.

"Wait and see," she told him.

14

Claire called on every society matron she knew and enlisted their aid. Fortunately it was one of the days set aside by Evelyn and her circle for being "at home" for visiting. Claire went first to Evelyn Paine's home.

Evelyn, fortunately alone, was tickled just at the thought of being a spy. "It's so exciting, Claire!" she exclaimed. "Imagine me, helping the Pinkertons!"

"Yes, but you mustn't let on to a soul!" Claire insisted.

"As if I would." Evelyn scoffed. "Do you know where he is, and where he's got the money?"

"I haven't a clue," Claire replied miserably. "But if it's a lot of money, and John said it's thousands of dollars, wouldn't it be bulky and hard to hide?"

"He might have it in a trunk," Evelyn suggested.

"That would be very easy to search."

"Surely," she said. "But what if his wife's clothes were in it?"

Claire was taken aback. John had said that Diane pretended to know nothing of Calverson's plans, but was that true? Or was Diane only helping the man hide his ill-gotten gains? She might not go into hiding with him, but she might be willing to help him get away for a percentage of his profits. Had John considered that?

"What if they were?" Claire thought aloud. "And while everyone's watching Mr. Calverson to see if he runs, it's Diane who has the money!"

"Claire, what a devious thought." Evelyn chuckled. "And a very good proposition, too. Now how do we get into Diane's trunks?"

"We may need a little help there," Claire said thoughtfully, and cringed as she realized who the very best person for the job would be. After all, who would Diane trust more than John?

The thing she didn't know was whether or not John would be willing to do something so underhanded to the love of his life. It made her sad to realize that if Diane indeed did have the money hidden away in those trunks, it would destroy John's opinion of her. But the alternative was to do nothing and let the Calversons get away with grand theft — while letting John go to prison. It was a thought that gave Claire goose bumps. Somehow, she had to make John see reason.

But it was harder than ever to talk to him when they were back at the apartment together. She dressed for dinner, and then worried about what to say. And there were things she couldn't bring herself to tell him just yet. She touched the belt at her waist, which she'd had to let out two notches. It was only a suspicion, but it seemed a logical one, that she was going to have John's child. How would he react to that? Were his feelings for Diane so strong that it wouldn't matter, or would guilt cause him to give up Diane because of the impending child? She had no idea. She wasn't sure she wanted an answer to the worrisome question.

He came out of his own room, immaculate and solemn. His gaze slid over Claire, noting how radiant she looked even though she wasn't smiling. He'd missed her more than he'd dreamed he could.

"Thank you," he said tersely.

"For what?"

"For making it possible for me to speak to my parents, among other things. I had thought never to see my father again in this life."

"Habit sometimes keeps us on paths we deplore," she said philosophically. "Your parents are wonderful people. They made me feel right at home. So did Emily and Jason."

He moved forward and took her hands gently into his big, warm ones. "I was worried to death about you," he confessed. "I lay awake nights, wondering if you were safe." He chuckled softly. "And you were with my people all the time. I had no idea that you even knew where my parents lived."

"You had told me they were in Savannah," she reminded him. "But they are acquaintances of Evelyn Paine's, and she introduced us."

"I see." He shook his head. "You are a surprising woman."

She searched his face, seeing new lines there. "I'm sorry to have left at such a bad time for you. I never dreamed that you would be accused of any shortfall at the bank," she said gently. "You are the most honest man I have ever known."

He smiled. "And you are the most honest woman I have ever known," he said, returning the compliment.

"As for the charges, we shall certainly

prove them false."

"As I heard you telling the mob outside." He shook his head, his eyes full of delight. "I was so proud of you. And not only then. I was proud of you for driving Chester through the flames to save me. Oh, Claire. The risk you took! I would never have permitted it if I had seen you in time."

His concern made her heart race. He was acting very different since her return, as if he liked her more than ever. But she was afraid to hope. She hadn't forgotten his coldness to her at their wedding, or his indifference for the first few weeks they were together. Perhaps most of all, she hadn't forgotten that kiss she'd witnessed in the kitchen of this very house.

She pulled her hands away slowly. "Has Diane been to see you in jail? I don't suppose she could, with her husband accusing you in all the newspapers."

He seemed saddened by her mention of the other woman. He made an odd movement with his shoulders. "Diane would hardly want to be seen with me at such a time," he said, and knew that it was the truth. Had Diane been free, she still would not have come near him. Certainly she wouldn't have defended him so bravely as Claire had against a potential lynch mob.

"We have to look forward, you know," he continued gently. "Diane is the past, Claire. You are the future."

She wanted — oh, so badly — to believe him. But past events had made her wary. Her gray eyes lifted to his. "This is not the time to speak of the future, John," she said solemnly. "So much depends on proving Mr. Calverson guilty."

He let go of her hands. "Indeed."

"His wife will surely know of his plans," she said, without looking at him. "How sad that we don't have her confidence."

He studied her for a moment — and it occurred to him that she was asking for his help, without actually putting it into words. She didn't trust him. Perhaps he could change her mind, show her that Diane no longer mattered. He moved away, considering possibilities.

Two days passed, during which John spent his time at the bank calming investors and reassuring coworkers; he and Claire passed their evenings at the hotel with his parents. The bank's customers seemed reassured by his continued presence there. Each morning, Eli Calverson sent his wife to open the bank's doors for him, making it obvious that he still didn't trust his vice president with the key. He was seen at his home, but he didn't approach the bank. Diane was flirtatious toward John — and she made suggestive remarks that he simply ignored, puzzling her.

The Pinkerton man, Matt Davis, had compared the entries in the bank's ledgers with both Calverson's signature and a sample of John's handwriting. He and the other Pinkerton man assigned to the case had no difficulty pointing out that Calverson had made the entries, and proving it to the police. Thank God, he told John, for scientific method and its application to law enforcement.

"And thank God you were in town when I needed you." John chuckled. "Chicago would be much too far away for you to work on a case like this." John stuck his hands in his pockets and paced his office. "Well, we can prove that Calverson forged the entries, but the money is still missing. Unless we can produce it, and tie it to Eli, and find Dawes to testify . . . well, I'm in a bad situation."

"Your wife's friends are busy watching the Calverson home. I've got men on the train depot. The only other way out of town is in a carriage or buggy, and I've got people watching at stables for those, too — in case

339

he tries to get to another town to board a train bound for Charleston."

"He'll have to try it eventually," John said. "Accusing me is obviously a stopgap measure until he can get away. But what if he lets Diane take the money away for him? What if she goes out of town with trunks supposedly full of clothing?"

"There are ways to find out what's in the trunks," Matt murmured dryly.

"I suppose so. But it might be easier if I went to see her myself."

"Would she be likely to let you in the door, if she's involved in this?"

"We've no way of knowing until we try," John reminded him. "She doesn't know that I suspect her."

"All right. But be careful," Matt cautioned. "Desperate men do desperate things."

"You'd know." John chuckled.

Matt didn't smile. His eyes were full of the past few years. His father had died at Little Bighorn. His mother had died at the Wounded Knee massacre, along with his young sisters. Matt himself had been badly wounded. The kindness of a white reservation doctor and his daughter's skilled nursing had spared Matt from life as a cripple. The doctor, afterward, had helped him to

Chicago, to find work at the Pinkerton detective agency through a boyhood friend. The past few years had been fruitful ones for the tall detective.

He lived in Chicago, and his appearance continued to raise eyebrows and comments about his ancestry, but no one dared tease him about it. He had a temper as formidable as his mind was keen. John was proud to call him friend. Matt, like John, had been a loner. His only other friend had been an attorney from New York, a mysterious man named Dunn with blue eyes that intimidated even hardened veterans. Those had been good days, John thought. But he had the hope of an even better life with Claire, if only he could tie the broken threads of his life together.

John called on Diane that very afternoon. She seemed taken aback to see him. First she was welcoming, and then all at once, she seemed afraid.

"You shouldn't have come," she said urgently, glancing around behind her. "John, this is not a good time for a social call."

Despite her maneuvers, John glimpsed two trunks through the front door. Both were tagged and waiting at the foot of the staircase, with a valise. He pretended not to notice.

"I thought you wanted to see me," he said softly.

She bit her lower lip. "I did. I do." She looked up with a worried frown. "John, it's all so upsetting. I don't know what to do. There's so little that I can do now." She put a hand on his chest. "Forgive me," she said huskily, glancing over her shoulder. "I must go."

"Shall I call again this evening?" he asked in a hushed tone, his eyes full of calculation that she was too upset to see.

Her whole face contorted. She seemed unusually pale. "No! I mean, no, John. Perhaps tomorrow evening. Yes. That would be very nice indeed. I'll have my sister come to play chaperon." She lowered her voice and attempted to look coquettish. "Will that do, my dear?"

"That certainly will do," he said, with forced tenderness. He touched her cheek. "I'm sorry for all the trouble you've had," he said, lying. "Until later, Diane."

"John?"

He turned.

"I understand that your father and mother have come from Savannah, and that Claire is with them," she said. "I'm very sorry for

342

all the trouble you've been subjected to. I hope —" she gnawed her lower lip "— I hope it will work out for you." Her eyes fluttered up and then down again. "I know that you didn't steal from the bank."

How sweetly concerned she seemed, when she was certainly buried in this foul matter up to her pretty neck. He didn't say a word. He only smiled, tipped his hat, and walked back down the sidewalk.

"Why didn't you get rid of him sooner?" the dirty little man Eli had hired raged as she closed the door. He came out of the parlor, wiping his sweaty brow. "What if he saw the trunks?"

"He couldn't have; I blocked the doorway," she murmured. She glanced at him impatiently. "Now do get these things loaded and go."

"You'll be on that train when it pulls out?" he asked.

The little man scared her. "Yes, Mr. O'Connor. I'll be on the train — just as I promised Eli I would. I'm not going to betray him now. I can't afford to," she added in a miserable, frightened tone.

"See that you are. Or he might send me back."

Eli had turned into a madman after the embezzlement came to light. Diane was actually afraid of him. John had wanted her once, but despite his tender tone today, it was painfully obvious that he no longer did. She'd seen John as the answer to her problems, but she'd lost him somehow. Now she had to do as Eli had demanded, even though her heart wasn't in it. His plan was devious and shrewd. But those Pinkertons were shrewd, too. She only hoped the deception would spare them an arrest. Otherwise, she was certain to go to jail with her thieving husband, a prospect that honestly terrified her. Her beautiful dresses and expensive jewels had carried a price tag that she'd never expected to have to pay. Her family would be disgraced and she would be a fugitive, tarnished beyond polishing. She shivered at the very thought of where her greed had led her.

John got back into his waiting carriage and directed the driver to go beside the house and around the block. He had a sneaking feeling that Eli was about to make a run for it. Sure enough, he spotted a freight wagon parked just behind the Calverson home. Even as he watched, a man came out the back door with one trunk on his shoulder. He put the trunk on the wagon where the valise stood, went back for the second trunk, loaded that on, and climbed up behind the horses.

So *that* was how Eli planned to get out of town, was it! Not as a passenger at all, but as freight. He was probably under one of those sacks in the back of the wagon and planned to hide himself inside one of the trunks. How very ingenious! And Diane herself had given away his travel plans. He was going today. Right now. No doubt he was on his way to the depot. How could John move fast enough in a carriage to intercept him?

And then it came to him. Claire had an automobile. Pray God she could get it running and had enough gasoline. That was going to be the swiftest way to tie all these loose ends together. It was highly unlikely that Calverson was armed, or that he would resort to violence, so he wouldn't be putting Claire at risk.

He had the carriage drop him off at Mrs. Dobbs's apartment house. He found Claire upstairs in their apartment, a charcoal pencil poised over a large drawing pad.

"I need you," he said quickly — and with a blinding smile that set her heart racing. "Can you get Chester running in a hurry?"

Claire threw down the pad, on which a dress was being sketched, and jumped up, her eyes bright with excitement. "Me? Why — why, I certainly can!" she exclaimed.

"Calverson is about to make a run for it in a freight wagon. I expect he's trying to ship himself to Charleston, along with the money. God, I hope I'm right!"

She didn't stop to ask questions. It was more than enough that John needed her. She grabbed her long cotton-duck duster and her goggles, then ran out the door that John was holding open. "I don't have one of these for you. I'm sorry," she said over her shoulder.

He chuckled. "I don't mind a little grease and dirt, Claire. Let's go!"

She cranked the car, thanking providence that she'd been tinkering with it just the day before to make sure it would run. She backed it into the road and put it into gear, with John holding on to his hat.

"Where to?" she asked him, shouting to make herself heard over the engine.

"The Morrison Hotel. We have to pick up Matt Davis to make the arrest."

"I can have you there in no time!"

She drove like a madwoman, racing over the rutted roads onto Peachtree Street, which was a little easier to traverse because the near end had a hard surface. She laughed at the sheer exhilaration of the experience, glancing once at her husband to find the same reckless light in his eyes. Yes, he was like her, she thought. He had the same passionate spirit. If only he could love her as he loved his Diane, what a pair they would make!

She pulled up at the entrance to the Morrison Hotel, frightening a carriage horse nearby. She grimaced and called an apology to the irritated driver as John leapt over the door and rushed into the hotel. Scant minutes later, he came out with Matt Davis running right behind him.

Davis skidded to a stop at the car, his black eyes wide with surprise. "I'm not getting in that thing!" he yelled.

"Oh, yes, you are," John said firmly. He dragged the taller man to the other side and almost pushed him into the seat. "Go, Claire. Go as fast as you can!"

John had jumped in, too. The three of them barely fit, but they managed to hang on as Claire raced the little car to the train depot a few blocks away.

"You can't mean that Mr. Calverson really intends to go to Charleston in a trunk!" Claire called.

"I certainly do. I saw the trunks and the freight wagon with my own eyes," John called back. "Claire, drive around behind the depot, behind that warehouse, and stop the car. We'll wait here until he turns up."

"What if he's already here?"

John scanned the freight wagons. "I don't see him —"

"Wait!" Matt interrupted, pointing. "Here comes another one."

"That's it," John replied, recognizing it immediately. "I saw it at his house, where that little weasel was loading the trunks on it. Claire, you stay here, out of harm's way," he said firmly, holding up a hand when she protested. "You've done your part. Now we'll do ours."

"Let me handle this," Matt said firmly. "I haven't forgotten your temper."

"I'm a changed man. I only want five minutes with him."

"Not on your life," came the droll reply. "I want him in one piece."

"Pity," John remarked as he followed the detective around the side of the building.

Claire didn't stay where she was told. She got out of the car and followed at a discreet distance. Along the way, she picked up a couple of big rocks and stuffed them in the pockets of her duster. She didn't think Calverson would put up a fight, but it was impossible to predict what a desperate man would do, especially one carrying large sums of cash.

Matt stopped the agent who had two men helping him get the trunks out of the wagon.

"We have reason to believe that stolen money is hidden in these trunks." He showed his identification to the man, who shrugged and stepped back, as if to say, *This isn't my problem.*

Matt instructed the two strong men to break the locks and open the trunks.

The first lid was pried open. Matt had his pistol in his hand and he nodded to John to draw the clothing out.

It was evening gowns, quite a few of them, and shoes. John plowed through them, but there was nothing hidden in the trunk under the clothing. No Eli, and no money.

Cursing, he moved to the other trunk. The depot agent shrugged and used the crowbar once more. The lock was sprung, the trunk opened.

"Something has to be in here," John muttered. He reached in. Yes, there was a bag. His heart began to race. He moved the dresses and undergarments aside and pulled out a gray bag. But inside it was an old quilt — and wrapped in that was a priceless Waterford crystal vase. John cursed viciously as he repacked it and put it back inside.

"Nothing!" he raged. He hit the lid of the trunk. "Damn it! He got away!"

"What about the driver?" Matt asked. "Maybe I can catch him if I hurry. He might be able to tell me something."

"But what about Eli?" John asked angrily. "And why are so many of Diane's gowns here in these trunks?"

The answer was that Diane must be thinking of going with her husband — or why would she ship her gowns to Charleston? Perhaps her husband was already safely out of town. With the very large sum of money missing from the bank, the Calversons could live handsomely for the rest of their lives if they got on a ship and sailed down into the Caribbean or to South America.

"And now here we've busted these locks for nothing," the station man said irritably. "You'll have to pay for this."

"I'll do it," John said. "It was my idea." He reached for his notecase, irritated beyond measure. He counted out several bills and handed them over. "Mrs. Calverson knows me. She can contact me if that isn't enough."

"Where is he, do you think?" John asked Matt Davis when they were walking back toward the automobile.

"God knows! Damn the luck! How many

trunks were there?"

"I saw only two," John said angrily. "But there might have been a third that he sent on later or earlier. God knows how he managed it! The only thing I'm certain of is that he's on his way to Charleston." He let out a long breath. "And that's where I'm going right now. I'll be damned if he's getting away with it!"

"I can't help you," Matt said, with concern. "I've got to leave in the morning, back to Chicago. But I can wire one of our men in Charleston to meet you at the depot."

"Do it," John said tersely.

"Meanwhile, I'll try to find that driver and see what I can shake out of him. What about your wife?"

As he spoke, Claire came around the corner with her duster pockets bulging with rocks.

"Where is he?" she asked, and pulled one of the rocks from the coat.

John's eyes twinkled. God, she was game! "On the train, we presume," he said. He moved forward, his voice soft as he spoke to her. "Listen, Claire, I'm going to Charleston after him. You take your automobile back home —"

"I will not!" she said firmly. "I'm going with you."

His eyes widened. "What about the auto-mobile?"

She turned to Matt Davis. "I know it's a presumption, but could you go around to Kenny Blake's men's shop and ask him to take it home for me? He and a couple of men can put it on a wagon and take it there. The shed's open — and he can close the lock afterward. And if you could also tell Mrs. Dobbs at our apartment house . . . and John's parents at the Aragon Hotel where we've gone?"

John chuckled at her efficiency. "She seems to have it all organized. Do you mind?" he asked his friend.

Matt smiled faintly. He didn't like white women as a rule, but this one had spunk. "I'll do it," he said, agreeing.

"Thank you, Mr. Davis," she said genuinely.

John shook hands with him. "If you'll have that man alerted to meet us at the depot in Charleston when we arrive, perhaps we can find Calverson before he makes a clean getaway with the loot."

"Nobody escapes the Pinkertons," Matt said, with tongue in cheek.

"Nobody escapes the Hawthorns, either," Claire assured him. "John, look! The train's getting ready to leave. We must fly!"

She grabbed his hand and spirited him toward the ticket office. He went with her, more elated and excited than he'd ever been in battle. The chase was on, the game was afoot, and he felt like a boy on a snipe hunt again. Except that this time, he wasn't looking for some mythical bird. He was hunting big game, and his whole future depended on finding it.

15

They managed, just, to get seats in a compartment that was empty. Claire took off her duster and put it aside, using her handkerchief to remove some of the grime from her dark dress and her face.

John stared at her from across the compartment on the seat facing hers. He smiled. "Why is it that you seem to be sewing all the time, yet you wear the same things over and over again? And don't tell me it's for Macy's. That really was a tall tale, Claire."

She looked up with lifted eyebrows. "I never lie. You know that."

He scowled and leaned forward. "You mean that it's true? You actually have sold gowns . . . to Macy's?"

"Indeed I have," she replied, ruffled. "I know that you wouldn't have heard of my gowns, but they're quite popular. A buyer from Macy's has just employed me to design a collection for the store. I also sew gowns for society ladies in Atlanta, notably Evelyn Paine and her friends. And I have been commissioned by your mother to sew Emily's coming-out gown for the spring debutantes' ball in Savannah."

He looked perplexed. "How long have you done this?"

"Since just after we married," she confessed. She toyed with the handkerchief. "I had plenty of time for such pursuits, and I wanted an independent income." She looked up. "After all, it seemed for a time as if you would divorce me and marry Diane at your earliest opportunity. I felt it would be politic of me to become self-sufficient as soon as possible."

He felt a sense of shame that he'd made her so insecure. "Well, at least it explains all that sewing," he remarked.

"Kenny introduced me to the buyer from Macy's. I had a sundae with him while we arranged for the designs to be sent to New York."

He let out a breath. "I see. So that's why you were in town with him. And I suppose it's why you met him the day of the bank riot and the fire?"

"Exactly. I took him some sketches to send to Mr. Stillwell, the buyer at Macy's."

"And you didn't feel you could explain

this to me, even when I charged you with infidelity?" he asked gently.

She shrugged delicately. "It hardly seemed the time to tell you that I was on the verge of becoming well off in my own right." She lifted her hands. "You must see that I had every reason not to trust you."

He grimaced. "I do. But that doesn't make it easier."

"It disturbs you that I shall be independent?" she asked, fishing.

He leaned back and crossed his long, powerful legs. He stared at her across the coach. "Not really. It's a good idea for you to have your own income. Not because I plan to divorce you," he added firmly, "but because you would be able to support yourself if anything happened to me."

"God forbid," she said, and felt a chill.

He smiled. "Really? At times it seemed to me that you wouldn't mind if I fell off a cliff. In fact, I feel certain that during our brief marriage, you were ready to push me off one a time or two."

Her eyes lowered to her long, dusty skirt. "I would mind, though." She lifted her eyes again. "You searched the trunks, didn't you? And neither Mr. Calverson nor the money was in them."

"You saw that?"

She smiled ruefully. "I was peering around the corner. I had rocks in my pockets, so that I could wade in and help if you needed me."

He chuckled with pure delight. "It's nice to know that you have my interests at heart."

"You are my husband, after all." She studied his face for a long moment. "What did you find in the trunks?"

He didn't want to tell her that just yet. He looked away. "Just some clothing. It seems that Eli plans to spend quite a lot of time either in Charleston or abroad and hopes I take his punishment for him."

She grimaced. "You thought better of him, I'm sure. I'm sorry."

"I'm not really surprised, you know," he said. "Eli was always one to put profit above friendship or compassion. Money is so unimportant in the great scheme of things, Claire. I've had money and I've been without it. I don't notice any real difference, except that I feel more comfortable making my own way in life, depending on my intelligence and my wits to keep me on the right track." He searched her eyes. "Yes, you understand that, don't you? Because you've never had money."

"That's so. I had Uncle Will and not much more. Except the automobile." Her face

357

broke into a grin. "Your friend Matt Davis is afraid of automobiles!" she said, with pure glee.

"Yes, I noticed," he said, chuckling. "If you knew anything of his true background, you might find it even more amusing."

"Do tell," she coaxed.

He chuckled. "One day, perhaps, not now."

"You said that he was Sioux."

"He is."

"It has something to do with General Custer's death, doesn't it?"

"Something," he said. "Because there was so much bad feeling toward his people after the event, for some time after he left South Dakota, Matt was sensitive about any reference to his race. Most people who know him are savvy enough not to take the risk of mentioning it. But in some ways, he's still sensitive about his identity. The accepted facade of the dumb Indian or the untamed savage infuriates him. He's a very educated man."

"I noticed that. But he doesn't seem to like women."

"White women," he said. His eyes went toward the coach window. "No, he doesn't."

"Why?"

"I don't know," he said honestly. "We

served together in different units in Cuba, and although we were friends, Matt was a private person. He kept his background very much to himself. I've never heard him called anything except Matt Davis, but I'm certain that it's an invented name, that he has another name altogether on the reservation."

"Do you have other friends besides him and your friend in the military who came to visit?"

"Quite a few. Some live in Texas, some in Florida, some in Charleston, and some in New York."

"Were they all in the military?"

"Not all. A few were friends I made at college."

"I just had a thought," she said. "If you were at the Citadel for a time, you must know Charleston fairly well."

He smiled. "Yes, I do. However, that isn't going to help us find Calverson."

"We could search the train," she suggested.

"How would we explain that to the porters? I have no credentials as a lawman."

"You could say that you were a Pinkerton man."

"And they'd telegraph the nearest office and discover that I was not. Modern communications make life hard for robbers, and that's a good thing."

She glowered at him. "While we sit here talking, Mr. Calverson is no doubt hidden — with his ill-gotten gains — somewhere on this very train!"

'I'm afraid that may be true," he replied. "But we'll have to wait until we get to Charleston to find out." He leaned back again. "You might as well rest while you can. Stretch out on the seat, if you like."

"It's rather chilly."

"Here." He took off his overcoat and handed it to her. She took it gingerly.

"It won't contaminate you," he said sharply.

She looked up. "I know that." Her shoulders moved. "I was just thinking about how it will be for Diane when she discovers that her husband has run away and left her behind to be gossiped about even more."

He didn't tell her what he suspected about Diane — that she was, in fact, running away with Eli. His lips pursed thoughtfully. "Yes. It will be bad for her, for a time."

She searched his eyes, but they gave nothing away.

He reached out and touched her cheek gently. "You care so much about people," he said slowly. "Even rivals. I never realized how warm your heart really was until we married. Warm, and very fragile."

The heart of which he spoke jumped sharply in her chest and began to beat recklessly.

He smiled. "And you still find me desirable, even though you can't manage to confess it," he added in a deep whisper, bending. "I find that . . . reassuring."

As she formulated words, his mouth gently settled on her own. She was too surprised to fight, or protest, she told herself. But that didn't explain her sudden desperation to be close to him, to incite him to ardor.

Her arms reached up blindly and pulled him down to her on the seat. He wrapped her up close, turning her so that she lay across his lap with the duster and his overcoat in a pile on the floor. He kissed her hungrily, with no thought for consequences or the unshuttered glass of the compartment, through which they could easily be seen.

"I can never get enough of your mouth," he said against her lips, his breath ragged. "I could die kissing you and die happy. Come closer!"

She kissed him back with a rough little moan, remembering the pleasures they'd shared in his bed in the darkness, the hunger of his body, the yielding submission of hers, the aching pleasure of ecstasy.

He lifted his mouth just a little, and his eyes were black with hunger. "I want you," he whispered unsteadily. "Here, on the bench, on the floor, anywhere! Oh, God. Claire!"

His mouth ground into hers again. His hand went between them to the soft curve of her breast and covered it. His thumb and forefinger traced it, teased it. She gasped and then moaned, and her fingers covered his, pressing them even closer to her aching flesh.

She tasted the coffee he'd had for breakfast on his mouth, breathed in the delicious scent of the bay rum cologne he was wearing, savored the raspy warmth of his face under her fingers. Marriage was still exciting and new, and she had a secret that he didn't know. She carried his child under the heart where his hand lay. If only she could tell him! But she wasn't sure of him — not until Eli Calverson was caught and returned to Atlanta . . . not until John's true feelings for Diane were known.

Even as their hunger threatened to go out of bounds, the door suddenly opened and an elderly face gaped at the two young people entwined on the seat.

"Well, I never did!" the elderly woman in a black dress and hat and veil exclaimed. "Such carrying on, in public!"

"This is hardly a public place, madam," John said, rising to his feet shakily but respectfully. "And the lady in question is my wife," he added, with a mischievous smile, "from whom I have been parted for some weeks."

The elderly face relaxed a little as it took in the young woman's red cheeks and demure glance. She smiled and made a little sound in her throat. "I see." She glanced from one to the other. "Are you on your honeymoon, then?"

"We've been married for several months," Claire responded.

"How lucky you are," the old woman said wistfully. "I have my husband of fifty years in a coffin in the mail car. I am taking him to Charleston to be buried with my family and his, in the old cemetery." Even through the veil her eyes were sad. "Forgive me for thrusting my sorrow upon such a young and obviously happy couple, but this seems to be the only vacant seat left. The train is quite crowded."

"Please sit down," John invited, moving beside Claire to give the elderly woman a seat. He picked up the duster and the overcoat and put them aside. Without a qualm, he reached for Claire's hand and held it warmly in his. "My wife and I are on holiday," he added untruthfully, and with a smile. "Charleston is a city I know well, having graduated from the Citadel."

"Did you really?" the old woman exclaimed, pushing back her veil to reveal warm, dark eyes. "My son was a student there. Perhaps you knew him: Clarence Cornwall?"

John hid a grin. "Yes," he said. "In fact, I did know him. He was in the class behind mine." He smiled. "I am John Hawthorn, and this is my wife, Claire."

"I am Prudence Cornwall," the widow said, introducing herself. "How very nice to meet you both." She sighed. "Clarence hated the Citadel, poor boy. He didn't graduate, I'm sorry to say. It was a great disappointment to my husband."

"What is Clarence doing now?"

"He's captain of a fishing boat. Isn't that ironic?"

"Indeed it is." John turned to Claire. "Clarence hated the water. He couldn't swim."

"He still can't." The widow Cornwall chuckled. "But he's very good at his job, and he earns his living from it. He married, John. He and Elise have six children."

"How fortunate for him," Claire said warmly. "He must be very happy indeed to have children."

John moved restlessly. He hadn't thought about a family at all. "I find children a bit unnerving," he remarked, without looking at his wife — which was, perhaps, a good thing. "It isn't something we have to consider right away, however."

He sounded as if he were relieved about that, and Claire began to worry. If he didn't want children, what would she do? And what about Diane? As John and the widow spoke of Charleston and old times, Claire stared out the window with her worries like a knot in her soft throat. She had plenty of problems — and not one single solution in sight.

The widow Cornwall tucked her veil back in place. "I wish I had a happier reason for going to Charleston," she said wistfully. "It is a sad trip for me. And for that other young woman, who refuses to leave the side of her dead husband. Poor dear. It must be so uncomfortable for her in the mail car. She did look well-to-do, but the coffin is only a pine box." She frowned. "Her husband must have been a very large man. I must say, I have never seen a coffin of such size. Still —" she dismissed it with a wave of her hand "— the shipping cost should not be monumental."

"Did the other widow board the train with you in Atlanta?" John asked, with unusual intentness.

"Why, no," she replied. "I did not board the train in Atlanta, but in Colbyville, where my husband and I were visiting his sister when he died suddenly. Although," she added, "at our stop in Atlanta, the young widow did have two trunks loaded into the mail car. But the coffin came aboard at Colbyville. That's why it has taken me so long to look for a seat," she added. "I did not feel comfortable leaving her there alone, even though she was anxious to be alone with the coffin."

John's eyes were wide and curious.

Claire looked at him. "You don't think . . . ?"

"Oh, don't I?" he murmured coldly. "Shall we go for a stroll, Claire?"

"I'd be delighted. You'll excuse us?" Claire asked the widow softly as they stood.

"Certainly. You go right ahead. I never like being cooped up in these compartments on such long journeys. I fear we will tire of each other's company long before we reach our destination!"

"And I'm certain that we will not," John said gallantly, smiling at the widow.

She laughed with enjoyment. "You're a flatterer, young man. Your wife will have to keep a close eye on you!"

"Indeed I will," Claire replied, reaching for John's hand in a shy attempt to maintain the fiction of togetherness.

If he was surprised at her action, he concealed it quite well. He returned the pressure of her soft fingers in their white glove and drew her from the compartment.

They were down the walkway a good piece before Claire spoke. John hadn't released her hand, and it thrilled her to feel its gentle pressure.

"Do you think it's Diane?" she asked warily, because even now, she wasn't sure of his feelings.

"Of course I do," he said, and sounded actually indifferent! "There were two trunks packed in the hall of her home earlier when I went there. Those were the ones Matt and I broke into at the station in Atlanta. I didn't tell you," he added, with a grin, "but they were full of Diane's gowns and dresses. I knew then that she was probably going to go with Eli." He chuckled wickedly. "Eli and the money, I should have said. Diane would have been hard-pressed to let him take the money and not her, as well."

"I'm very sorry, John," she said, with genuine regret. "I know that she . . . means a lot to you."

He slowed, looking down at her with tenderness in his dark eyes. "She *did*," he said, emphasizing the past tense. But while Claire hung there with bated breath, and before he could enlarge on that, the porter came past. John stopped him.

"Where is the mail car?" he asked. "A friend of ours is there with her late husband. We wanted to pay our respects."

"Mail car's that way, sir. Just go down through the passenger compartment and out the door. It's the car just behind this one. Watch your step, now," he added, and smiled at them.

"Thank you."

They walked through the rows of passenger seats and to the back of the swaying car until they reached the platform.

"I wish Matt could have come with us," John murmured. "I don't know what Diane will say when she sees us."

"She needn't see us," Claire replied. "Can't you peer through the door and see if it's really her?"

"Not if the shade is drawn," he said. "But

I'll try. You stay here."

He crossed to the next car, looking around to make sure there was no one observing them. He stood beside the door. The curtain was drawn all right, but the swaying of the cars on the tracks made it swing back and forth. He glimpsed two coffins through it — one ornate and one a pine box. And he saw Diane, in widow's weeds with a black veil momentarily lifted from her face, sitting beside a coffin whose lid was open; Eli Calverson's bald head was just visible above it. He was obviously discussing something with Diane, who looked worried and out of sorts. He moved quickly away and back to Claire, chuckling as he bustled her inside the passenger car.

"It's them," he said gaily. "Now if we can just find the Pinkerton man in Charleston . . ." He paused, snapping his fingers. "Claire, we'll stop over in Augusta on the way! I'll rush in at the next stop and telegraph the Pinkerton office and have them meet the train at Augusta! If the money's in that coffin, we'll have Eli dead to rights!"

"What if it's not?" Claire asked worriedly. "What if he sent it on another train, or if it's in a trunk he left behind?"

"We'll have to take the chance. But he wouldn't be likely to leave that much money

369

behind," he said. "And Diane wouldn't be with him if he had, either."

"You sound so bitter."

"I am." He glanced down at her with regret. "I was obsessed with her for years, and in all that time, I never once let myself see what she really was. I've wasted part of my life chasing fox fire."

Her heart jumped with renewed hope. "No time is wasted if we learn a lesson from how we spend it, John," she said solemnly. "But it must be hard for you, all the same, to have to see her arrested."

He glanced at her. "In a way it is, Claire," he said, smiling. "But by and large, people get what they deserve, sooner or later."

Claire thought very hard for a moment. "Is there a reward for capturing someone who embezzles money from a bank?"

"Yes. The reward would be paid by our bank."

She smiled. "Let me try something, then."

"What?"

"Let me talk to Diane."

"Absolutely not," he said shortly. "I won't put you at risk. He might have a gun, for all I know."

His concern flattered her. "I would do nothing to put myself at risk," she said at once, thinking of the tiny life inside her that he didn't know about, and might not even want. "I think I might be able to speak to her alone. I think I have an idea that might work. I can sit there in the back of the passenger car and watch for her to come out."

"Alone? Oh, no." His fingers tightened on hers. "I'm not letting you out of my sight, Mrs. Hawthorn. I'll wait with you."

She grinned at him, overcome with delight. "Don't you want to talk to Mrs. Cornwall?"

"I do not!"

She chuckled. "Then I would be glad of your company. Some people must be in the dining car, or there would be no seats here. And it may not be long before they return."

"Then we'll have to hope that she comes through here soon."

Claire was betting on it, because there wasn't a restroom in the baggage car. Perhaps there were restrooms farther down the train, but this would be closer. She had to hope that Diane would arrive long before any other passengers came to reclaim their seats.

John retained her small gloved hand when they sat down, fascinated with its smallness and strength.

"I like your hands," he remarked. "They're very capable little hands, too. They can even fix automobiles."

She smiled up at him, her face radiant and adoring. "They can fix meals, as well." Her smile faltered a little and she looked away. "Of course, there's no need, since Mrs. Dobbs does it so well."

He watched her averted face with disquiet. His hands tightened on hers as he saw the pain there. "Claire, I never even asked if you might prefer a house of our own. Would you?"

She tried to speak and couldn't.

"Oh, my dear," he said softly, and bent to kiss her eyes closed. "Of course you would." He answered his own question. "We can start looking when we get back," he said firmly. "I know of at least two small houses near Mrs. Dobbs. Unless you want something elaborate?" he added, smiling with barely contained excitement. "We could have one with gingerbread trim and crystal chandeliers, if you like."

She laughed with such joy that she felt she might burst. "Oh, no. Crystal chandeliers are far too grand for me! But I would like a small house," she said. "If you're sure that you want to live in it with me," she added, with a painful lack of self-confidence.

His arm went around her thin shoulders and drew her close, easing her head back so that he could search her radiant face with quick, possessive eyes. His breath warmed her face. "Yes, I want to live with you," he whispered ardently. "But not as we have. I want a much closer marriage." His arm contracted. "I want to be your husband, my darling, in every way there is. I want to hold you in my arms every night and wake up beside you every morning of my life."

Tears pricked at her eyes. "Oh, I want that, too!" she said huskily. Her gloved fingers touched his firm mouth. They trembled with the depth of her feelings. "John, I love you so!" she whispered.

Without caring about their fellow passengers, he bent and kissed her mouth with such tenderness that she shivered in his arms.

He smiled against her welcoming lips, so overcome with joy at her words that he could barely breathe. "And I love you," he whispered back, to her surprised delight. "With all my heart. With all my soul. With all that I am, or ever will be." He whispered the last words against her mouth as he kissed her again, a kiss that was more than a touching of lips. It was a vow.

Murmured laughter caught his attention and he lifted his head to meet indulgent smiles from the people around them. His cheeks actually flushed, and he chuckled self-consciously as he sat up, still possessing Claire's small hands.

"The rest will have to wait," he whispered with a wicked grin. "This is hardly the place to discuss our whole future, and we're stuck here."

She beamed at him. "It will only be for a little while, though. In fact —"

The door to the car opened; Diane came in. She didn't look to the left or right, passing by their seat without even noticing them. Claire pressed John's fingers, got out of the seat quickly, before he could protest, and followed Diane right down to the restroom. When Diane went inside, Claire pushed right in behind her and shut the door, closing them in together.

"What . . . ?" Diane exclaimed, grabbing her throat.

"Don't be afraid. It's only me," Claire said gently. "You're in a lot of trouble. We know that your husband is hidden in a coffin in the luggage car. A Pinkerton man will be waiting for both of you at the next station," she lied. "We arranged it in Atlanta."

Diane leaned her head against the wall and let out a ragged sob. "I knew this would happen! I told him. I told him it wouldn't work!" she wailed. "He dragged me into this

374

and made me help him. He hasn't been the same since he took the money. He threatened me if I didn't go along with it. He said that he would provide for me handsomely if I helped him, but that I would be in great danger from that little weasel-faced man he employs if I didn't. I was afraid of him," she confessed, her eyes meeting Claire's. "He has been cruel — and I was weak and I agreed to help him. I am lost, you see! I am disgraced, and so is my family — all because I couldn't bear to be poor!"

"Listen to me," Claire said earnestly. "There's a reward for Eli's capture and the return of the money. It's a very large reward."

"Blood money." Diane sniffed. Her lovely eyes filled with tears.

"No. A reward for catching a criminal who stole money from innocent investors in his bank," Claire replied. Her voice was earnest and quick, because John's whole future depended on gaining this old rival's help. "Think of it, Diane. You'd be a heroine. People would like you as well as pity you, because of what you endured. They would respect you for having the courage to turn in your husband, despite your fear of him."

Diane stopped sniffling and stared at Claire with red-rimmed blue eyes. "They would?" she asked, surprised.

"Of course they would."

Diane fiddled with a handkerchief, her eyes downcast. "It's a large reward?"

"Very large."

"But I went with him. I'm an accomplice. I'll go to jail!"

"No, you won't. If you turn him in, you can tell them the truth — that he forced you to help him by threatening you. That's the truth."

"Well, yes, it is. I suppose I could." She eyed Claire suspiciously. "Why are you willing to help me? You do know that your husband is in love with me? And that when I'm free of Eli, he's going to leave you and marry me?"

Claire knew better than that, thank God, but she didn't dare admit it just now. "If you don't turn in your husband, John might go to prison," Claire pointed out. She took a slow breath and waited. As she did, she thought about John's child, and the way his face had looked when he confessed his love. She loved him — and would have sacrificed her own happiness to give him to Diane, if that had been what he wanted. She thanked God that it would not be necessary. She contrived a wistful smile as Diane wavered, and added calculatingly, "I'd rather see him with you, you know, if that's what he really wants, than see him go to jail for another man's crime."

"You're very unselfish," Diane said after a minute. "I'm not. I like being rich. I like having pretty things." Her shoulders shrugged. "I thought John would be poor, and I'd had enough of living hand-to-mouth and having my sisters depend on me for a living when they were between lovers. I married Eli because he was wealthy." She sighed. "I never loved him. I loved John." She looked up. "But I never loved him quite enough, did I, Claire? And I think that you do. I'm sorry he doesn't love you."

"That doesn't matter," Claire said, keeping her delightful secret. "Keeping him out of jail is my only desire at the moment. Will you help?"

Diane hesitated. But she really had no choice. "Yes," she said. "I'll help you. What do you want me to do?"

16

A small town called liberty was along the route the train took to Augusta. While the engine stopped to take on passengers, John dashed into the station and sent a wire to Augusta, to the sheriff.

Diane went back to the mail car, carefully closed the door, and made sure the shade was down. She went and sat down beside the coffin as if nothing had happened.

"Is it all right?" Eli asked, peeping over the edge of the coffin. "You didn't see anyone you knew?"

"Of course not," she lied prettily. She'd had plenty of practice. She even smiled. "But the train is very crowded."

"That won't matter. The people will get off at stops all along the way. As soon as we get across the state line into South Carolina, I can get out of this thing. I'm terribly uncomfortable. I'm not wanted in South Carolina."

She glanced into the coffin, at the bags of money. There were several, all of them stuffed full. It was a king's ransom, and she'd just agreed to help the bank recover it. Well, she sighed, there was a reward. She wouldn't have to go to prison. She'd be free of Eli. And she'd even be able to get John back. Claire was no match for her. She smiled.

"You look very smug," Eli muttered, wiping his sweaty brow.

"Everything is going our way, isn't it?" she asked cheerfully, and stared out the window at the passing scenery as she began to work out a happier future in the privacy of her mind.

When the train pulled in to the Augusta station, several men in suits rushed forward, and John went out to meet them. While Claire watched from the compartment she was still sharing with Mrs. Cornwall, the men came aboard the train. Minutes later, she saw a shocked, defeated-looking Eli Calverson being led away in handcuffs. Beside him, a man wearing a star on his lapel was carrying several bags of the sort used by banks.

John came back into the compartment quickly. "Sorry to leave you here, Mrs.

Cornwall, but Claire and I must get off the train and go back to Atlanta at once. Come, dearest," he added, dragging Claire up by the hand. "Have a pleasant trip," he told Mrs. Cornwall.

"Thank you, young man. I hope things go well for both of you," the widow said.

They waved to her as they rushed down through the passenger car, out the back door, and down the steps to the platform. Diane was standing a little apart with two uniformed men, weeping noiselessly into a handkerchief while her husband looked back with furious anger and outrage as he was spirited away.

"My poor, poor Eli." Diane sniffed. "Oh, his poor mind was so twisted. He couldn't have known what he was doing, could he?" She looked up at the impressionable young lawman with a face that would have melted stone.

The young man patted her gloved hand. "Of course not. Now, don't you worry, Mrs. Calverson. We'll take excellent care of you. Here, let us get tickets for you on the train back to Atlanta."

"Not on the same train with my husband?" she asked, with real fear. "Oh, I simply couldn't bear it!"

"No, ma'am. He'll be going on a special

train," he replied. "Don't you worry about that. We'll take care of everything. Oh, Mr. Hawthorn," he called to John, grinning. "Are you and your wife traveling back with us, too?"

"Indeed we are," John said. He smiled at Diane, but he had Claire by the hand and showed no sign of letting go.

If Diane was surprised by the attention he showed Claire, she handled it well. She managed a weak smile for the Hawthorns and then linked her arm with that of the young Pinkerton man and walked into the depot with him. It was understandable that John wouldn't approach her in public, she supposed. After all, they had to keep up appearances. Surely that was his rationale, as well. She smiled prettily at the young Pinkerton man, who beamed back at her and began to talk about himself.

She encouraged him. She knew how to handle men, and this one was no challenge at all. Men could always be flattered into doing anything if one appealed to their vanity by asking them about their jobs or their lives. It was really amazing how much unwanted information came flowing out.

She went with him to a seat on the train — far removed from the ones that John and Claire were able to get. It didn't seem to take so long to get back to Atlanta as it had to reach Liberty. In a very short time, it seemed, they pulled up under the Spanish facade of the Atlanta railroad station depot and passengers began to disembark on the platform.

Pinkertons met the train, among them Matt Davis, who hadn't yet left for the home office in Chicago. But instead of taking charge of the prisoner, which another senior agent might have done, he let the young arresting Pinkerton officer take Calverson into the local jail. It made the young man dizzy with self-esteem and amused Claire, who watched him lead his prisoner away as if he'd won at the races.

"And now I really am going home," Matt told John, his eyes twinkling with amusement. "He wasn't in the trunks, so where was he?"

"He was hidden in a coffin, of all places!" John chuckled. "With his wife in the mail car beside it playing the part of the grieving widow. It might have worked, except that a real widow came and sat with Claire and me and mentioned the beautiful young widow in the mail car whose husband's coffin came aboard at Colbyville." He shook his head. "She didn't realize that she was solving a robbery. I suppose we should have told her. It would have made her day."

Matt glanced past John and Claire at the dispossessed widow, around whom two other Pinkerton men swarmed helpfully. "And what about her?" he asked.

"She'll get the reward," John said. "Afterward, I daresay she'll land on her feet."

Matt nodded. "There's quite a sizable reward, put up by the board of directors of the bank," he said. "I suppose you knew?"

"Yes," John said. "They weren't too warm with their welcomes after I was released from jail," he added darkly, "but they did bend enough to tell me about the reward they'd posted for return of the money. They seemed fairly certain that I'd miraculously produce it, given enough incentive."

"This should satisfy them," Matt said. He glanced past John's shoulder. "And some more reassurance is forthcoming."

Even as he spoke, reporters from the local paper and two out-of-town ones, alerted to the railroad chase by someone in city government, rushed forward with their pads and pencils — ready to take down whatever answers they could get to their questions.

John told the story succinctly, aided by Matt Davis, and, almost at once, Diane, whose fair beauty made her the heroine of the story. At least it did until Claire's part in the chase became clear.

"You have a motorcar?" one young reporter exclaimed. "And you drove it here to the depot? May we see it?"

"Certainly you may," Claire said, beaming. "It's at our apartment house."

John's arm came around his wife. "And there's something else you should know about my wife," he added proudly. "She's just contracted with Macy's department store of New York City to design a line of women's evening gowns for them."

"Under your own name, ma'am?" one reporter asked.

"No," Claire replied. "I use the name 'Magnolia' on my gowns."

There was a gasp from Diane, who went pale as she realized that the designer whose elegant creations she'd so coveted was someone she actually knew. What a pity that it turned out to be John's wife!

John himself was impressed. He'd had no idea of the name Claire used on her designs, but he'd heard enough of "Magnolia's" fame to make him feel very like strutting. The woman he loved was indeed a woman of parts. He grinned at her with pure pride. She intercepted that look and her hand tightened in his.

" 'Magnolia.' How very Southern," another reporter said. "And now, Mrs. Hawthorn, let's go and see that automobile!"

The press followed Claire and John back to Mrs. Dobbs's and photographed Claire sitting in the seat of the pretty little black Oldsmobile with her fingers on the steering knob. She arranged to have Mrs. Dobbs in a photograph with the two of them, and the motorcar, which made the little woman's day. The reporter who was the most interested in her turned out to be the only one who'd maintained John's innocence and had mentioned the charge of embezzlement in Calverson's past. Claire liked him at once and thanked him heartily for his defense of her husband.

That evening, Claire and John dined with his mother and father at the hotel. Maude Hawthorn was full of the excitement of the day, and she ran out of breath asking questions about the mad chase to Augusta to recover the stolen bank money and catch the thief.

"I still can't believe it," she said, shaking her head. "You two are lunatics, do you know that? What if he'd been armed?"

"I had rocks in my duster pocket," Claire volunteered.

John chuckled. "And I had a .32 Smith & Wesson revolver tucked in my belt," he added, glancing at his wife's shocked face. "No, I didn't tell you, did I? I thought you were better off not knowing. And as things turned out, I didn't have to use it."

"I seem to recall that you won awards in the service for pistol marksmanship," Clayton Hawthorn interjected. He was still having a hard time talking to his son, but he'd relaxed a little this evening. He looked as if he were desperately trying to rebuild their relationship.

"I did. I miss the service from time to time."

"My boy," Clayton said quietly, "why don't you reenlist?"

That, coming from his father, was almost an apology. He smiled. "I don't know that I'd be happy in the service again, although I have thought about it," John had to admit. He looked at Claire and smiled gently. "At first, I had doubts about settling into life as a banker."

Claire didn't bat an eyelash. "I'm quite happy to go wherever you want to go," she said happily, still keeping her precious secret about her child.

"Your good name will be cleared when the newspapers hit the street corners tomorrow," his mother added. "And you do look so handsome in uniform."

He smiled. "Thank you, Mother. But there's still some action in the Philippines," he said, glancing at Claire. "There's no guarantee that I wouldn't be sent there. I shouldn't like to take my bride into a war zone, especially when she has a whole new career opening up for her. I did mention, I hope, that I'm very proud of you, Claire?"

She colored. "No, you didn't."

"Then this is a good time to tell you that I am," he replied, his dark eyes warm on her face. "So, it's rather an inopportune time to reenlist just yet." He reached for Claire's hand and brought it to his lips gently. His eyes made hungry promises. "I have enough to do right here. I won't have it said that I ran, after the slur Calverson made against my character. I want to stay here at least until the scandal dies down again. Then, Claire and I will decide what we both want to do."

Clayton cleared his throat. "Well, I'd be very happy if you both came to Savannah; you could take over the presidency of my bank when old Marvis retires." He shifted. "That's not a bribe. I guess it sounds like one."

John studied his father carefully. "I'd like

387

to be near you and Mother. I'll consider it."

Clayton looked shocked. "You will?"

"Would you like to live in Savannah?" he asked Claire, with a loving smile.

She beamed. "Yes. I adore it," she said. "There's so much history there. And it's right on the ocean, as well. You could force yourself to go sailing with Jason and your father. I heard about the seasickness," she added, with a grin.

"You know about that?" he said teasingly.

She smiled. "Yes. I heard all about it in Savannah. As well as a few other things," she added wickedly. "Like about the frog you hid in your mother's sewing basket and the worm you put down the back of Emily's dress at church. At church, of all places!"

"It livened up the service." John chuckled, his eyes twinkling as he looked at his wife.

She was beginning to realize how little of the real man she'd ever seen. He was mischievous, she saw, and the amusement in his eyes delighted her with its promise.

She looked down at their linked hands. "But, as you said, we can talk about where to live later."

His fingers contracted.

"And from now on, whatever you want to do with your life will be fine with me," Clayton Hawthorn said, lifting his chin.

"I'm . . . quite proud of you, John — and quite ashamed of myself and the two years I've wasted. I never should have blamed you for something that was an act of God, my boy. I've accepted that now. I'm sure you grieved as much as I did."

"That's quite true," John said, agreeing, and his eyes were sad. "But those years did teach me how much my family meant to me. Perhaps they weren't wasted."

Clayton's jaw tautened. "You could come and visit."

John smiled. "I could come for Christmas, and bring Claire."

The old man's eyes twinkled in a radiant face. "So you could!"

"You must," Maude entreated. "It will be the most joyous Christmas, to have all my family with me!"

John searched his wife's eyes. "Shall we go home and pack?"

Her breath caught in her throat. "You mean it?"

"Of course I do!"

She jumped up, oblivious to the amused looks of fellow diners. "May we go now? Right now?"

John chuckled. "Indeed we may! If we can conclude all our business, we can leave with you at midday tomorrow, if that suits you?"

he asked his father.

"It suits me very well. Come and have a late breakfast with us in the morning, and we'll purchase our tickets afterward."

But the packing didn't get done. After they fielded Mrs. Dobbs's excited questions, John locked Claire in their suite and carried her to bed. They loved as they never had before, tenderly and slowly, with such exquisite fulfillment that Claire was breathless and exhausted and hopelessly enthralled.

Later, they slept — and then woke early the next morning and made love again, even more fervently than before.

They got up and dressed; Claire was just finishing her coiffure when Mrs. Dobbs tapped gently on the door.

"I'm sorry to wake you," she called, "but Mr. Hawthorn has a visitor. It's that Mrs. Calverson," she added, with distaste.

Claire glanced toward John, whose face was cold.

"Do go down, darling," she invited softly, reaching up to kiss his firm mouth. "I still have my hair to finish."

"Claire . . ." he began hesitantly.

She lifted both eyebrows mischievously. "Yes?"

He chuckled, brought her close, and

kissed her hungrily, and then again, with breathless tenderness. "Come down when you're ready," he whispered. "And don't worry!"

"I'm not worried. Not after yesterday. And last night," she added demurely, blushing.

"It was good, wasn't it?" he asked huskily. "Don't blush if Mrs. Dobbs asks you if you heard screams last night, or you'll give the game away." He kissed her gasping mouth slowly. "No, don't be embarrassed," he whispered, his arms tightening. "I cried out, too, at the last. I couldn't get close enough to you, deep enough inside you, to touch you as I yearned to." He actually shivered. "Claire, no two people ever were so intimate as we were then."

"Yes." She pressed close, her own body trembling with the memory of it. She had lost consciousness as they strained together in that shattering ecstasy. The memory of it was still a little frightening.

His cheek drew against her own, his breath hot and quick at her ear. "I never had intimacy with Diane," he confessed as he lifted his head and searched her eyes. "I lied about that. I'm ashamed that I did."

Her eyes brightened. "Thank you for telling me."

"It was necessary," he said simply, tracing

her mouth with a long forefinger. "A man must have no secrets from a beloved wife."

She smiled again, sighing her pleasure as he pressed one last kiss on her soft mouth and let her go.

She watched him out the door, convinced that he was about to be offered Diane on a platter, unless she missed her guess. She wondered how he was going to send her on her way, because she had no doubts at all about his fidelity now. She touched her thickening waist with a smile. She still had one last secret to share with him. And she would, as soon as their unwanted guest left.

She was right about his feelings. He wasn't happy to see Diane. If anything, he was annoyed. Although she did look beautiful in a blue suit with frilly white lace and a jaunty hat, he had to admit. But she didn't even make his heart flutter now. He thought of Claire and his blood sang through his veins.

"What can I do for you, Diane?" he asked politely.

She seemed taken aback. "Why, John. I thought you would have expected me. I mean, Eli will certainly go to jail now. I will testify against him, Dawes has been found and made another confession, and they have the money and Eli's reluctant confession, as well. The bank's funds will be restored, and everyone knows now that you were an innocent victim of Eli's greed. Mr. Whitfield has even agreed to go ahead with the merger, in light of this development. Of course, that will be up to you, now, since you will almost certainly become president of the bank with Eli's conviction. Everything is back the way it was. So I thought — that is . . . I thought you wanted me."

He drew her out onto the porch and closed the door behind them.

"Shall we be completely honest with each other?" he asked quietly. "I loved you once. But you wanted more than I could give you, and you married another man. Perhaps I tendered hopes even then. But I can assure you now, with all my heart, that the woman I want most in the world is upstairs in our apartment waiting for me. I didn't realize until recently just how long she's been waiting. I've hurt her. I don't intend to ever hurt her again."

"You don't love me?" Diane sounded plaintive.

"I'm quite fond of you," he said, with a smile. "I always will be. But I love Claire, you see."

She smiled sadly. "So she's won. I was afraid that she would. I could see quite clearly that she loved you enough to give you up. I didn't."

His eyebrows met above the high bridge of his nose. "I don't understand."

"We had a conversation just before I agreed to help you catch Eli," she confessed. "Claire said that if you loved me, she would never hinder you in any way. I knew then that her love for you was greater than mine. You see, I would never have let you go to another woman without a fight."

He searched her eyes. No, she wouldn't. Her vanity would have prevented her from letting go. Claire was made of softer stuff, but in its way, much stronger.

"I'm sorry, Diane," he said.

She waved a hand. "Oh, pooh," she said languidly. "I think I knew it was over when you married. I just didn't want to accept it. Well, I'll have the reward — and there are plenty of men who would be willing to marry a young, rich woman." She smiled. "Even a 'disgraced' divorcée."

"Be happy."

She shrugged. "Happiness isn't my lot. But I'll be content. Goodbye, John."

"Goodbye, Diane."

She walked back to her waiting carriage, and John watched her. But his eyes weren't filled with either longing or regret. He was impatient for her to be gone.

When she was out of sight, he went back into the house and took the steps two at a time in his eagerness to reach Claire. The night before was still in his mind, in his heart. In bed, she was more than he could ever have hoped for. Even out of bed, she filled his heart, his life. He adored her. He wanted no one else.

He opened the door and went in, to find Claire standing at the window, looking out at the backyard. It reminded him of the early days of their marriage, when she stood here alone and thought sad thoughts.

"She's gone," he said.

She turned and smiled. "Is she truly, John?"

He moved close to her and framed her face in his hands. "Truly. I sent her away, Claire," he said softly. "And not out of self-sacrifice or duty or shame. I sent her away because whatever I felt for her is long gone. Dead. Finished." He took her in his arms and hugged her close with a long sigh. "I adore you," he whispered, dizzy with pleasure. "I want to hold you and kiss you all the time. I want to be with you always, in every way. God, Claire. I would have nothing without you. I love you," he whispered, and kissed her.

"I know. I love you, too." She chuckled under his mouth, kissing him back with all the joy within her, all the years of longing, all the hopes and delight. But then she remembered something that she'd forgotten in her joy, and she pulled her lips from under his.

"Oh, John. Stop." She moaned. "There's something I have to tell you. You may not want to stay with me."

"Imagine that!" He laughed.

"I'm serious!" She put her small hands on his chest and held him away, her eyes troubled. "John, I am . . . that is, I think . . . I'm carrying your child."

His face was a living portrait of shock. He didn't even seem to breathe. "You are . . . *what?*"

"Yes. And you said — that is, you told Mrs. Cornwall that children unnerved you, so I was afraid to tell you . . . Oh, dear," she added worriedly at the look on his face. "I'm so sorry!"

"Sorry?" He let out the breath that had all but choked him. His eyes glittered. His face became radiant. "Sorry?" He lifted her and whirled her around, laughing like a madman. "Sorry? Oh, you witch, you witch. Come here!"

He pulled her close and kissed her again,

396

hungrily and then tenderly, so tenderly.

"Claire, I want our children more than you'll ever know," he whispered into her lips. "I want sons and daughters and then, eventually, grandchildren. Claire, what a sweet, sweet surprise."

She was breathless, overwhelmed. She reached up to him; he kissed her again. Only then did he pull back and grimace. "And I said . . ." His breath jerked out. "Forgive me. I spoke rashly and without thinking, on the train. I do want children. It's only that I never considered what it would be like to actually have a baby in the house." His eyes became dreamy. "We must buy a house, Claire. A nice, big house that we can fill with children and the love we bear each other."

She pushed close into his arms and held him. "Oh, my dear," she whispered huskily. "My dear. I can't bear the happiness!"

"Neither can I. But I think we'll manage," he added on a laugh. "What a Christmas it will be. Have you thought about it? Between us, we have the most wonderful present that any two people could ever anticipate. We have the promise of a child!"

She pressed closer to him, shivering with joy. "We'll go home with your parents?"

"Yes, we will. And I can promise you the

most joyous Christmas you've ever known."
He lifted his head and looked down into
her beautiful gray eyes with exultation.
"Claire," he exclaimed, "it's going to be
glorious!"

And it was.

ABOUT THE AUTHOR

The prolific author of over 100 books, **Diana Palmer** got her start as a newspaper reporter. A multi-*New York Times* bestselling author and one of the top ten romance writers in America, she has a gift for telling the most sensual tales with charm and humor. Diana lives with her husband in northeast Georgia.